Gangster in our Midst

First Edition: August 5, 2017, Book1One.com
Second Edition: April 10, 2018 (re-edited to accommodate additional stories)
Third Edition: January 15, 2019 (modified front & back book covers)

ISBN: 978-0-9992635-3-2 (Paperback)
ISBN: 978-0-9992635-2-5 (E-Book)
ISBN: 978-0-9992635-4-9 (Large Print)

Library of Congress cataloging-in-Publication Data available upon request.

Printed in the U.S.A

Book cover and interior: Lance Buckley Design
Map by Betty Brandt Passick

This book is a work of fiction. Names, characters, places, and incidents either are products of the author's imagination or are used fictitiously. Any resemblance to actual events or locales or persons, living or dead, is entirely coincidental.

Read more about historical Fairbank, Iowa, the town that inspired Oxbow, at www.bettybrandtpassick.com.

GANGSTER
in our
MIDST

an historical novel

BETTY BRANDT PASSICK

Dedicated to the brave and courageous people worldwide who live, work and raise families amidst criminal elements and war.

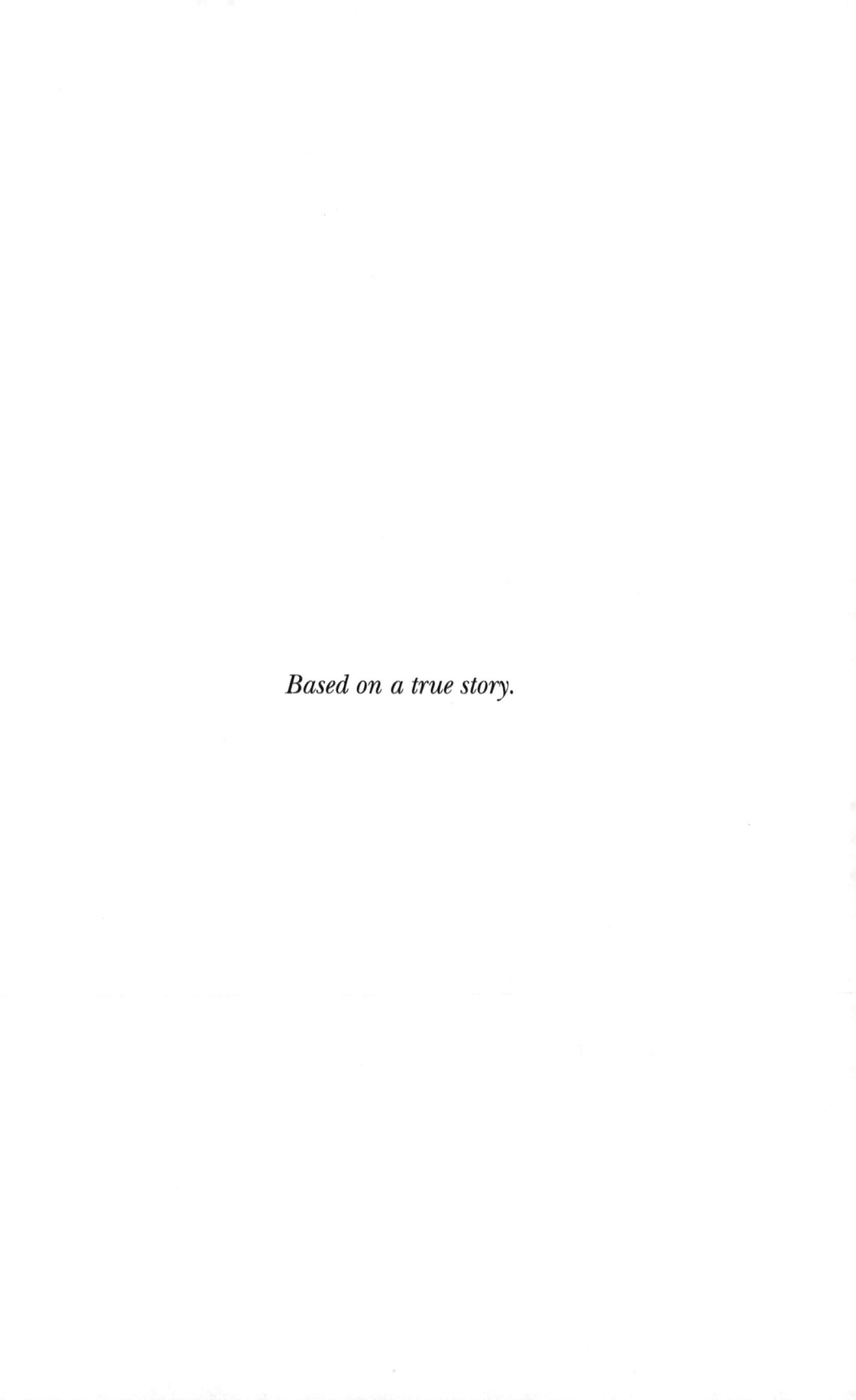

Based on a true story.

CONTENTS

CAST OF CHARACTERS

1928

Tuffy Adams (Evelyn, wife): *Oxbow Creamery owners*

Ed Allen: *Bon Ton owner*

Albert Anselmi: *One of the Chicago Outfit's most successful hitmen in Prohibition-era Chicago; he and Giovanni "John" Scalise were known as the "killer twins," believed to have killed Capone's gangster rival Dion O'Banion in 1924*

"Baby": *Marshall Delaney's Ford Model T car*

Robert Bentley: *Old Grist Mill owner*

Emma Bierkoff (Walter, husband; sons: Leonard & Samuel): *Farmers wife (with tuberculosis)*

John Bierkoff (Onnallee, wife; brother to Walter Bierkoff): *Farming neighbor to Walter & Emma Bierkoff*

Leonard Bierkoff: *Eldest son of Walter & Emma Bierkoff, brother to Samuel; I.C. school student/baseball pitcher*

Walter Bierkoff (Emma, wife; sons: Leonard & Samuel): *Farmer*

John Bierkoff (Onnallee, wife; brother to Walter Bierkoff): *Farming neighbor to Walter & Emma Bierkoff*

Bill Biggs: *Bon Ton employee-baker; baseball umpire*

Billy Bundy (Gina, sister): *I.C. school student*

Alphonse "Scarface" Capone (Mary Mae, wife; "Sunny," son): *Chicago Outfit Don (1925-1931)*

i

Frank Capone (Al Capone's brother): *Gangster (killed in 1924 Chicago election skirmish)*

Ralph "Bottles" Capone (Al Capone's older brother): *Gangster (best known for his Cotton Club in Chicago)*

"Fats" Arnold Coffin (Gert, wife): *Barber Shop co-owner/barber*

Aunt Gert Coffin (Arnold, husband): *Coffin Cafe co-owner*

Calvin Coolidge: *30th President of the United States (1923–1929)*

Mrs. Crawley: *Leehey's Cash Store employee*

Vera Cummings: *Oxbow public school student*

Phillip D'Andrea: *Gangster (Al Capone's private bodyguard)*

Olivia Delaney (Sweeney, husband; Vanessa, daughter): *Coffin Café employee; president of Phythian Sisters*

Sweeney Delaney (Olivia, wife; Vanessa, daughter): *Oxbow town marshal (1916-1949)*

Vanessa Delaney (Sweeney & Olivia, parents): *Oxbow public school student*

Emmett Durham (Son of Frank Durham): *Oxbow public school student; newspaper delivery boy*

Frank "Francis" Durham (Father of Emmett Durham): *Emerson Grain Co./John Deere Implement owner-manager*

Dr. G. C. Eickelberg: *Oxbow dentist*

Clara Fenne: *Oxbow pharmacist*

Barney Finkle: *Farmer (neighbor to Bierkoffs and Schumers)*

John Gardner: *Oxbow mayor (1927-1936); Stockyards owner*

Charles Grantham (Bethel, wife): *Oxbow Opera House owner; Oxbow View newspaper owner-publisher; boxing promoter: patent holder*

Jake "Greasy Thumb" Gusik: *Gangster (Al Capone's most trusted advisor and brains of the Chicago Outfit, treasurer and financial genius*

Delbert Habercamp: *Farmer*

Fr. John Q. Halpin: *I.C. Church priest (1915-1931)*

Herbert Hoover: *31st President of the United States (1929–1933)*

Mary Huegnot: *Oxbow beauty shop owner*

Capt. Michael Hughes: *Chicago Police Department chief (promoted to chief following the gang murder of Dion O'Banion in 1924)*

M. E. "Bee" Leehey (Georgiana, wife): *Leehey's Cash Store owners*

Louie La Cava (Josephine "Jess," wife; eldest son of Pasquale "Patrick" and Maria Tripol La Cava): *Gangster (secretary, bookkeeper, lieutenant, and hit man for Al Capone & John Torrio)*

Geraldine Lehmkuhl: *Daughter of Melvin Lehmkuhl, whose family lived above family-owned Lehmkuhl Hardware*

William "Bill" Lehmkuhl: *Lehmkuhl Hardware owner; Marshal Delaney's poker buddy*

Joe Levendusky (Rose, wife): *Josephine La Cava's brother-in-law and sister*

Jake Lingle: *Chicago Tribune reporter (gang murdered in 1930)*

Danny Little: *I.C. school student/baseball pitcher*

Dr. Paul T. Logue: *Oxbow physician and surgeon (1926-lifetime)*

Antonio "Tony the Scourge" Lombardo: *Gangster (Chicago Unione Siciliana 3rd president)*

Charles Luciana: *Gangster (known for establishment of first Commission; also first official boss of the modern Genovese crime family, and instrumental in the development of the National Crime Syndicate)*

"Maggie": *Walter Bierkoff's Ford Model T car*

Jason McCuniff: *I.C. school student/baseball catcher*

William H. McSwiggin: *Chicago Assistant State's Attorney (gang murdered in 1926)*

Louis J. Miller: *Miller Blacksmith shop owner*

Lucy Ann Dean Wiltse Minton (Husband, Jacob): *Wiltse Hotel & Minton Sinclair Gas founder-owners*

George "Bugs" Moran: *Gangster (Leader of what had been Deon O'Banion's Chicago North Side gang; seven of his gang members were gunned down in St. Valentine's Day massacre on the orders of Al Capone)*

Adolph H. Nieman: *Oxbow State Bank, president*

Frank "The Enforcer" Nitti: *Gangster (Director of Al Capone's homicide squad, also in charge of whisky and alcohol operations)*

Dean "Dion" O'Banion: *Gangster (Founder and leader of Chicago North Side gang; he was murdered, reportedly by Frankie Yale, John Scalise and Albert Anselmi)*

John O'Conner: *O'Conner's Grocery owner*

Lawrence O'Malley (Mary, wife): *Josephine La Cava's sister and brother-in-law*

Gayle Peick: *Oxbow public school coach*

Walt Polege: *Oxbow town maintenance man*

Bill Rechkemmer: *Oxbow Ford-Jewitt dealership owner*

Franklin D. Roosevelt: *32nd President of the United States (1933-1945)*

Giovanni "John" Scalise: *One of the Chicago Outfit's most successful hitmen in Prohibition-era Chicago, he and Alberto Anselmi were known as the "killer twins," believed to have killed Capone's gangster rival Dion O'Banion in 1924 Meryl Sharp: Local boxer (semiprofessional)/winner of "Golden Glove" award*

Ed Schumer (Noritta, wife; Victor, son): *Farmer (neighbor to Bierkoffs)*

Sister Keith: *I.C. school teacher/Holy Ghost sister*

Sister Mary Margaret: *I.C. school principal/Holy Ghost sister*

Alice Skinny: *Free Will Baptist Society Church member*

Charles Slutter: *Farmer (south of Oxbow)*

Dave Spankey: *Oelwein Sacred Heart school student/baseball pitcher*

Miss Lil Thompson: *Oxbow Opera House pianist*

William "Big Bill" Thompson: *Republican mayor of Chicago for three terms (1915-1923; 1927-1931)*

Tommy Thunker: *Oelwein Sacred Heart school student/baseball best hitter*

Fr. W. J. Torpey: *I.C. Church priest (1931-1952)*

Johnny "The Fox" Torrio (Anna, wife): *Gangster (New York Mafia Kingpin who took over Chicago crime gangs, then relinquished the business to Al Capone before reestablishing his business in New York/ leader of Big Seven Cosa Nostra on the east coast)*

Agnes Triggers: *Oxbow Telephone Exchange operator*

Dr. Lorraine W. Ward: *Physician (office was above grist mill; served as company doctor for the CGW railroad in Oelwein)*

George Weiland: *Oxbow local; Marshal Delaney's poker buddy*

Earl "Hymie" Weiss (aka Henry Earl J. Wojciechowski): *Gangster (became a leader of the Prohibition-era North Side Gang and a bitter rival of Al Capone; known as 'the only man Al Capone feared)*

Lewis Robert "Hack" Wilson: *American Major League Baseball player/ power hitter during '20s and '30s*

Harry Willey: *Buchanan County sheriff*

Rev. A. Van Benschoten: *Free Will Baptist Society Church pastor (1924-1929)*

Frank Wilson: *Agent of the Treasury Department's Bureau of Internal Revenue (1920-1931)*

Dr. W. W. Wilson: *Oxbow veterinarian*

Francesco "Frankie" Yale: *Gangster from Brooklyn (part of cosa nostra; Al Capone's boyhood friend from Five Points gang)*

Jack Zuta: *Gangster (vice lord of Chicago North Side Moran-Aiello gang before becoming political "fixer" for the Chicago Outfit)*

1936

John D. Agostino: *John Torrio's accomplice from Egg Harbor City, N. J.*

Earl Bentley: *B & R Motor Service, co-owner with Claire Rechkemmer*

Buckmaster Twins (Doc Buckmaster's sons): *Local amateur boxers (lightweight)*

Dustin Cobbledick (Phyllis, wife; Mikey, son): *Responsible for Weibel Hardware break-in*

Charles Daniels: *Oxbow CGW depot agent*

"Dynamite" Dunn: *Local boxer (amateur heavyweight)*

Arthur "Dutch Schultz" Flegenheimer (Frances, wife): *Gangster (leader in Big Seven cosa nostra on east coast/John Torrio's bail bonds business partner)*

Rev. George Gaide: *Methodist Church pastor (1961-1964)*

John Gipper (Pearl, wife): *Wiltse Hotel owners (1939-1963)*

Rev. H. J. Heilmann: *St. John's Lutheran Church pastor (1930-1960)*

Jacob "Yasha" Katzenberg: *European booze and narcotics peddler*

Neil King: *Local boxer (amateur heavyweight)*

Seymour Klein: *Assistant U.S. attorney (presented the government in the prosecution of John Torrio on tax evasion in 1939)*

Joseph La Cava (3rd son of Pasquale "Patrick" and Maria Tripol La Cava): *Among the La Cava brothers listed in a Federal document "Who's Who of Organized Crime in Chicago"*

Dutch Marsh: *Local boxer (amateur heavyweight)*

Frank Miller: *Miller Plumbing & Heating owner; fire chief*

John Byron "Bud" Murphy: *Oxbow postmaster*

Robert P. Patterson: *U. S. District Judge of the U. S. District Court for the Southern District of New York (presided over John Torrio tax evasion trial in 1939)*

Claire Rechkemmer: *B & R Motor Service co-owner with Earl Bentley*

Mrs. Clarence Soden: *Wife of Rev. Clarence Soden, pastor, First Baptist Church (1943-1945)*

Max D. Steuer: *Counsel for William Stockblower and John Torrio in the 1939 John Torrio tax evasion trial*

Harry S. Truman: *33rd President of the United States (1945-1953)*

Cash "Baby Grand" Ward: *Local boxer (amateur heavyweight)*

Griffy Ward: *Local boxer (amateur heavyweight)*

Rev. C. C. Winter: *Methodist Church pastor (1937-1943)*

1968

Kurt Lehmkuhl: *Paperboy who delivered newspapers to La Cavas at their house built in 1968 on the north end of Oxbow*

Bob Maricle: *Maricle Body Shop owner (1960s)*

1981

Earl Bellis: *Oxbow public school and Commercial Club president*

Gracie Failes: *Oelwein hitchhiker*

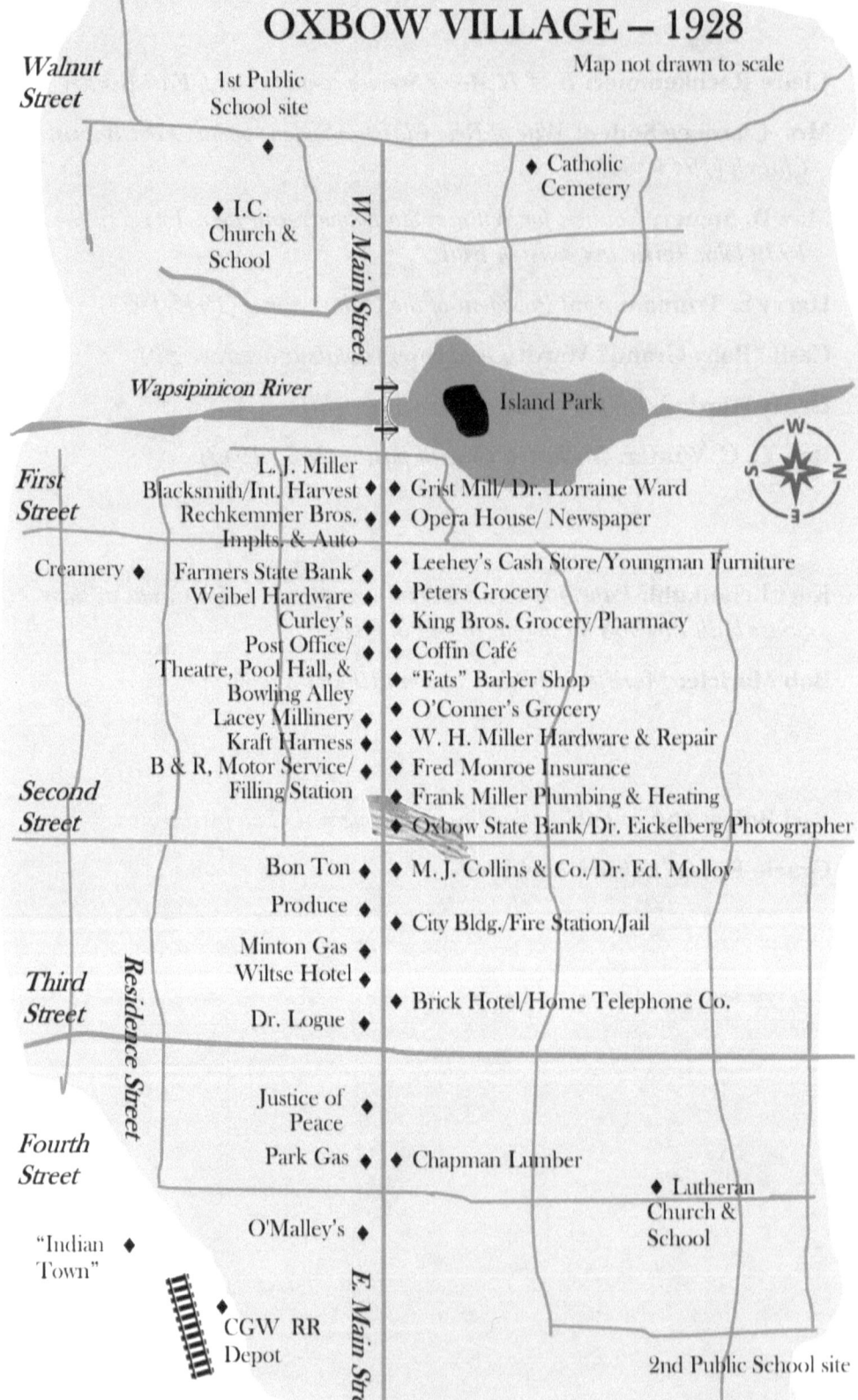

OXBOW VILLAGE — 1928

Map not drawn to scale

Walnut Street

1st Public School site

♦ Catholic Cemetery

♦ I.C. Church & School

W. Main Street

Wapsipinicon River

Island Park

First Street

L. J. Miller Blacksmith/Int. Harvest ♦
Rechkemmer Bros. ♦
Implts. & Auto

♦ Grist Mill/ Dr. Lorraine Ward
♦ Opera House/ Newspaper

Creamery ♦

Farmers State Bank ♦
Weibel Hardware ♦
Curley's ♦
Post Office/ ♦
Theatre, Pool Hall, & Bowling Alley
Lacey Millinery ♦
Kraft Harness ♦
B & R, Motor Service/ ♦
Filling Station

♦ Leehey's Cash Store/Youngman Furniture
♦ Peters Grocery
♦ King Bros. Grocery/Pharmacy
♦ Coffin Café
♦ "Fats" Barber Shop
♦ O'Conner's Grocery
♦ W. H. Miller Hardware & Repair
♦ Fred Monroe Insurance
♦ Frank Miller Plumbing & Heating
♦ Oxbow State Bank/Dr. Eickelberg/Photographer

Second Street

Bon Ton ♦
Produce ♦
Minton Gas ♦
Wiltse Hotel ♦
Dr. Logue ♦

♦ M. J. Collins & Co./Dr. Ed. Molloy
♦ City Bldg./Fire Station/Jail
♦ Brick Hotel/Home Telephone Co.

Third Street

Residence Street

Justice of Peace ♦
Park Gas ♦

♦ Chapman Lumber
♦ Lutheran Church & School

Fourth Street

O'Malley's ♦

"Indian Town" ♦

♦ CGW RR Depot

E. Main Street

2nd Public School site ♦

PROLOGUE

The vast majority of the Americans were dead set against Prohibition, when, on January 17, 1920, Congress casually voted to ratify the 18th Amendment to the Constitution, prohibiting the manufacture, sale and transport of alcoholic beverages. However, it remained legal to drink and buy liquor. This created one hell of a mess.

Overnight, thousands of legalized drinking establishments closed, while hundreds of small-fry bootleggers leapt in to partake of the bootlegging gold rush to meet the needs of its thirsty citizenry. The most ruthless and cunning embraced the opportunity to organize illegal manufacture, distribution and sale of beer and booze. Chicago quickly gained a reputation for its underworld jungle—its Big Three bosses: Johnny "The Fox" Torrio and General Al "Scarface" Capone, old pals from the New York Italian Five Points gang; and Dean "Dion" O'Banion, a Chicago-born lad, the dominant force controlling Cook County's nine hundred square miles.

The murder and mayhem on the streets of Chicago seemed a long way from the bustling Village of Oxbow, Iowa, some two hundred sixty miles to the southwest—at least until two area teenaged sisters dropped out of school and ran away to Chicago looking for work, each also finding a husband.

As best as the phlegmatic Marshal Sweeney Delaney could recall, the younger sister, Josephine—and her new husband—first showed up in Oxbow sometime in the early 1920s. Sweeney stood outside the city building on the boardwalk as a big shiny black Lincoln crept to a stop outside the Coffin Café. A well-heeled man, clearly not from these parts, got out and strolled to the passenger side. Josephine emerged through the open door.

A short time later Sweeney received a police bulletin warning of an armed and dangerous man; he'd robbed and shot someone in Chicago.

Sweeney soon suspected the town's "mystery man" of being a gangster. So did Walter Bierkoff, a farmer and man of keen curiosity; also the perspicacious Father John Halpin, priest at Immaculate Conception Catholic Church, where Josephine's family attended.

CHAPTER ONE

Three Fingers

July 1, 1928—Frank Yale was found slumped over the wheel of his new Lincoln near his New York home, gunned down by four men in a black Nash sedan dispensing one hundred .45 caliber bullets into his car. The police found Yale, diamonds, ring and belt buckle intact, his .32 still in his coat pocket. He had double-crossed Capone. The automatic revolver and sawed-off shotgun inside the car were identified as belonging to Capone. When police reached Capone, he said he was on vacation in Florida at the time.

From the kitchen table, Louie La Cava heard the timid knock at the front door of the O'Malley house. He'd gotten out of the habit of answering the door, any door, ever since '24 when a car exploded in front of his Chicago duplex. That day the raps on the door had been furious, demanding. He opened it slightly, and finding no one there, ran out onto the sidewalk, eying the street up and down in search of the caller. When the bomb went off a hundred feet away, he was knocked to the ground, fire raining down upon him. He knew his cover was blown as an anonymous cigar salesman.

The knocking persisted. He was the only one at home. Shortly after sunrise, his brother-in-law Lawrence O'Malley caught a freight train at the depot a block from the house that took him to his switchman job at the CGW yards in Oelwein, a larger town about ten miles east of Oxbow. Later he delivered his sister-in-law, Mary O'Malley, and Jess to their sister Rose and brother-in-law Joe Levendusky's farm near Independence for the day.

1

Louie looked up from the pile of receipts on the table, laid down the pencil and quietly pushed back the chair. Avoiding floor boards that notoriously squeaked, he stole across the living room floor to the bay window and peered out onto the open porch through the thin space between the window frame and drapery. It was that scrawny kid, Emmett Durham, who delivered the Des Moines paper. Probably here to collect.

He turned the key in the lock and wrenched the door ajar while his eyes canvassed the area around and past the boy.

"Good morning, Mr. La Cava!" Emmett said. "I'm glad I caught you at home. Been delivering the Sunday paper regular…you're a few weeks behind in payment. Would you like to take care of this, or should I come back and collect from the O'Malleys?"

Louie rolled the stump of the smoking cigar with his tongue to one corner of his mouth and swung open the door by two-thirds. "Sure you don't wait to see Lincoln parked in front of house before you knock at door?"

"No, Mr. La Cava—honest, I don't," Emmett said.

"What's your dad Francis up to? Ask if he will go for drive again some night. We talk about at tavern dis afternoon when play cards."

"I will, Mr. La Cava."

Louie watched the boy tear a perforated section of a ticket dangling from the silver ring he held in one hand. He grabbed the strip from the boy, discarded it on the lamp table near the door, reached with his right hand into a pant pocket, hauled out a handful of coins, selected a silver dollar and flipped it to the boy.

The toss caught Emmett by surprise. The coin bounced off the tips of his fingers and onto the weathered porch floor.

Louie smirked as the kid waited for the coin to stop rolling before bending over to pick it up.

"Looks like you have future as outfielder with da Cubs!"

"Aw, Mr. La Cava, the Cubbies are gonna come back and win the World Series again one of these years." Emmett said, as he descended the porch steps leading to the narrow stone sidewalk where Louie's Lincoln was parked.

GANGSTER *in our* MIDST

"Tell your friends I take to da movies Saturday night—anyone who wish go!"

"Thanks, Mr. La Cava," Emmett said, scrutinizing the Lincoln's interior as he passed by and, Louie surmised, probably wondering what it was like to ride in car with L Head V-8 engine.

Louie shut and locked the front door on his way to the kitchen. The wall telephone chimes had begun to vibrate. The O'Malley's ring was two longs and one short. With one hand he lifted the receiver to his ear, while adjusting the hinged mouthpiece with the other.

"I have a call from a Mr. G in Chicago—for Luigi," the operator said.

"Speakin'!" Louie said, waiting for the connection to be made.

"Three Fingers Luigi! How ya doin' back in Iowa? Boss said I'd find ya at dis number."

Louie knew the caller as Jake "Greasy Thumb" Guzik. He'd been Capone's sidekick ever since Capone discovered his gift as treasurer and financial wizard in da Torrio-Capone days. *It is insult to have to deal with Guzik*, he thought. *A man incapable of killin' even a fly.*

"Boss wishes me inform you he's sendin' familiar face your way first of next week," Guzik continued. "Find nice place for him to hole up few days while you conduct some business. Says he's waitin' for your monthly report, too. Wants to know if it be on time…gettin' pressure from da owners, you understand? Also, double, triple check numbers so all da percentages are right."

"Thanks, Jake da Jew. I know you don't care for dat name," Louie said. "Assure boss report will be on time, done right, unlike some. And I will get room for guest. And tell boss may have new booze market for him in Oxbow area—will be in touch with Nitti, if worth his time."

"Oh, and another thing," Guzik added. "Boss says after meetin' next week, you should hightail back. Something big in da works."

Louie hung up the receiver and sat back down at the table, his mind in a cloud of incredulity. *All dis happen too soon after Frankie Yale killin'*, he thought. *Police findin' guns in Yale's car bought by Capone will bring heat for long time. Cazzata! Chicago police still in revolt over da McSwiggin murder—and he not even da guy we was after. Suppose dis visitor comin' to Oxbow is followed by goons from New York, or da Feds. Boss could be puttin' Jess and family in jeopardy. But Al Brown, or whatever he call himself now, is probably chompin' at bit to get back to business. And no one disappoints da boss.*

He felt the sting of an old wound. Old injuries bleed at the slightest touch, he'd found. In '24 he first went to work for Capone, and ended up fleeing for his life. Twelve months later he was back in Capone's employment. Now he divided his time between three gambling establishments, giving daily updates to Capone, Jake Guzik, Ralph Capone and Frank Nitti on bets placed over the wire and depositing daily receipts into Capone's bank account. Over time, Jess's interrogations became unrelenting, and he confessed to working for Capone: "I do Capone's books, but only for good side of business, all da millions he gives to charities," he had told her. But Capone was no Robin Hood. And by then, he'd resumed fixing other things for Capone.

His mind flicked back to Lawrence O'Malley's fiasco from earlier that morning. Mary, Jess and he had watched from the kitchen window as Lawrence waited for the rattler on the depot platform. His stance was that of a defeated man. During breakfast he spoke of new railroad executive threats of furloughs and cut wages. It hadn't helped when the government took over the railroad business during the Great War, but the misery began in earnest with President Harding's anti-labor attitude that brought strikes in the early '20s. Perhaps he should speak to Lawrence about getting into the business. Bootlegging with Joe Levendusky was other option. Surely Nitti could send some business Joe's way.

He touched the pot with the back of three fingers, reached for a match from the tin box on the wall, struck it on the stove top and lit the burner. The heat from the flame reminded him he felt no remorse for Frankie Yale—*dat happen when anyone betray Capone. Not boss's fault Yale get bump off, and Feds ought to understand. Da U. S. government order Louie to kill in Great War—what different 'bout Yale's death? All just war.*

The eleven o'clock passenger train was due. The acid in his belly mounted and he let go of a gigantic belch. He needed to get to work. He extinguished the flame under the coffee, lifted his suitcoat from the chair back and slid it on while coasting toward the front door, noticing the quiet street as he passed the window. He turned the lock, grabbed his hat from the coat tree, and hustled to the Lincoln.

Two blocks later he pulled the car beneath the overhang of Minton Sinclair Gas. Jacob Minton advanced from inside the station. He was a dapper little man who wore a long-sleeved plaid shirt and striped denim bib overalls far too long for him, requiring him to turn up the cuffs several inches. Still, he was a friendly bird.

"Fill 'er up, Jacob!" Louie said, getting out of the car. "Got business with da missus in hotel—won't be long."

"Get you a bottle of Coca-Cola, or maybe a bag of fresh popcorn from inside? How about an oil change?"

"Next time," Louie said, as he passed beneath the white sign hovering on six-foot stilts above the sidewalk leading to the hotel's front porch. Hotel Wiltse, run by Lucy Minton, was one of the better class of smaller hostelries of the state, according to Francis Durham during one of their late-night rides in the township.

Pushing open the front door, he was startled by a caged green and yellow parrot across the way calling out, "Polly wants a cracker!"

On the other side of the small lobby, he spied a petite, aged woman standing behind the mahogany reception desk. Her no-nonsense face stared back at his. He sauntered toward her. With one hand he buttoned his suit coat while the other rose to remove the fedora from his head.

"Good morning, Mr. La Cava, what can I do for you?"

Surprised she knew him, he hesitated before speaking.

"Mrs. Minton, don't believe had pleasure to meet. Am here inquire 'bouta room. Will have guest first of next week...wonder if have single room, one or two day only."

"Let me check my book." She flipped forward a few pages in the registry then stared dismally at her findings. "Sorry, I'm booked all next week... mostly salesmen. The last rooms went a week ago...cattlemen coming to town for a stockyard sale."

"Then, wonder if have vacant room to see for next time have guest in town. Will send business yer way, if possible."

"Follow me," she said, walking briskly from behind the desk toward the open staircase leading to the second story.

The parrot let out a shrill whistle as the two began to ascend the stairs.

"How much longer are you in town?"

"Uncertain yet," he said.

At the landing, she followed the worn wool runner in the center of the wooden floored hallway. Midway, she stopped in front of a varnished pine door, twisted the white porcelain knob and thrust it open, inviting his examination.

"This is the bath," she said, moving aside. "All guests share this facility. Nice white porcelain tub…washbasin, too. Outhouse is back of the hotel."

Louie peeked into the room with its plain accommodations and nodded.

She closed the bath door and continued toward the far end of the hall. At a second door, she stopped, stepped inside, and gestured for Louie to pass in front of her.

"This room was vacated early this morning. I haven't had time to tidy it up yet. It's a bit chilly this far from the staircase in the winter, but I get no complaints the rest of the year. Comes with heavy quilt, fresh linens and towels, and chamber pot…for nighttime use only, please. All my rooms are clean. Windows open to let in fresh air. Still get a lot of street noise even after the Prohibition…drunken fights have been known to keep my guests awake on occasion. Can't say I approve, but what's to be done? All rooms come with nice desk and chair…dresser, too. I will apologize in advance for the top drawer on this one."

She walked over and pulled on two wooden knobs to withdraw the drawer, pointing to its backside.

"I musta had a gangster in here at some time or other. It's the only reason I came up with why someone would remove a big piece from the corner. Probably brought in a Tommy gun and wanted to stash it out of sight. I get all kinds. You never know what folks are carrying in bags brought into a hotel."

She glanced into Louie's eyes, then looked away.

Louie stepped forward to look inside the drawer. "Likely was Dillinger, Tommy Carroll, or da like.... Hear Dillinger gang came 'round dis parts. Dey call Carroll 'lantern-jaw', onetime boxer—believe."

"It could have been one of Dillinger's gang. Listen, Mr. La Cava, I'll give it to you straight. I've been through a war in my lifetime, and I'm puttin' you on notice. I don't take damage to my hotel lying down. If you put someone up here and something gets broken, I'll hold you personally responsible. I believe I know where to find you."

She stepped back into the hall and waited for him to follow before closing the door behind him.

"And I failed to tell you. The hotel kitchen is open for breakfast, dinner and supper. Best home-cooked meals in town."

At the bottom of the staircase, Jacob waited at the registration desk.

"The Lincoln's filled to the top, Mr. La Cava. You can pay me outside," Jacob said, before exiting through the front door.

Louie turned to follow him. "Thank you, Mrs. Minton. Next time have guest in town, I return."

"You might try Hotel Mealey in Oelwein for your guest. I'm sure they'll have a room. It's a little newer, but not by much."

"Stool-pigeon...he's packin' heat!" the parrot called out as Louie neared the front door.

Lucy gasped. "Jacob thought it would be clever to get Bogart to say that. Say it again, Bogart: Stool-pigeon...."

CHAPTER TWO

Mystery Man

Walter Bierkoff had been passing down his wisdom to his sons as long as Leonard could remember; he was now nine, and his brother, Samuel, was four. He could recite several of his father's sayings at will: "We expect God to show up in life—and do stuff. This is how we make sense of the world. Expecting God to be there, and active."

And another: "Whoever we are, whatever we make of ourselves, is all we will ever have—and that, in its profound simplicity, is the meaning of life."

His father's words mirrored how people observed him live his life. His was the religion of a simple man.

He also said he liked messy people who didn't fit in. Leonard figured God must've taken that as a challenge, as Walter still didn't know what to do about the gangster who had again holed up in Oxbow Village.

Today marked Leonard's start at Immaculate Conception school. It was the twenty-seventh day of August 1928. Leonard watched from the farmhouse window as Walter started the Model T, which Walter lovingly called "Maggie," named after his saintly mother, Margarete, who'd passed away two years earlier. In the Catholic tradition, saints helped the faithful reach sanctity, and Maggie, too, had proven trustworthy.

Walter turned the key and withdrew the choke on the dashboard, then walked to the nose of the car, inserted the crank and gave it a few turns. More adjustments at the dashboard, another turn-and-a-half on the crank, one final adjustment of the spark, and Maggie began her "hymn of liberation," as Walter called it.

Leonard scrambled from the house, book bag and lunch pail in hand, and climbed aboard Maggie, ready for his first day of fourth grade at the Catholic school. Dust from the balloon tires swirled as she rolled across the baked dirt yard, a waft of wind lifting the curled tail of the long red ribbon inscribed "Mother" tied to the driver's door handle. Leonard looked back to see his mother and little brother waving from the screened porch at the side of the house. This place had been farmed by Walter's father, and his father before that. Since 1868, all had lived and died by whatever the land supplied. Leonard expected it would be his and Samuel's one day. Walter had told them the weathered boards of the house used to be painted white, and Leonard often wondered if this meant his family was poor.

Normally a quiet, soft-spoken man, Walter only raised his voice when the ruts in the dirt road and rattles from Maggie's tin frame threatened to drown out his epic words. Or when the dust so enveloped the car's cabin and his lungs he had to forcibly expel the words from his arid throat. On this morning, Leonard heard his father inhale and hold onto his breath for a very long time, which made his heart race with anticipation. The moment reminded him of the story of Moses at Mount Sinai, when the Israelites waited for him to deliver the Ten Commandments.

At long last, Walter spoke: "Leonard, your mother and the Catholic Church think it's time for you to start at the I.C. school..."

Interrupting the thought, his father turned right to wave at Ed Schumer standing next to the side barn door directing milk cows out to pasture. Walter had commented at breakfast his intent to stop by on his way home to give Ed a hand with delivery of a calf, if it hadn't already happened overnight.

Walter turned Maggie east onto the gravel road and slid the lever right of the steering wheel all the way forward. The old tin can surged to her top speed of forty miles per hour. Oxbow would soon be in sight.

Leonard yet waited for his father to finish his initial thought, as Walter plucked a handkerchief from a pocket to expel the collection of morning dew and dust from his nostrils.

Finally, he continued his thought.

"You can still make your own decision about your faith when you're older. Roman Catholic, or something else—it's up to you."

Leonard knew his mother expected he'd be forever wholly and utterly Roman Catholic and hoped one of her sons would become a priest.

Then, Walter—always expressing another way to view religion, along with most everything else in life—concluded the conversation with an adage Leonard had heard a hundred times:

"The best policy is to leave the barn door open a bit, to let fresh air in and the stale air out."

The words reminded Leonard he had inherited his father curse: Being born a thinker. Walter ruminated about everything, much like a cow moving its food back and forth among its four stomachs; the idea being that eventually it all got sorted out.

At the western edge of town, Walter slowed as he passed the empty lot on the right, where the old Oxbow schoolhouse once stood. Leonard watched his father, wondering if he could see children playing on the lawn at recess from years gone by.

As for himself, beginning fourth grade at the I.C. school meant one of his fondest desires had just slid out of reach—forever. He'd dreamed of playing baseball and becoming a pitcher like Sweeney Delaney, a lefty, who'd chewed slippery elm, his top-secret weapon in putting the old spit ball just where he wanted it, and with all the speed he could muster. After high school, Sweeney went on to pitch in amateur leagues for Oxbow and other nearby towns. If he pitched for your team, you could bet on winning. Sweeney had quit pitching years ago, but many a star-struck boy still idolized the ground his cleats walked upon. There were flickering moments when Leonard wished he'd been born a Methodist. The Catholics offered baseball, but he knew if he went to the I.C. school he'd never play competitively, not in the same league as Sweeney and other public school kids.

His father stopped Maggie near the front entrance of the school on the west lawn of the I.C. Church. Leonard withdrew from the car and ran inside. He had attended Saturday confirmation classes for a long time, and always knew Catholic school was on his horizon. A promise had been made. And that was that.

—

Walter lingered in the car. His Grandfather Johann had helped build this church in 1868. His team of horses dragged hand-cut native stone from the cavernous lime quarry south of the parish grounds. And he had helped with construction of the Academy-Convent built in 1896. That building was destroyed by a fire in December 1916. People still spoke of the inferno visible for miles.

His mind looped to the Great War begun in 1914, when the town's young men, so handsome and full of promise, went off to fight, doing what their country asked of them. So many came home laid out in austere wooden boxes. Walter still felt the sting of death of those who'd grown to manhood alongside him whenever he drove by the quarry, the place he and the deceased had played as boys.

That alone would have endured as a painful memory. But the yellow paint splashed on his family's farm buildings at the height of anti-German sentiment had turned his life upside down.

Most recently another conflict captivated his mind: Prohibition.

From newspapers Walter ascertained ratification of the 18th Amendment to the Constitution sprouted from well-meaning women of faith, those who'd lived with and seen the effects of drunkenness on families. Initially a few states adopted Prohibition laws. Finally, on January 17, 1920, the entire country went dry—when the bootlegging war began in earnest. Eventually everyone got caught up in it, in one way or another.

He endeavored to keep a journal of the war raging in Carl Sandburg's magnificent "City of Big Shoulders." He pulled the journal from a rear pant pocket and searched the pages. In 1923, Chicago had about one hundred thirty gangster killings. The big three bosses: Southside leaders, Johnny Torrio and Al Capone; and leader of the Northside, Dion O'Banion. An early entry, dated November 10, 1924, noted the murder of O'Banion: His body was placed in a ten-thousand-dollar aluminum and silver casket laid in gangster state in the chapel of an alleged gangster-owned undertaking establishment. Truckloads of flowers arrived, one gargantuan spray with a card signed "from Al."

Another entry: Furious offenses launched by O'Banion's gang; Johnny Torrio, seriously injured, fled to his native Italy. Capone, too, undergoes attacks. Carloads of machine-gun squads and sawed-off shotgun crews poured a thousand slugs and bullets at six hundred rounds a minute into his bulletproof armored car. Capone, a Catholic, claimed the rosary he carried had been his protection.

A subset notation followed: Capone, 25, sole survivor of the Bootleg Battle of Chicago, runs the Outfit from his garrison: the Hawthorne Hotel on West 22nd Street, the true city hall in Cicero. One day hotel windows, covered by bullet-proof shutters, took a thousand rounds during a drive-by during Capone's lunch. Capone survived unharmed.

He'd recorded a Chicago Tribune reporter's comment: About half of city, county and state employees and politicians are on Capone's payroll, including Chicago Mayor William Thompson. Capone thugs strong-arm legitimate businesses, too, including mom-and-pop shops, grocery stores, junk dealers, laundry services. Everyone pays the ante, or is maimed or murdered.

His eureka moment happened around April 1926.

He, along with Leonard, looking over his shoulder, had been reading an article about a triple killing, which included the young Assistant State's Attorney of Cook County, William 'Billy' H. McSwiggin, a renowned crime-fighting Chicago prosecutor, and the man who'd publicly stated his determination to convict and send Capone to Alcatraz.

That day Walter laid down the newspaper, his eyes fixated somewhere in the space of sixteen inches between heaven and hell.

It was then he realized Oxbow's mystery man...was a gangster!

—

Inside the school, Leonard dropped off his book bag and lunch in the classroom before clumping down the basement stairs for morning Mass. There, gaggles of boisterous boys and giggling girls genuflected and crossed themselves and searched for seats in rows of barren wooden pews. Once seated, the girls, prayer books and black rosaries in hand, began to adjust the black veils pinned atop their heads. Six Holy Ghost sisters, dressed in full black habit and white coif, exposing only their pale, stern faces, filled in around them. Leonard often wondered: *What color hair did they have under there? What were their real names? Why had they become nuns?*

Father Halpin entered the front of the room in his black cassock, genuflected and made the sign of the cross on his head and chest, then bowed midway before the small altar. Earlier, Billy Bundy had lit two white candles on the altar. Leonard knew Billy. They were among a half-dozen recent recruits who'd signed up as altar boys. Their job was to help the priest at Mass with moving and holding the missal, and anything else he might need. The priest now took his place. The students dropped onto wooden kneelers, and all clamor ceased.

Father Halpin began: "In the name of the Father, and of the Son and of the Holy Ghost." Everyone crossed themselves again and in unison repeated with the priest, "Amen."

After Mass was over, Leonard and the rest of the students filed to their classrooms. The daily curriculum, taught by the nuns, would be the same as country school—plus religion, the fundamentals of the Catholic faith, and Latin. Understanding the Bible fell to Pope Pius XI, Father Halpin, and the nuns. Catholic kids were only required to memorize The Lord's Prayer. Second graders could expect the nuns to ask for a show of hands of anyone who had a Bible at home. Those who presented their Bibles to the nuns never got them back. Aware of the practice, Leonard had avoided disclosing his family's King James Bible. It occupied the shelf at home in the parlor next to a Charles Dickens' book.

Leonard tucked his rosary in a pocket, took a middle seat in a row of wooden desks, removed the items from his bookbag, and placed them on the desktop. He counted nine children in his class, if one included Victor, Ed and Noritta Schumer's son. Victor sat at an orphaned desk in the rear of the room and rocked in his seat.

Sister Mary Margaret came into the room and everyone stood at attention. Almost immediately her eyes diverted to Victor.

"Victor, Victor! Why aren't you standing with the others?" she said.

CHAPTER THREE

Oxbow Village —1928

A fetus male child, around five and a-half months was found on the banks of the Little Wapsipinicon River by the new public school superintendent. He had gone there to drown a litter of kittens born at his home a short time before. At the edge of the water, his attention was attracted to a package covered with a towel. He investigated, and inside, wrapped in common brown wrapping paper, he discovered the body. He notified the mayor who called the sheriff and coroner. Dr. Ward was of the opinion the body had been in the water for a number of hours and that the child had been born dead.

Walter maneuvered Maggie east toward downtown. The steel bridge rumbled as she traversed its thick plank floor. He turned south to Farmer's Creamery Co. The thick, sour smell of whey greeted him as he pulled up next to the stark wooden structure. Typically, the wait to unload was long. He and Charles Slutter, second in line, struck up a conversation. Charles had a small farm south of town, but Walter was unsure of its exact location.

"The mystery guy's still in town," Charles said. "Been here quite a while."

"You mean the *gangster?*" Walter said, glancing over his shoulder to see who might have overheard his comment.

"Saw him in the barber chair yesterday. Came in for his usual morning shave... Dressed to kill! Heard he's staying with the wife's family again over on the east end of Main Street," Charles said. "Not from around these parts, that's for sure. Ever seen him? Tan complexion, black wavy hair—looks like a foreigner."

"Seen him, though have yet to meet to the guy," Walter said.

The traffic outside the creamery moved forward. Slutter moved his unit under the single-vehicle, stilted wooden overhang, and bustled to unload his ten-gallon steel cans, then drove off. Walter pulled Maggie forward. The creamery owner, Tuffy Adams, approached to give him a hand unloading.

"What's new, Tuffy?" Walter said, grabbing the first can and, in one uninterrupted motion, swinging it from Maggie's rear to the new raised concrete slab along the side of the creamery.

"Business is sure good."

Walter was aware, after five years as owner, Tuffy had doubled his production of butter and cheese he sold to grocery stores in town and to locals. Still, creameries were competitive, and farmers picked one based on which paid the most for their milk and cream and highest percentage of profits at yearend. That decision came easy for Walter: The Oxbow Farmer's Creamery was where his father and grandfather had brought their milk.

"I'm on my way to Ed Schumer's place to give him a hand pulling a calf...the cow never had a problem before," Walter said.

Tuffy nodded. "Haven't seen Ed in here yet this morning. That probably explains it."

Walter hoisted the last can onto the platform and climbed back into Maggie. Leaning toward the open passenger window, he shouted at Tuffy: "Could be I'll be back with Ed's milk later."

As Maggie rolled past the creamery, Walter noticed the back-up of traffic included more humble Model Ts, plus several horse-and-wagon units, a few driven by Amish neighbors. Decades earlier, a small group of them had split from the Anabaptists by Cedar Rapids and relocated to the Oxbow area. Their numbers had increased substantially, just like the Germans, Irish and Swedes who'd settled here.

Walter steered Maggie east for three blocks south on Residence Street in the direction of Indian Town, the site of the town's Civil War monument. The woody area included a few shacks, including the residence of Dr. W. W. Wilson, the veterinarian. Walter noticed the absence of Doc's car.

He swung around to Fourth Street driving north; a block later took a left onto Main Street so as to pass by the entire four blocks of Oxbow's bustling storefronts, the same tour he took most mornings. On his left, Phil Riggs lifted the hose to handpump gas for a customer at Park Gas. Across the street, F.A. Klinger, manager of Chapman Lumber, examined a stack of planed oak with a customer. The Hotel Wiltse occupied most of the next block; next door was Minton Gas, both owned by Lucy and Jacob Minton. Across the street, two gents in suits, white shirts and ties gabbed outside the front door of the Brick Hotel.

Walter slowed Maggie at Second and Main to maneuver around the town's flagpole in the middle of the intersection. Passing Fats' Barber Shop in the third block, he detected Marshal Sweeney Delaney in the barber chair talking to a captivated audience, including the newly elected Mayor John Gardner. Sweeney was probably jawing about the fetus found on the riverbank in recent days, which reminded Walter he wanted to press Sweeney about the town's gangster who had now lingered in Oxbow for over a month. *Was he hiding out here? Might other thugs follow him? Was the community in danger?* he wondered. He'd catch up with Sweeney another time. Right now, he'd go directly to the Schumer place.

In the middle of the steel bridge, he checked the level of the mercurial Little Wapsipinicon River beneath, then glanced north past the log dam at the renowned island park, the scene of baptisms, picnics and amateur boxing matches, now only accessible by boat since high water washed out the pontoon foot bridge a few years earlier.

At this point, he turned Maggie loose, whisking past several west side businesses. Fifteen minutes later he pulled onto Ed's farm, parking next to Doc Wilson's car adjacent to Ed's immense red barn. He found the vet and Ed standing in a partitioned corner bay, the pen strewn with fresh hay and an awkward newborn bull calf nursing at its mother's teats.

"Morning, Walter," said Ed.

"I'm just finishing up, Walter," Doc said. "We almost lost both cow and calf. Probably shouldn't breed this cow any longer, Ed. She's getting up there in years. I need to get going now…got three other calls to make yet this morning."

"He's a real beauty," Walter said, brushing past the hind quarters of the calf still shimmering with sticky wetness.

"Thought I'd stop by to pick up your milk and take it into town, Ed. You've pretty much had your hands full this morning," Walter said.

"Job's already done… You probably crossed paths on the road with Barney Finkle. He stopped by earlier this morning."

Walter nodded.

"Noritta's got the coffee on at the house, got a minute?"

"Sounds good," Walter said.

The two had been friends since boyhood. Most farms in the township were about a hundred acres. Ed's farm was half timberland; nonetheless, he and Noritta made a decent living. Last year she inherited her father's farm near Westgate after her parents died suddenly, both from pneumonia. They'd found a good renter for the farm, and the extra income was welcome help after years of Victor's doctor bills. The outbreaks of anger, screaming and thrashing started when Victor was about three. He'd been back and forth to doctors. Ed and Noritta had even taken him to the Mayo Clinic in Rochester, Minnesota. Noritta believed Victor wanted to communicate and got frustrated he couldn't speak. She read to him, treated him as she would have treated any other child. He was learning, she was certain. How they loved the boy. Everyone could see he was the joy of their lives.

Noritta greeted Walter with her usual welcoming smile. Swinging wide the narrow front porch door, she motioned for him to pass into the kitchen.

"Morning, Walter! Saw you pull in… Drop Leonard off at school okay this morning? Can you believe our boys are starting fourth grade together? Sit down at the table next to Ed. I'll have your coffee to you in a second. Isn't it a beautiful day? God is good, isn't he!"

Walter nodded as he squared his body into the straight-back chair closest to the door.

"Shoulda taken off my boots in the porch. I've come from the barn."

"No worries, Walter. Any update on Emma's health?"

"She's still sickly, coughing, having trouble sleeping. She'll see Doc Ward again in a couple days if she doesn't improve. The Doc's good, but he's kept pretty busy with doctoring those Chicago Great Western men in Oelwein."

Walter watched as Noritta reached for dishes from a small wooden cupboard above the white cast-iron sink and set three cups and saucers on the table. A small plate with a few slices of Noritta's black walnut-zucchini bread followed, and a generous square of golden yellow butter on another, the same spread he had watched Emma put out countless times when neighbors called at their farm.

"Drop off Samuel anytime, Walter. I'm always here. And Victor's grateful for the boys' company on evenings, too."

For the next thirty minutes, Noritta replenished the cups with freshly perked coffee from the well-used pot on the cookstove, while the three talked about the prospects for the fall crop of corn and soybeans, gossiped about the progress of new farming techniques being tried by neighbors, finally getting around to considering the kind of president Herbert Clark Hoover, son of a Quaker blacksmith, would make. As head of the U. S. Food Administration, he'd been hailed worldwide as the Great Humanitarian for feeding war-torn Europe, and now Coolidge was recommending him as the next Republican president. Since Hoover was an Iowa-born boy, the choice seemed clear.

"Don't need to know about a person's religion, political party or anything else—character is integrity, morality, honesty and generosity. It's about how someone treats others, especially in the worst of times. Hoover will do well as president," Walter said.

He forked the final crumbs of bread from his plate to his mouth and pushed back his chair from the table before announcing: "Got to go. Thanks much for the coffee and bread. Emma will be in touch, Noritta."

Ed and Walter walked side by side toward the barn, parting company next to Maggie.

Mid-morning now, a hot southern breeze had come up to gently lift the black chariot, and soon would propel her homeward.

CHAPTER FOUR

Marshal Sweeney Delaney

Sweeney's day as town marshal normally started at one p.m. He had an hour off for supper, finished sometime around five or six in the morning, then went home to bed. Not today. It was nine a.m. and he was on his way back to his office in the city building. Reaching for the brass doorknob on the old weathered door, he could hear the vibrating silver bells at the top of the oak coffin box on the wall inside: two longs and two shorts, followed by another long. He had put a call into the police commissioner in Chicago after receiving a news bulletin a few days earlier, along with scads of alerts in the past month, seeking information about criminals wanted for questioning by Chicago police.

He lifted the receiver to one ear.

"Sweeney," he said.

"I have a phone call from the Chicago police commissioner," said Agnes Triggers, the operator from the Telephone Exchange next door.

"Thank you, Agnes," he said, waiting to hear the click on her end before proceeding, though he still couldn't be sure she wasn't eavesdropping. He once overheard her conversation with a local about a toggle switch that allowed her to listen in without anyone being the wiser.

Sweeney's first contact with Captain Michael Hughes, appointed police commissioner following the gang murder of the mobster Dion O'Banion, came in '27, shortly after he read a newspaper account where Hughes stated his plan to drive Capone out of Chicago and Cook County. That still hadn't come to fruition. Nonetheless, Sweeney thought it a gutsy edict at a time when allegedly half of those sworn to uphold and preserve law and order throughout metropolitan Chicago were getting graft payments from

19

Capone. His first call to the captain had been to probe for information about the mystery man who'd showed up in Oxbow, a guy with peculiar mannerisms and steely way about him. Sweeney and the captain had been in touch ever since.

"Hoping you could find the time to call me back, Captain Hughes. I've received the most recent police bulletins. Wondering if you can tell me who exactly might show up in Oxbow?"

"Wish I could tell you—unconfirmed yet who's involved in the O'Banion or McSwiggin killings. Capone's behind 'em, for sure! Mostly it's been the Italians and Irish involved in this bloodbath since about '23. Chicago police are especially interested in talking to the likes of Frank Nitti, Jake 'Greasy Thumb' Gusik, and Jack Zuta; plus 'Bugs' Moran, and the Aiellos—four brothers, plus a bunch of cousins, the last of O'Banion's Northside gang. You're getting all the picture profiles from the Buchanan County sheriff's office, right?"

"Got 'em lined up on the wall in front of me."

"Somebody new in town, Sweeney?" Captain Hughes continued. "Check out the bulging hip. Most use a shoulder harness with a .45. A smaller one in a coat pocket. More in other pouches. They get coats made special for them. Keep an eye on anyone standing around with one hand in a pocket. The heavy stuff—Tommy guns and sawed-off shotguns—those'll be in the back seat or trunk of a car.

"Gangsters looking to find a hole until things cool down scatter to big cities, but small towns like yours, too, any place they have a personal connection. In St. Paul, they offer safe haven to thugs, as long as they check in upon arrival and promise not to do their business there. And go to St. Paul they have! Did ya hear about the clever guys who put machine guns in a couple banjo cases then strolled around pretending to be musicians? Strolled right into a bank and robbed the place. No one was the wiser 'til the bullets started flying. Killed a police officer."

"I read about it," Sweeney replied. "They must stay up nights thinkin' about ways to pull off their next job. Some of them are likely bright guys—most of 'em, though, thick in the head."

Realizing the captain's call might go long again, Sweeney shifted the receiver to his other ear, dragged a nearby stool to the phone and sat down.

"Remember the Pole, Hymie Weiss, from a few years back? He engineered a way to make murder a real charismatic experience," Captain Hughes added. "Befriends a total stranger, and one day invites the guy to go on a nice ride in a stolen car. At some point: a bullet to the head. Called a 'torpedo'. Expect he gets upwards of thirty gran' per killin'. Yup, these are real nice guys. Get close enough to any of 'em and you'll see they have eyes like a dead carp.

"A lot of them are snappy dressers. Enjoy the opera, spend a quiet day at the horse or dog track, take in professional fights, baseball games, too. And real nice manners, like they went to some charm school. Things will likely get pretty hot in the next months… Hoover and the Bureau of Investigation have launched an investigation into gangster activity across the country. Guess someone in Washington ultimately got the message: there's a whole lot more of them out there than us good guys. Capone's the rising star on the Public Enemy list, along with another twenty-seven goons. Feds are really putting the screws to the big shot. Started following his every move, squad cars sitting nonstop outside his house and businesses. How's everything where you are, Sweeney?"

"My mystery man reappeared in Oxbow about a month ago—usually he's only in town a few days. Told you his wife's family lives here. Been watching him real close. Comes and goes from Chicago, New York, too. Keeps a low profile. Fits the description though. Any idea behind his extended stay in Oxbow?"

"Frank Yale is my best guess…some big mobster from New York who recently met his maker. Capone owned the guns police found in Yale's car…could be your guy is hidin' out in Oxbow after the killin'.

"One more thing—the Intelligence Unit recently sicced their bulldog Special Agent Frank Wilson on Capone, checking him out for tax evasion. Wilson has taken another look at the report filed by Chicago police back in May '25 when police raided a Capone gambling establishment, the Hawthorne Smoke Shop. Hauled away slot machines, roulette wheels, and a lot of other gambling and racketeering stuff, plus they seized a bunch of records, including a cloth-bound book, a kind of ledger. Special Agent Wilson found your guy was named in that police report as the one who'd phoned Capone during the raid. The big guy appeared in French silk pajamas under his trench coat, demanding police return all that expensive equipment, pronto. Your guy was listed as a bookkeeper and manager in the ledger. Likely he's doing other business for Capone. Be careful, be very careful, Sweeney."

"Manky! I'll keep a close eye on him. He stops in to talk to me on occasion during the night shift. On the surface, seems like a personable guy. Say, we got lots of bootlegging going on around here, too. Pretty much everybody's involved. A few guys got the monopoly. They think I'm not on to them, but most days I still need to get other parts of my job done. Like reading water meters."

"Right, right...but if you come across something out of the ordinary, don't try and take on some guy alone, Sweeney. Call Sheriff Harry Willey in Independence for backup. And call me if you hear of anything big happening. Winds of change are blowing. Lotta families moved out of Cicero for fear of being killed, and now the citizenry has had enough of Capone's stranglehold. The Feds are puttin' the pieces together. I believe Capone's indictment could be somewhere in the near future."

"Thanks for the call. Appreciate the update!"

Sweeney hung up the phone, rolled his body off the stool and walked to the slat back chair next to his desk and sat down. He pulled a Chesterfield from the pack in his shirt pocket, stuck one end of the white stick in his mouth, struck a match, and sucked until the tip glowed red. Intoxicating smoke flooded his lungs as he stared at the wall of shame across from his desk, contemplating the unsettling thought of coming face to face with any of the assassins staring back into his own baby blues. Most stunning was what he'd learned of his mystery man, Louie La Cava—a confirmed member of Capone's gang. More dangerous than he wanted to believe. Though the guy had the bulge. And eyes, such that when Sweeney peered deeply into them seemed void of any emotion.

Sweeney's mind wandered back to the day a dozen-plus years earlier when he'd been hired by the town council. Job description: town marshal and water superintendent. Salary: seventy-five bucks a month. Besides keys to the city building, engine house and well shed, he'd been assigned a nine-inch Biffar billy club and .38 Special snubnose revolver to carry at night. He still hadn't fired the gun except for a little target practice, whenever he could find the time.

The water meter book on the desk caught his eye. The meters would have to wait. He stood up, pulled down the cotton shade on the window and crossed to the door. Outside, the heat of the late August sun bore down on him as he twisted the long key in the lock. He would avoid Main Street this morning. It would take less than seven minutes to reach his house on Residence Street. He felt his billy club wobbling against his side and saw glimpses of white wispy smoke curling 'round his cheek and over his shoulder with each stride.

Home was the bottom level of a duplex on the town's south side. The in-laws lived upstairs. He kicked off his boots at the door and put the billy club, heavy leather gloves, and silver star from his shirt on the pretty tray on top of the refrigerator. On the stovetop, he found a covered dish of fried bacon, eggs sunny-side-up, and buttered toast. Olivia had gone to her job at the café; the girls were in school. He heated the coffee in the pot on the stove while washing his hands at the sink, then seated himself at the table and enjoyed his breakfast in silence. When every morsel had been consumed, he stacked the dirty dishes on the linoleum covered countertop next to the sink. Once more he revisited the tabletop to gently brush the crumbs with his left hand into his right one before depositing them in the wastebasket on the floor next to the cupboard.

In the bedroom, he found Olivia and Vanessa and the girls had made the bed after they crawled out. She'd remembered to lay out his cotton pajamas. His work clothes dropped to the floor. He picked them up, neatly folded each piece, set the pile on the straight-back chair by the bed, slipped into the pajamas, pulled back the soft-pink chenille bedspread and crawled between the crisp cotton sheets, feet over-reaching the foot of the bed.

A minute later he heard the neighbor's dog. *Judas Priest!* he thought. *That damn dog starts barking every morning as soon as I crawl into bed.* He rolled over on his side facing away from the open window, lace curtains hanging listlessly alongside its frame. For the millionth time, he wished the room had a southern-facing window to catch a breeze.

He waited for the Peters Grocery & Milk delivery wagon to pass the block. Silence prevailing once more, he soon floated off to that peaceful place, where only good guys triumphed in the world; kids had endless days frolicking outdoors in the sun; he was able to keep up with watering down Main Street, at least enough to keep business owners, and customers from complaining about the dust. And all the water meters got read, on time.

CHAPTER FIVE

Coffin Café

Olivia Delaney started work at the Coffin Café by six most mornings. Her attire: a freshly ironed and starched, loosely-fitted gingham print dress and fresh white apron tied tightly around her slender waist. White cotton stockings wrapped her thin legs, polished white shoes swathed her feet. Her hair was freshly styled like the prominent ladies in the township who came into the beauty shop. She worked there several days a month, too.

At age twenty, she and her family had relocated to Oxbow after living in neighboring states. They'd owned the Brick Hotel a couple times, living in a couple rooms in the back; traveling salesmen stayed in upstairs rooms. In time, the Telephone Exchange took over the east side of the Brick. She gained experience waiting tables there, then added working at the Wiltse across the street.

By the time she was twenty-five, she'd married Sweeney Delaney, a fallen-away Catholic, church never really his yoke, he said. They'd married at the Methodist church parsonage a few months before his thirtieth birthday. Sweeney had been born in a shack on the south side of town by the railroad tracks; his parents still lived there. His favorite pastimes were fishing, hunting, and ice skating on mill pond… He still enjoyed skating as much as the kids. A dozen years ago he became the town cop. Daughter Vanessa was born a year after they'd married. She'd hoped for more children, but Sweeney's job kept him away from home most days. They only saw each other at supper and on Sundays. He'd yet to miss a day of work for sickness, but talked about taking the family on a nice vacation.

He just couldn't think of anywhere he really wanted to visit.

A half-dozen men waited to enter the café by the time Olivia flipped the sign in the door window to OPEN. How she loved the gentle tinkle of the tiny black bell above the door that sounded each time a patron entered and left. Farmers wore overalls, plaid shirts and tall black boots; the Amish stood out in their plain blue or black garb, all smelling of barns, animals, and manure. Salesmen sported three-piece vested suits; neckties, short and mostly unseen; glossy polished shoes; and slicked-back hair reeking of tonic water. Almost everyone smoked, requiring Olivia to zigzag between booths, tables and counter in a thick fog; more so if smoke-ring competitions were underway to see whose was bigger and held together the longest.

Seeing the glass case on the counter was nearly empty, Olivia gathered plates and carried them to the kitchen for a refill of homemade dough-nuts and cinnamon rolls. She found her dear Aunt Gert scraping fried potato pieces, bacon grease and buttermilk pancake drippings from the grill. A twenty-cup tin pot of drip coffee sat on a rear burner. She'd stacked thick slices of smoked bacon and ham on a single giant platter. Within easy reach: salt, flour and sugar canisters; a heaping bowl of boiled white pota-toes; and cardboard trays of farm fresh eggs stacked four-high. Platters, bowls, cups and saucers balanced delicately on wall shelving. A side table cradled freshly baked loaves of crusty white bread at the ready of a sharp serrated knife, along with a large bowl of fresh yellow creamery butter, plus an assortment of jams and jellies. Toaster, too. Aunt Gert knew how people wanted their food: simple, cooked homestyle. Served by the sort of people they'd find at home.

"Busy day already," Olivia said.

"That it is! Temperature's not bad in this kitchen yet…can't think what it will be by noon; hope I don't pass out. I'm not as young as I used to be," Aunt Gert said, brushing her forehead eyebrow to eyebrow with a corner of her soiled apron.

"Sit down and take a rest now," Olivia urged.

Instead, Aunt Gert picked up a full coffee carafe, and handed it to her, saying: "Here, they'll be wanting a hot topping-off."

Olivia waited for her to take a seat on the stool next to the stove before returning to the dining room, replenished plates of pastry lining one arm, carafe in the other hand. As she pushed open the café doors, she heard the tinkle of the bell.

The first time Louie came into the café she knew him only as the mystery man. He lingered barely inside the glass door, the reverberations of the bell finishing as he scoped out the clientele, front to back. He wore a black fedora hat with its nice gutter dent, tipped forward on his head of thick black hair; dark suit coat and pants; white shirt and nice tie and clasp; a belt buckle that sparkled like diamonds. Stocky, about five-foot five, olive skin, late-thirties; a fat lit Cuban cigar between his thick lips.

He nodded and muttered a distant "good morning" to anyone who glanced in his direction, and that morning everyone had stopped everything to look at the stranger who'd entered the café. His was an edgy beginning in a town priding itself on friendliness. Olivia thought he had the presence of a wealthy man. She had looked around him to see if his big fancy black car was parked out front. It was there.

Today he took his usual seat in a booth at the rear of the café, facing the front door and the plate glass window overlooking Main Street.

"I'll be right with you, Louie," Olivia said, as she moved among patrons with the carafe and a small pitcher of cream. Most had finished their meal and declined another hit of coffee, though still finishing up the last morsels of prattle. Finally, she pulled checks from her apron pocket, fingered through them and placed each next to its owner.

"Appreciate the business, fellas," she said with a warm smile.

She moved to a spot behind the counter, where four of her regulars occupied red-capped stools, to top off their cups.

"What night should Sweeney expect you to stop by for poker this week?" she said. All had graduated high school with Sweeney. Most had town jobs—no farmers here. One was a maintenance man at the Chevy dealership. His clothes pretty much appeared to be clean but smelled of motor oil. Olivia knew some odors didn't come out with soap, even after a whole day of hanging in the sunshine. Another owned a hardware store, his gloves smelling of steel wire and cardboard boxes. She thought every trade came with an aroma. She could tell most days when Sweeney came home for supper if his day involved reading meters, or trimming trees around creosote electric poles, or greasing a water pump. Conversely, he could identify the café's daily specials lingering on her clothes and hair.

Once a week the guys played poker with Sweeney at the engine house, usually gambling long into the night. George Weiland reliably brought the booze. Sweeney often jailed at least one of them to keep from hurting himself, or others—and more often than not, it was George who got sozzled.

At last George responded for the group: "Tell Sweeney Friday night sounds good to us. We'll let Coach Peick know, too."

Olivia made her way to Louie's table. "What can I get for you this morning?" she said.

"Believe I take da special," he said, glancing up at the chalk board above the cash register. "Pancakes, eggs over easy, ham and toast. Coffee, too, please."

He had a strong trace of an Italian accent which stood out among the other ethnicities in the township. Since the first day he walked into the place, she looked forward to hearing him speak. Louie always smelled of witch hazel.

"I wonder you got da blueberry preserve dis morning, Olivia? Big spoonful onna pancake would be nice!"

"Out of the blueberries, sorry."

"Bring me whatever you got then. Next time you got blueberry, save me some. I pay ahead if you wish. Told Jess how big they are—real juicy, too."

She smiled and nodded while pouring his coffee, then deposited the cream pitcher on the tabletop, and pushed the sugar bowl toward him.

"Order up!" she said, tearing the order from the pad and sliding it across the counter toward Aunt Gert. Soon bacon drippings sizzled on the hot grill, a wide-enough swath to cook eggs, ham and pancakes side by side. Olivia detected a lineup next to the cash register and returned to the dining room to ring up orders. Each patron waited patiently as she counted out the exact change into a waiting hand. Since her first day working in cafés, she'd hoped for a tip. Anything. Nothing yet to report.

"Thanks for coming in," she said with an appreciative smile.

Most men acknowledged Louie before departing the café, tipping a hat if they'd worn one, saying: "Morning, Louie." He responded in kind, and seemingly made trite conversation about things Olivia was unable to overhear while moving about the café stacking dirty dishes.

"Got a copy of *The Oxbow View* here, Louie, if you'd care to glance at it," she said, aware they were now the only two people in the room.

"Sure, love to read," he said. She handed it to him before returning to the kitchen, noticing he quickly flipped to the back page for the I.C. Church's order of service. If he was looking for changes, he'd find none.

> *On all Sundays and Holy Days an obligation low Mass with sermon at 8:00 a.m., high Mass with sermon; Benediction of the Blessed Sacrament at 10:00 a.m. Confession every Saturday and on the eve of Holy Days at 8:00 p.m. Religious instruction for children not attending Catholic school every Saturday at 10:00 a.m. Other services during the year as announced on Sundays.*
>
> *Rev. John Halpin, Pastor*

Olivia reappeared with a large pan for depositing dirty dishes. Filled, she transported the dishes to the kitchen and exchanged the pan for a pail of hot soapy water and dishcloth to wipe down the booths.

"See inna paper da Opera House has new moving picture on Saturday, Olivia. Think daughter Vanessa like to go? Imma gonna take kids in town—anyone who want can come."

"She'd like that very much. That's very kind of you, Louie."

A familiar twinge of unrest came over her. How had she first learned of Louie? Sweeney had told her and the girls over dinner one evening he'd received a police bulletin, to "beware a man in the area who was part of a big mob, a bad man; he'd robbed and shot someone." Sweeney also passed the word to a few locals. Then a mystery man arrived in town on the arm of Josephine Necker, an area farmgirl. Word quickly spread of Louie's mobster ties, and at first people were really scared of him. He and Josephine attended I.C. Church, and it wasn't long before a few Catholics noted he was friendly, plus he hadn't caused any trouble.

At some point, the town kids probably endeared Louie to the adults. The first time he invited a few kids to the Opera House to see a movie, his treat, Vanessa had asked if she could go. "Absolutely not!" Olivia remembered saying. A week later, Louie stopped by the café. She dawdled at his booth that day, gazed into his face, and listened to him talk, about hunting pheasants, as she recalled. Something he said compelled a change of mind. Maybe she would let Vanessa give the movies a try, but with rules. Next time he invited the kids to see a movie, Olivia acquiesced. Still, it was never far from her thoughts: Louie was a killer and member of a gang—Al Capone's gang, she subsequently learned from Sweeney.

"I see advertisement," Louie said, reading portions of it out loud:

Warning—all intoxicating liquors strictly forbidden on this place at these dances. An officer will attend these dances.

Russell's Orchestra plays at the hall four miles west of Oxbow.

Ed Allen

"Ever go to dance, Olivia?"

"Heavens no, we're good Methodists—no dancing for us. You're in the heart of the Bible Belt of the Midwest, in case you didn't know. Interested in taking it in?"

"Ed Allen—he big time operator dis area?"

"Probably as big as they get. Pretty good turnouts, I believe... Converted a machine shed into a dance hall."

"Could be I check it out."

Olivia heard the hand bell go off in the kitchen signaling Louie's order was up. She retrieved the platter of food and placed it front of him and refilled his cup with hot coffee. "Get you anything else?"

"No, I good—dis look real tasty."

"Interested in the boxing matches while you're in town? Still held on Saturday nights in Oran. Charles Grantham at the Opera House has details. They started as street fights between Oran and Oxbow kids. Organizing the fights seemed a better way to let 'em get it out of their system. They get a different mix of kids every week—a few who just want to try the sport."

"I like fights with burly guys...Cash Ward, Neil King, "Dynamite" Dunn, Dutch Marsh. Merle Sharp, too—heard he got amateur Golden Glove Award."

"Here's your check... I'll leave it with you in case I get busy."

"Don't leave—I get for you now." He checked the bill, reached into his pocket, pulled out a few coins, and counted out the exact change into Olivia's waiting hand.

"Thank you, Louie. Have a good day!" she said.

CHAPTER SIX

Dirt Roads

Everything Jess love in life is at da end of dis dirt road, Louie thought, as he pointed the Lincoln in a southeasterly direction, buried the accelerator into the floorboard, and watched in the rear view mirror as Oxbow and the back half of the black car disappeared in a veil of grey powdery dust.

Her Christian name was Josephine; he'd shortened it to Jess. She and Mary, her sister, had been close all their lives, only a year apart in age, two among a dozen siblings. As young girls, Mary had insisted on waiting a year so the two could make the Sacrament of Confirmation together at St. John's Catholic Church. Over the years, they found toiling side by side, morning to dusk, on the family farm grueling work: caring for animals—milking, feeding, pitching manure, pasturing—birthing and burying, too, plus planting and harvesting crops, gardening and canning.

Jess told him how it happened she and Mary had run away from home: Shortly after dawn one spring day in their teens, while picking up rocks in a newly plowed field, Mary had asked Jess: "What would we do if weren't afraid to live own lives?" Their talk hatched a plan...to abscond, leave everything and go to Chicago. Jess later recounted...the idea emerge in fertile field, warm by da first rays of daylight, nourish by dewy dust at their feet.

Jess was poetic like dat in everything she said, he reminisced.

Mary was first to marry, meeting future husband Lawrence O'Malley at the drugstore where she found work. He slogged for the railroad and was the one to introduce the bashful Josephine to Louie. The two exchanged manacles a few months later. He was still vague at times about whether she fell in love with him, or with the rolls of dough he flashed back then. Initially, he thought her a bunny, an easy mark, naïve about things, like no one earns boatloads of money without getting on the wrong side of the law. After their wedding, he took her to live in a nice flat with his parents in Manhattan.

Lawrence got transferred to the big CGW railroad hub in Oelwein, when he and Mary bought a house in nearby Oxbow. Louie and Jess stayed with them when his travels took him to the Midwest, though usually he traveled alone. When Jess came along, the girls spent time at the ancestral farm, now inhabited by Joe and Rose and their brood.

Eighteen miles later, he pulled into Joe's farmyard by Independence. He parked the Lincoln a few feet from the windmill and lingered in the bucket a minute waiting for the dust to lift. Inside the house, he'd find Jess playing games with nieces and nephews. Not being able to have children had created a gulf between them. Whenever he had a disturbing dream that included Jess, it was about her having another miscarriage. Plus, she'd never gotten used to living in Manhattan. "Once a farm girl, always a farm girl," she would remind him.

Over the years, he tried to compensate, *poco a poco*, little by little.

He stepped outside the car. The creaking windmill triggered a look heavenward, where spinning blades at the top pulled cold water from deep within the earth and wooden troughs channeled the water to a tank by the barn. There, he noticed the tailgate of Joe's truck.

He began the hike to the farmhouse, passing beneath a spindly wooden trellis covered over by a blooming pink rose vine; and beyond that, across field boulders buried in the lawn leading to the front door. Jess mentioned their allure with each visit to her birthplace.

"Ciao!" he called out as he opened the porch door and stepped inside, first wiping his feet on the corded rug at his feet. From the dining room on the other side of the second door, he heard laughter.

Jess lifted her eyes as he entered the room, and immediately rushed over to give him a peck on the cheek. "What did you do with your day?" she asked warmly, reaching for his hand.

"Journal...errands...play cards at old tavern—da usual."

A rise of laughter tumbled out into the room from around the table where the kids and Mary played a card game. Louie eyed them, inquiring: "Whatcha playin'?"

Mary shouted out: "Crazy eights. Wanna play?"

"Believe will pass," he said. The children hardly looked up.

Rose called out from the kitchen, "Come on in, Louie…I'm fixin' supper. Joe's down at the barn. Should be back to the house in the next half hour or so. Lawrence and most of the rest of the clan are on their way. Make yourself comfortable."

"Think Jess and I drive back early. Will grab bite to eat at Mealey, then we stop see friend in Oelwein."

"But it's the weekend and the children are not in school. We planned to spend the evening together," Jess said.

"Sorry, Jess. Must finish up little business tonight."

"It'll only take a moment to get my things, Lou," Jess said, reaching for her purse on the old dish bureau. Then, taking a step in the direction of the kitchen, she spoke to Rose: "Lou and I won't be staying for supper after all. He has business in Oelwein. I'll return tomorrow, dear."

Rose emerged through the kitchen door. The two embraced. "It's okay, I understand. See you tomorrow, love."

"I don't understand why you have to leave right this very minute," Joe Jr. said, running to Jess and throwing his arms around her. The other children quickly followed his lead.

Lifting Joe Jr.'s face with her hand, Jess looked into his eyes. "I'm fortunate to have made the trip with Lou, with him being such a busy man and all. We have to settle for seeing each other when we can. I'll return tomorrow. Lou, how many more days do you expect we'll be here?"

"Few," he said.

"Well, goodbye for now," Jess said, staring into the cherubic faces of the children before turning toward the door. Louie followed on her heels, giving a hasty wave with a few fingers as he closed the door behind him.

Stepping out onto the lawn in the late afternoon sun, Jess stopped abruptly. Her attention was on the setting sun.

"Just look at that red sun. What does it mean, Lou? Doesn't red sun at sunset mean...'sailors take warning?'"

—

At ten forty-three that evening, Louie crept the stately Lincoln to a stop behind the O'Malley's flivver. He and Jess singly departed the car, meeting beyond the front bumper, where they joined arms and walked together in the moonlight across the lawn and up the porch steps.

They had ordered a fine dinner at the Mealey. Within minutes, the waiter seated an Oxbow family at a table next to them. Jess overheard the father instruct his children to look away and not to speak to them. Jess fell silent after that, but Louie believed inside she was probably screaming.

Louie released Jess's arm to unlock the O'Malley's front door. Inside, he keyed the lock again and set the deadbolt, before they tiptoed up the stairs to the back bedroom of the house. At the landing, she waited for him to pass into the dark bedroom. He stumbled forward, one hand extended, in search of the ceiling light cord dangling mid-air over the bed. He kicked a box of dishes at his feet.

"Mannaggia!" he said, a cuss word he knew she would not approve of.

When the light came on, Jess examined the contents of the box to see if anything had been broken, and indicated all was fine. Louie studied the jumble of boxes sitting along the floor's perimeter, packed with family heirlooms, pots and pans and dishes; a closed ironing board tilted warily along a wall; a pile of Lawrence's railroad rags in need of repair piled on a straight-back chair next to Mary's sewing machine; and next to that, a small table balancing a tray of thread, thimbles, needles, scissors, buttons, and the like. He was grateful whenever he managed not to upset that tray.

"Wish Mary would clean up da place," he whispered.

"It's not her fault the spare bedroom has to double as storage," Jess said, her whisper quieter than his. "You know Mary would rather concentrate on caring for people than having everything tidy and in order. It's a good trait—according to Jesus."

Louie removed his suitcoat, folded it in half and laid it across the end of the bed before walking toward the half-opened screened window facing the back yard. The scene included a two-seater outhouse next to the alley.

"And when will dis town get modern plumb? You not live in squalor in New York."

"Did everything go okay for you today, dear?"

"Yes, everything fine, fine," he said, returning to the other side of the room, passing between her and the foot of the bed, taking care to not scuff the polka dot heels on her feet.

At the closet door, he withdrew a clothes hanger before twisting around to reach across the bed for his suit coat. He saw his hat sitting on the bed, Instinctively, he bent down and wrenched the hat to his chest. He glanced at Jess. She thought it silly for grown man to believe putting a hat on a bed portends an early grave. But he'd experienced things she did not know of.

She stole to her side of the bed, lifted the pillow to retrieve her cotton nightgown, and pulled down the blanket and sheet.

"Lou," she said, in an agreeable tone, which meant she was about to make a sensitive request of him. "When you meet with Mr. Capone, as you do on occasion, I hope you use your influence for good. People who choose violence do so to get their own way, but Mr. Capone must be a very intelligent man who could run any other business he set his mind on."

His back to her, he let several seconds transpire before responding.

"I make you happy, Jess?"

"Why do you ask such a thing?" she said, turning her back to him as she changed into her nightgown.

"We not have children, as you would like, but we still have good marriage, no?"

"We've had many blessings, Lou, for which I am grateful."

When she finished dressing, she turned back around, took several steps in his direction, and reached for his face that she cupped in her hands. "I've been meaning to talk to you about a dream you had the other night. You were mumbling in your sleep, sweating…and your words were muffled, though it seemed like you were saying something about a man lying face down in a river. You were quite dazed, until I managed to shake you out of it. I'm wondering...if perhaps you have something on your conscience. Even if it's nothing, Lou, maybe it would be good for your soul to go see Father Halpin."

Louie turned away and walked to the sewing machine chair, where he draped his suit coat across its back and gently tossed the wooden hanger in a box on the floor.

"I will, Jess...soon."

"Are you going out yet tonight, dear?"

"I make plan with Francis Durham to go for short drive—he manage grainery by depot...only gone hour or so. He interesting fella. Know township like back of hand."

"Please don't wake me when you return. Rose's children really tired me out. I'm thinking...it's probably a good thing we didn't have children. I don't think you care to be around them very much at all."

—

Louie sprinted to the Lincoln. He noticed the evening air had grown rancid from the thick smell of manure coming from the stockyards just beyond the depot.

Francis lived in a two-story pink house on the northeast part of town. Louie crept the car into the driveway, leaving the headlights on and engine running as he lit a fresh cigar. Through the lighted kitchen window, he watched for movement. Several minutes went by before Francis emerged on the porch and roved to the car. He swung open the passenger door, bent down far enough to stick his head inside, and grumbled: "Are we still on for tonight? Thought you forgot all about me!"

"Not forget, Francis. Which direction I drive tonight?"

"Thought I'd show you old Indian Town," Francis said, climbing inside.

"What there?"

"Only a big piece of the town's earliest history. Take Fourth Street south 'til you pass by my Baptist Church, crossover the railroad tracks, take a left and after another block, you'll be there."

Louie spun the bus around and headed south.

"I stop by Hotel Wiltse today," Louie said. "Met Mrs. Lucy Minton. Real tough broad. Where she from?"

"Maiden name was Lacey, I believe. Her mother owned a hotel somewhere out east. The circumstances of how she ended up in Iowa are a mystery. But she did pretty well for herself considering she married Dr. Wiltse, part of a prominent family in Fayette, a town northeast of here. She talked him into building the hotel in Oxbow. Everything was going fine on the surface. After a few years, they divorced. Never did hear what provoked the split, but something sure-the-hell happened. I thought it might be because they never had any kids."

"Maiden name, Lacey?" Louie said. "I know Irishman in Manhattan, name Lacey…spirited mick for Worker's Union. Wonder if related?"

"Can't say. Don't know much more beyond what I've told you."

"Dis Indian Town?" Louie said, as he slowed the Lincoln in a desolate section of the township. Only a couple shacks skirted its northern edge.

"Park over there and turn your lights so they shine on the front of the Soldier's Monument. This part of the township is named after the Sioux, Fox and Ojibwe Indians who once had temporary settlements in Oxbow, at least as far back as 1855 when the village was organized. Oxbow in Ojibwe means 'u-shaped bend in the course of a river.'

"The names of the killed and missin' in action in the Civil War are listed before you on that monument. We lost a lotta good men from the township, those who stood face to face, but a few feet apart—our blue clad Union soldiers firing muskets loaded with lead balls at Confederates in grey. Dammed miracle anyone survived! Many who made it back home died weeks or months later from lead poisoning, disease or malnutrition. Still have a few old guys around here who never recovered from shellshock, not much good as husbands or fathers after the war, their wounds getting passed down to the next generations."

"I serve in Great War… War is great moral dilemma," Louie said. "Wonder how does government justify slaughter of native sons?"

Louie took a long drag on his cigar and expelled a thick cloud of smoke.

Francis began to cough and frantically cranked the window down, all the while nodding in agreement with Louie's statement.

"Ready drive on?" Louie said.

Francis took another minute to recover from his coughing jag before responding.

"I thought next you might like to visit a cemetery or two. While stories vary of how the deceased lived...in the end, everyone ends up laid out in a box, facing heavenward...ready to meet his maker. And while most say cemeteries contain the town's history, I say history doesn't lie in the past at all. We keep livin' it over and over and over, like God's hopin' at some point in His grand experiment we'll get it right!"

"You right 'bout history, Francis... lives of boys made and unmade by fate."

Louie slowly backed the Lincoln away from the memorial, stopping when the car lights fell onto a large buck deer staring from the edge of the tree line.

"You long-time friend with Sweeney?"

"Since we was kids."

"Sweeney ever break da law? Maybe, bootleg a little?"

"Nah, pretty much he's a straight shooter. Never saw him look the other way for anyone."

The deer disappeared into the trees. Again, Louie exhaled a large plume of smoke from the cigar and blew it in Francis's direction, and his hacking resumed with gusto.

"Will ya cut that out!" Francis said.

Louie reached over and patted Francis on the back, thinking: *Next time we take drive Chicago I point out graves down dark roads... Bet stories will make you squirm, Francis.*

"Which way I drive next?" Louie said.

"Go back the way you come from!" Francis said, still sucking in fresh air from the open window.

CHAPTER SEVEN

The Arrangement

Walter had read enough novels by Charles Dickens to know that an awful lot of his characters died of illness; tuberculosis, in particular. Emma's condition steadily worsened. Night sweats. Fever. Doc Ward prescribed bed rest; said to be careful not to cough near Walter or the boys. She'd begun to cough up blood. He made another appointment with Doc for four o'clock on Thursday. They'd drop Samuel at the Schumers' farm, and Walter thought her spirits might be lifted if she shopped for a new dress at Leehey's beforehand, if she felt up to it.

"I do feel a little stronger today, Walter," she said. "I think it's a sign I'm getting better. And shopping for a dress, what a lovely thought."

He finished part of his evening farm chores before the three of them boarded Maggie and headed to Oxbow.

"Will you die?" Samuel said, looking intently into Emma's eyes from his seat on her lap.

She looked with bewilderment at her younger son.

"Why no, Samuel. What makes you say such a thing?" she said in her softest voice, wrapping her arms around him and pulling him close.

"Leonard said Gina's momma died."

Walter knew what he had heard was true. Every day, since Leonard began attending I.C. school, he came home bubbling over with news of his new classmates. Gina Bundy, a girl from Oran, told him her mother had died, and she and her brothers lived with a grandmother. Gina sometimes cried at school. The story had saddened one and all.

"No, mommy is going to be fine. I have a cough, and Doc Ward is going to give me medicine to help me feel better."

"Okay—will you bring me candy from town then?" Samuel asked.

"We sure will, and some for Leonard and Victor, too."

Noritta was watching from the porch as Maggie pulled into the farm and quickly made her way to Emma's side of the car. Samuel nearly flew into Noritta's arms as the car came to a stop and the door opened. In recent months, he'd come to know the Schumer farm almost as well as his own. Victor's tricycle, still practically new, had become Samuel's favorite toy. He called the three-wheeler, "Maggie." And Victor was a calmer child whenever Samuel was his play companion.

"Come into the house, Samuel. We're going to have cookies and milk then walk to the barn to see the new bull calf. We still haven't named him—what do you think we should name him? He's going to be a big bruiser!"

Walter interrupted, "We should pick up Samuel by five-thirty or so, Noritta. I told Leonard to walk downtown after school and we'd meet him at the Bon Ton. What are your plans for picking up Victor from school?"

"Ed will do that...take your time. We'll be thinking of you, Emma, at Doc's today...saying the rosary several times a day just for you. God will hear our prayers, you wait and see."

In town, Walter parked Maggie along the west side of Leehey's Cash Store in the first block of East Main Street.

"I don't believe I've been in the store to shop for a dress since Samuel's baptism. I love seeing the latest fashions. A dress in the window has caught my eye," Emma said.

Owner Michael "Bee" Leehey and Mrs. Crawley, the dress saleslady, saw Emma and Walter approach from the boardwalk, and greeted them as they entered the store. Bee's wife, Georgiana, taught at the public school.

"Glad to see your sunshiny face again, Emma," Mrs. Crawley said, trying not to appear to notice Emma's pale complexion and thin frame. "Looking for something special today?"

"Walter has decided it's time for a pretty frock, Mrs. Crawley," Emma said, raising a hankie to cover her mouth as she spoke.

Mrs. Crawley directed Emma across the expansive wooden floor of the mercantile store to the ladies' apparel section next to dry goods.

"Come over here and let me show you what we've got. The hemlines are a little shorter these days. Flapper dresses are popular. I can order from a catalogue out of New York or Chicago, but don't have any in the store to try on."

"Nothing too fancy for me. Something nice for church is all I hope for, the normal price range. I kind of like the one in the window. Where do I try it on?"

"Follow me," said Mrs. Crawley, directing Emma toward the rear of the store.

Walter stepped back out onto the boardwalk to take in the view of the island park across the way. Bee quickly followed.

"Too bad there's no way to get over to the island these days except by boat," said Walter. "Emma loved our picnics...the boys too. My father told me the story of the day they dredged the river in that spot. He said: 'The island just appeared out of nowhere.'"

"True story," Bee said. "And hopefully we'll get a new walk bridge soon. Charles Grantham tells me he's working on a design...only needs funding."

Walter and Bee walked back inside just as Emma emerged from the dressing room.

"I think I like this one, Walter—what do you think?"

"Soft pink is your color, Emma, and nice lace. Still the beautiful woman I married."

"But I'm afraid it's a lot of money," Emma whispered to Walter.

He found the price tag dangling from the cuff and examined it.

"That's exactly what I planned to spend."

"Well then, I'll take it, Mrs. Crawley. I'll change back into my dress. Will you wrap it up? We'll wait to take it with us."

Mrs. Crawley soon returned with the dress. Bee wrapped it in brown paper, bound it neatly with white string, and set it on the counter in front of Walter.

"Thank you for your fine help with my lady," Walter said, taking out his wallet to pay the invoice.

He checked his timepiece, noticing they still had a few minutes before Emma's appointment. When she returned to his side, the two departed the store. He dropped off the dress at the car then guided her across the way to the river's edge.

"Come and look at the island park, Emma. Sounds like maybe there might be a walk bridge to the island by next summer, so we can continue our family picnics."

"That would be nice...the boys so love to play and fish there."

Standing along the Wapsie's eastern bank, they listened to the quiet hum of the tributary to the Mississippi River, and watched the light of the afternoon sun scatter and reflect in its gentle flow. A few yards down river, water plummeted over the twelve-foot-high log dam and splashed into the pool below.

"That river is certainly calm today," Emma said. "Wouldn't it be nice if it meandered full and wide like this year-round?"

"Oh, Emma, that's the beauty of life. The ebb and flow. The changing seasons. The prosperity and lean times. It's all a gift, don't you see? A beautiful thing is never perfect."

"Walter, you are so wise... How I treasure every day we've had together. You are my prince. You truly are my prince."

"And, Emma, you are my beauty, my everlasting beauty. Whom I treasure beyond all else."

Walter lifted the face of his timepiece once more. "Emma, look at the time! School's been let out... Let's wave to Leonard and call to him as he crosses over on the bridge."

Moments later, the first of the Catholic children appeared from the west, keeping to the south side of the bridge. Then came the public school kids from the east, traversing the bridge's north side.

Walter's grandfather had told him of the arrangement put in place soon after the turn of the century. One day on the center of the bridge, a Protestant child allegedly had taunted a Catholic child: "You're going to hell, Catholics! Worshiping Mary instead of God!"

"What would you know about God, Luther lover?" a Catholic boy said. "You'd know nothing about God if it wasn't for us Catholics!"

Words turned into hurled rocks. Brawls erupted. Children hitting, kicking, hurting one another, all under the banner of faith.

Eventually a town order was put in place: Catholics would walk home from school on one side of Main Street; Protestants on the other. Eyes straight ahead. Go home, go straight home. Don't talk about religion when in mixed company. Stay within your own group.

Thus began the uneasy truce in Oxbow. People carefully negotiating every conversation and bond, intolerance just under the surface. Like circumventing a flag cemented in the middle of Main Street.

In the glow of the afternoon sun, Walter and Emma spied Leonard's slender frame on the bridge and Walter called out to him.

"Leonard, we'll meet you later at the Bon Ton."

Leonard waved, and shouted: "See you there!"

Walter intended to add…and we'll plan to throw a few balls as soon as we get home, but Leonard was quickly out of earshot. Baseball was important to the boy, though he sure wasn't in the right school to realize his dream of becoming a pitcher the likes of Sweeney Delaney. Still, Walter was determined to do whatever he could for the boy.

Nearing four o'clock now, they headed to Doc Ward's office. Walter helped Emma climb the steep, shaky outside stairs to the top floor of the old grist mill. Twice she stopped to lean up against its heavy timber frame, wheezing to catch a breath.

At last they reached Doc's door. Walter turned the old brass doorknob and the two stepped inside. The room was lit only by the rays of dusty sunshine pouring through a single-paned window, and smelled of antiseptic, ground corn and old timber.

"Good to see you, Emma. How are you doing today?" Doc Ward said, calling to her from the room beyond a second set of doors.

Walter held steady to Emma's arm as she teetered toward Doc and climbed onto the examination table.

"Why, I believe I'm feeling a little better," she said, raising her hankie to her lips as she spoke.

"That's great. Let's just take a look at you now."

He placed his stethoscope on her chest and listened, then moved it several times, front to back, and listened a few minutes longer.

"Your heart sounds labored, and I hear congestion. Any new symptoms, Emma?"

"Sometimes I cough up a little blood...that's not bad is it? I mean, that's gotta happen when you cough as hard as I do from time to time. I've had a little fever off and on, mostly I'm really feeling better today."

"Been getting your rest like I told you? And keeping your coughs contained?"

"I have...I truly have. All of it!"

Doc turned to Walter. "I'm afraid I don't see any improvement. I'm going to suggest a sanatorium, one in Waverly Hills. I've heard good reports. The sooner Emma goes, the faster she can get the treatment she needs."

"But what's wrong? What's your diagnosis...influenza, consumption? "

"I think Emma has tuberculosis, though it'll take a month before tests come back to confirm. A place like Waverly Hills is the best place for her right now. It's her best remedy."

"Well, Doc, that's not what we were expecting to hear. Emma says she's feeling better. How can this be?"

"She'll likely feel worse not too far down the road. It's time to make a plan to help regain her health. This has been going on a long time. I've seen other cases. If you catch it in time...."

"We can't afford a sanatorium, Doc," Emma interrupted.

"We can! I've saved some money. Emma, we can do this, " Walter said.

"Thanks, Doc," Walter continued. "Make the arrangements and let us know when we need to get Emma there...but where exactly is she going? Waverly Hills... Is that near here?"

"It's in Kentucky in the Cumberland Mountains. Patients spend their days outside in the sunshine. It's rejuvenating. In the winter, they sit in glassed-in porches. Special diet too. It may take a year or more."

"We should go now," Walter said. "We are meeting Leonard at the Bon Ton."

"Wish I had better news, Emma," Doc said. "I know it'll be hard to be away from Walter and the boys... I'm afraid your family won't be able to visit."

Walter helped Emma down from the table, and together they tottered back down the outside stairs and across the street to Maggie.

"We'll get through this, Emma," Walter said. "Now let's go see Leonard and have some ice cream."

He drove Maggie east two blocks to the Bon Ton where Leonard was pacing along the boardwalk.

"What did Doc say?" Leonard said, as Walter finished parking the car.

"We'll talk about that after we have some ice cream, doesn't that sound good?"

Inside the Bon Ton, Leonard quickly announced to Vera Cummings: "I'll have a chocolate sundae, please."

Vera had worked at the Bon Ton the last couple years. Everyone knew her for her tenacity on the girls' basketball team. She was one of Coach Gayle Peick's girls.

"And, I'd like a cherry on top, or could I have two?" Leonard added, matching his request with a giant smile.

"We'll all have the same," Emma said, being careful to remain several feet back from the counter.

"Order coming right up...two cherries on top!" said Vera.

"Plus, we're going to need some of that licorice in the jar... Put a few pieces in three small bags," Emma said.

Mr. Bill Biggs, the baker, appeared from a curtained doorway at the back of the store, and hastily interjected himself into the room and conversation.

"And put four of those bakery items left over from this morning in another bag."

Mr. Biggs was a large man whose waistline had grown incrementally month by month since under the employment of Ed Allen, the Bon Ton manager. "It's a hardship of the job," Mr. Biggs one day had readily acknowledged to Walter. "Being around food all the time makes one fat."

But Walter knew Biggs also liked to dispense a little mischief from time to time, though it was hard actually pinning anything on him.

"Been to see Doc Ward today, Emma? How 'ya feelin'?"

Walter glanced at Emma, who always seemed surprised how quickly news spread in a small town.

"I'm somewhat improved, I believe. Thank you for asking…and thank you kindly for the treats."

Then, feeling a coughing attack arising in her chest, she asked Walter to take her outside to the boardwalk.

Mr. Biggs rushed to open the door, watching through the window as she coughed and hacked, her frail body struggling to catch a breath.

Walter was certain Mr. Biggs wondered what she was coughing into her hankie with the delicate tatted edges. He hoped that Mr. Biggs, strain as he might, could not see.

—

Edging Maggie past the I.C. Church marquee, Walter caught the words, scribed in Latin, which he knew preempted the homily for Sunday Mass: "The Catholic Church is above the Bible."

The Catholic Church dominated in size amongst the other churches in town, boasting of 130 families and 600 German and Irish communicants when they organized. The Lutherische St. Johannes Germeinde Church, organized about the same time, located on the far north end of Fourth Street, had half the membership. The Methodists and Baptists laid hold to the rest of the consciences of the people in the township, and beyond.

Normally Walter dropped off Emma and the boys near the front steps of the Catholic church before continuing on to the Lutheran Divine service, which also started at ten. But today he and Emma would first speak to the priest to arrange a time for Father Halpin to come to the farm, as there was much to consider before Emma's departure. The priest said he'd watch for them outside the main entrance.

The rear car doors flew open almost before Maggie's wheels came to a stop. The boys quickly skipped ahead, disappearing inside beyond the massive wooden double doors. Together Emma and Walter walked toward the priest. Walter couldn't help but notice the very tall nun next to the priest.

"Good morning," Father Halpin said. "Heard, Emma, you've been to see Doc Ward about going away for a time to regain your health. I'd like to stop by first thing Monday morning, if it's all right with you."

"That would be most comforting, Father, wouldn't it, Walter?" she said, keeping a small distance between herself and the priest.

"It would indeed…what about ten o'clock?"

"Now that's settled, let me take a moment to introduce you to Sister Keith, who's been sent to us from the Archdiocese of Dubuque," Father Halpin said. "Sister Keith will be one of the nuns teaching fourth-through sixth grades. I'm certain Leonard is going to like her very much. And I do hope it won't be long before Samuel joins his brother at the school. Country school can't give him what Catholic school can offer."

"Nice to meet you, Sister Keith," said Walter and Emma, almost in unison.

"I look forward to helping Leonard progress in his studies, and I should also like to join Father Halpin when he comes to your home tomorrow, if it would be all right. Your illness has been a hardship for all of you. I'd like to help where I might—a woman's touch, you know."

"That really won't be necessary, Sister," said Father Halpin.

"Why, I'd appreciate it very much," Emma said. "What a nice gesture."

The Schumers approached just as Sister Mary Margaret, the school principal, took her place next to the priest. The sister was the priest's timekeeper for Mass, alerting him when it was time to put on his vestments and to make other final preparations.

Before departing, Father Halpin made the introductions. "Sister Keith, I'd like you to also meet Ed and Noritta Schumer—and their son Victor. Their farm is near the Bierkoff's, west of town."

Victor stood between his parents, his eyes fixated on the vigorous movement of his hands and fingers cupped together at his waist.

"I'm very pleased to meet you, though I've already met Victor. I would like to schedule a time, if you agree, to begin to meet with you in advance of school conferences, as I have some ideas for your special requirements."

"I would like that very much," Noritta said.

Father Halpin and Sister Keith walked back inside the church, as Sister Mary Margaret continued to greet those already at the door, keeping the line moving, in full accordance with her stern, brash reputation.

"Good morning, Mr. and Mrs. Schumer," Sister Mary Margaret said, pausing briefly, then adding, "and may I take this moment to remind you Victor continues to cause a lot of disruption in the classroom and impedes the learning of other students. You really should institutionalize him. He can't learn like normal children, as you well know."

"Morning, Sister," Noritta said, as she and Ed held fast to Victor's hand and pushed past the sister into the vestibule. Stopping at the holy water font, she realized she'd forgotten her veil, and pulled a fresh white hankie from her black purse and placed it atop her head.

The boys reappeared at Emma's side, and Walter directed them to a pew along the back wall of the nave. There, he lingered for a few moments longer. He had spied a big black Lincoln parked beneath the row of bur oak trees in the parking lot, and now scanned the backs of heads and shoulders of kneeling, faceless figures hoping for a glimpse of the gangster.

Instead, above the parishioners he glimpsed the statue of Christ on a gilded cross strung high above the altar; then another, a near-life-size of the blue-mantled Blessed Virgin Mary set closer to the people, with Joseph close by. His eyes moved to the weighty ornate altar made of stone covered with an altar cloth, and on it—the Lectionary, illuminated with candles on eighteen-inch gilded candelabra. Behind them, the tabernacle.

Large frescoes adorned the ceiling and walls of saints, apostles and others: Mary and Martha, a virgin and an old woman—two implausible mothers; Joseph bringing Jesus as an infant to the Jewish temple; the stable scene at the birth of the Christ Child; Jesus teaching as a child at the temple; the appearance of Jesus on the Emmaus Road. Along the side aisles were fourteen figurines, the Stations of the Cross, illustrating the story of Christ's crucifixion. Immense rectangle windows made of colored shards of glass let in refracted light, as music floated from the rear balcony, where a soprano voice sang a Latin chant.

Finally, the priest crossed over the rail into the sanctuary, his back to the people, and he began to say Mass in Latin. It brought to mind the day Walter and Emma had spoken their marriage vows, the ceremony taking place in the rectory, the only place a Catholic and a Lutheran were permitted to marry. It was a day like this, a hot August day... *I, Walter Bierkoff, promise to Almighty God, to the Blessed Virgin Mary, to St. Joseph, and to all the saints, and to you my love...*

His eyes filled with tears...his Emma, his dear, dear Emma...

Mass now underway, he turned to leave, just as Sister Mary Margaret prepared to close the front doors. Abruptly two silhouettes materialized in the doorway before the glare of the golden morning sun, a single hand appearing first, resisting the closing door, then a hatted man and woman hastily entered.

"Good morning," Sister Mary Margaret whispered. "We're happy to see you. Shall I tell Father Halpin when he might expect you to make confession while you're in town, Louie?"

"Morning, Sister," both responded while sweeping past the sister.

Walter's eyes were still adjusting as the two shadowy people vanished into the interior. He pushed through the partially open door. The heat of the day swiftly encrusted his wetted cheeks. In the background, he could hear the priest speaking from the lectern.

"The New Testament reading is taken from Galatians 1:15-16. Paul was a Pharisee, from the isle of Cyprus, who had not personally known the living Christ, as had the apostles; but God gave Paul a vision, and Paul, obeying, without consulting with the apostles, took the gospel to the Jews and Gentiles as the fulfillment of Christ.

"Thus, the Word was carried throughout the world. Protestants eventually accepted the Bible, observed the Sunday Sabbath, and in keeping Christmas and Easter, thereby accepted the authority of the spokesman for the church—the Pope. Sunday is our mark of authority... The Catholic Church is above the Bible, and the observance of the Sunday as Sabbath is proof of that fact."

CHAPTER EIGHT

At The Opera House

Olivia's faith informed her people are basically good, and everyone has a monster within. The difference was in the degree. That's how she'd reconciled living her life in a town with good people, whose actions on any given day were often misdirected, sometimes senseless, obnoxious, even immoral. What surprised her was her faith in mankind overflowed to a gangster...believing, over time, the good people of Oxbow would bring out the good in him.

Whenever Louie was in town, he told the kids to pass the word in his broken-English, sprinkled with an occasional Italian word: "I take any *bambino* to cinema Saturday night—I pay!" He could be hard to understand any day, but the kids seemed to know what he meant, even if he slipped and spoke entirely in his native tongue: "*Prendo ogni bambino al cinema sabato sera, pago!*"

The boxy two-story Opera House had entertained families since 1894. Its current owners, Charles Grantham and his wife, Bethel, kept the house immaculately clean. Charles was passionate about showing movies. On the day of the flick, he'd preview it on the projector to remedy any broken pieces with banana glue.

Vanessa, intrigued by the projectors, frequently stopped by to see what Charles was up to, one time inquiring, "Did they really make that glue out of bananas?"

"No. It's just a glue that has an odor of bananas. Some think it also smells like pears," Charles had said.

At least a half-dozen eager boys and girls typically showed up outside the O'Malley house by 6:30. Regulars included Vanessa Delaney, Emmett

Durham, Vera Cummings, and Mary Curley, whom Vanessa considered Louie's favorite.

As soon as Louie joined them on the lawn, the group shifted to the center of Main Street to begin the five-block trek to the Opera House. Theirs was a peculiar parade: Louie with his strut in the center of the mix, in a three-piece suit and fedora hat, puffing away on a chunky cigar, amidst encircling car and horse-and-buggy traffic. Along the way, people stopped whatever they were doing to stare, but that's how he had walked downtown since the day he first arrived in the village.

The bizarre display reinforced the impression he was a gangster, a man who feared he might have been followed from Chicago by the mafia and sought fortification of the town's children. He also had bulges, though no one had confirmed actually seeing a gun in the holster under his arm, the one in the right front trouser pocket, or another in the left outside coat pocket. Vanessa did tell Sweeney once she thought she might have seen the butt of Louie's holster gun, but couldn't be sure. And Emmett reported: "I once saw a machine gun in Louie's trunk, I think."

Inside the doorway, Miss Lil Thompson, a spinster, sold ten-cent tickets in a booth from behind a makeshift banker's window. Ticketholders followed the steep wooden staircase to the top floor which opened to an oak-floored auditorium, holding rows of wooden folding chairs seating a hundred. At the foot of the walled screen, Miss Vera Damge, the town's piano virtuoso, seated on the bench before an upright black piano, awaited a cue from Charles to begin playing. Each film came with special sheet music... soft and tinkly for the romantic scenes, bold and raucous for the dramatic ones. Mostly she played from the page, though she improvised throughout the film without anyone being the wiser.

Vanessa and her friends sought the best seats directly in front of the screen, and Louie never defected from plugging himself in the middle of the group. In time, the house lights went down, replaced by the flicker of the projector light, and up came the music from Miss Damge's slender fingers gliding across the ivories.

If Louie La Cava was fearful of being followed in the dark shadows and molested by individuals ready to do him harm, he was correct in thinking so. There were those who bought a ticket at the very last moment and took a seat at the rear of the auditorium, their children never out of sight. Olivia was among them. She made no bones about it: trust had to be earned.

The grainy gray newsreel began, its stories told through title cards:

∞ *China is still reeling following the May 1927 earthquake measuring 8.6 on the Richter scale, killing 200,000. The Chinese Autumn Harvest uprising followed, with Chinese gun batteries attacking British and U.S. shipping. The rebellion shows no end in sight.*

∞ *In January 1928, Joseph Stalin expelled Leon Trotsky from the Communist Party and took control in Russia.*

∞ *In February 1928, The Olympic Winter Games will be held in St. Moritz, Switzerland.*

∞ *In the United Kingdom, the Spanish influenza epidemic, which a year earlier killed a thousand people a week, finally is subsiding—the same disease, during the Great War, which led to fatalities of fifty to one hundred million, more than the war itself.*

∞ *In America, work is beginning on Mount Rushmore. Amelia Earhart publicized plans to become the first woman to successfully fly solo across the Atlantic Ocean. And Agent Eliot Ness now leads the F.B.I. Prohibition unit in Chicago.*

∞ *And coming soon to American theaters everywhere: 'Metropolis,' which debuted in Berlin, Germany—a science fiction film conspiracy revolving around an ultramodern Utopian city where all was not as it appeared.*

Eventually the box office hit "It" commenced and the movie-goers settled in. Clara Bow, playing Betty Lou Spence, a young woman from a small town arrived in the big city with big dreams, and adeptly found employment as a shop girl…and just as fast, fell in love with store owner Cyrus Waltham, Jr., played by the handsome Antonio "Tony" Moreno.

Olivia's rule for Vanessa about going to the Opera House with Louie was simple: she had to come straight home at the movie's end. And by the time she walked through the kitchen door, Olivia was back home seated in the stuffed arm chair in their tiny living room, appearing to have been enjoying a few moments of quiet time to read a book, only lifting her head at Vanessa's appearance to inquire, "What movie did you see tonight, dear?" Then for the next hour, she listened as a giddy young girl carried on about her bee's knees night out with friends, and Louie.

"I know exactly the next dress I want to buy," Vanessa exclaimed. "One like Clara Bow wore tonight. And I'll paint my nails, not red, of course, as that would be far too bold, and I wouldn't do that for Sunday church, because when I play piano for the Sunday school hour, I don't want to take anything away from worship of God."

Vanessa's ramblings transported Olivia's thoughts back to the day when Vanessa was in third grade and John Youngman's red pickup delivered an upright walnut piano to their house, after which Vanessa started taking piano lessons. Now, she played for the Methodist church services, and in her first year of high school would accompany small groups, instrumental and vocal soloists. She'd also started playing basketball for Coach Peick, though he required her to wear a wire mask because of her eyeglasses. This was one embarrassment; the other was Olivia's requirement Vanessa had to wear a union suit, long cotton underwear with a trap drawer in the back. Vanessa soon realized her classmates didn't have to wear long underwear beneath their school dresses, so she began hiding hers under her mattress. Olivia found it one day when turning the mattress, and never again insisted Vanessa had to wear one.

On that day, Olivia realized, Vanessa's life had gotten easier.

Vanessa stopped speaking at some point, realizing Olivia's mind was elsewhere. Eventually Olivia returned her attention to her daughter, saying, "Before I forget to tell you, dear, whenever you go to the movies with Louie, try not to sit in the seat right next to him. You should give him a wide berth, so he can really enjoy the picture."

—

Departing the Opera House, Walter and Leonard claimed a spot on the boardwalk just beyond the front door. He had seen Louie La Cava inside the theater, a bad person relying on the acquiescence of simple virtuous people to allow him to continue with his immoral ways.

Well past twilight now, Walter pointed out the fireflies glowing in ripples a few feet off the ground next to the bridge along the river.

"It appears from the movie people live differently in the big city than we do—huh, Leonard? Take those fireflies…I imagine Clara Bow doesn't have any of those bugs where she lives."

"I would imagine there are lightning bugs everywhere in the world, wherever there is water, Father," Leonard said.

The house emptied and movie-goers swarmed the boardwalk. Walter convinced Leonard to move to a space under the corner streetlight, where Reverend Van Benschoten, the Baptist preacher, held firmly to the collar of his yellow Labrador.

"Good evening, Walter," said the Reverend, scrutinizing father and son.

"Surprised to see you outside the movie house, Reverend," Walter said.

"I walk my dog most evenings and pass by this way…part of my job as spiritual leader of my flock. I say: 'Every coin spent on seeing a movie puts money directly in the pocket of the devil.'"

His oration was abruptly halted by a violent coughing spell.

"Emma and I went to see Doc Ward this week. He informed us Doc Logue's been treating you for a bad cough for months," Walter said.

"Got acute bronchitis. Doc wanted to give me a prescription for whiskey…said it would also be good for my heart. But true to my principles, and a good Prohibitionist myself, as God is my witness, I refused the stuff. People have known me to walk into taverns and dancehalls, Lizzy at my side, the men putting down their drinks when I show my face, out of respect, I imagine. Doc Logue, being understanding, wrote a prescription. Next day our own pharmacist Clara Fenne delivered to the parsonage a medicine bottle filled with green liquid. I faithfully take several teaspoons every day. I admit it's helped with the cough and I seem to sleep better."

"Heard the green mixture's been prescribed for others. What'ya think is in the stuff?" Walter said.

"Mostly water, sugar and a little food coloring," the Reverend said with a chuckle.

"Say, Leonard…my wife and I organized a Boys' Brigade to teach resourcefulness. Started after the Great War, because it seemed an awful lot of young lads who went off to fight didn't even know basic wilderness survival skills."

"Commendable, but we'll have to think about the brigade. Leonard keeps pretty busy between school and the farm," Walter said.

"My own boy signed up to serve in the U. S. Army—behind my back; knew I forbid it! I refused to speak to him the day he left," the Reverend said, his voice dropping off. "Never saw him alive after that. Then I became an enthusiastic supporter of the troops and war effort. Now I teach survival skills."

"I imagine one never gets over losing a son," Walter said. "I felt the same way about our nation's involvement in the war, but ultimately, we got caught up in it, too…the war to end all wars.

"Next, the U.S. Congress deemed we should try for utopia…sobriety for one and all. But it sure doesn't appear Prohibition was very well thought out. Seems the government chose to close down the huge alcohol production industry…and give it to criminals. They sold us on Prohibition as a patriotic, grain-saving measure. But an awfully lot of perfectly good corn has gone into stills."

"It's probably done more to hasten the revolution in decay of manners and morals than at any other time in history," the Reverend said. "Real change begins at conversion. The Baptist church's got a big baptismal tank inside. Immersion of a man or woman in that water, infused with the mighty workin' of the Holy Spirit, and full submission to the Lordship of Jesus Christ. Well, the combination has the powerful potential to turn any a life around for good."

"I've heard it's happened," Walter said.

"Hate to cut this short, but the missus is waitin' up for me. Nice seeing you, Walter. We have a missionary coming. Watch for the advertisement in the paper."

The Reverend and his dog hastily moved outside the glow of the streetlight and vanished into the black night.

Walter and Leonard observed the last stragglers emerging from the movie house, a cluster of animated high-schoolers, followed by Louie La Cava.

The troop came to a halt near the edge of the boardwalk.

"Hi, Leonard!" Mary Curley called out from the group.

"Hi Mary," Leonard said. "It was a good movie—did you like it?"

"It was a darb! How's your mom doing?"

"She's doin' pretty well...hopin' to hear more from Doc Ward soon."

"Well, I'll see you at school on Monday," she said, before returning to her unit.

Walter watched as La Cava appeared to scan the surrounding area, then heard him call out, "Pronto!" apparently the signal for the small band to begin the walk home.

"Walk to O'Malley house, then go home," Louie said, as the procession began its march back down the center of Main Street.

Walter thought: *La Cava—the tasseled corn stalk in a field of the unpollinated. The fox in the hen house. A shard of glass at the feet of barefoot children.*

"I'm ready to go home, too, Father," Leonard said. "Mother will be wondering where we are."

They headed toward Maggie parked a half block north of the movie house.

"I thought it was a good-enough movie," Walter said, "about smart and sophisticated people, many who probably came from small towns. I imagine people go to big cities for the same reasons as you and I might, mostly to make a new life for themselves; along the way, hopin' to find *Mehr Licht*—more light, as my Grandfather Johann used to say.

"It's just not usually the other way around."

CHAPTER NINE

Visitor At Three A.M.

Al Capone moves about cities and countries in a steelclad car weighing seven tons, and costing about twenty- thousand dollars, always accompanied by eighteen smartly dressed gentlemen in waiting, more bodyguards than the President of the United States. He is the object of a sort of hero worship in America, rising up from an indigent life and "making good." His eleven-and-a-half carat diamond ring is believed valued at $50K. People go out of their way to shake hands with him. He receives privileged treatment wherever he goes.

Sweeney put down the newspaper on the workbench in the new engine house, ran his fingers through his thick red hair and stared at the front page photo and caption of Al Capone standing next to his armored car with a bodyguard. The article noted newspapers in London, Berlin, Paris, Edinburgh, and Rome had carried the photo.

Capone contradicted Sweeney's basic belief in mankind. He believed most people are basically good, but sometimes do bad stuff. Many had strong urges they struggled to control. Only a few were mean-spirited and didn't seem to give a crap about the havoc they cause. He might have met one person who was truly evil, who held that bad is good.

The recent downward spiral of mankind could be directly linked with passage of the Eighteenth Amendment, intended to prevent people from drinking alcohol. Instead, it fostered intemperance and excess. Overnight, Christian teetotalers and law-abiding folks bought stills from hardware stores and learned to make and sell booze. Hearing of distilleries blowing up wasn't uncommon. No one hereabouts had died from tainted alcohol yet, at least no one he knew of.

A few local bootleggers held dreams of becoming millionaires: Levendusky, Allen, Fink, and McCuniff. All charged up to ten times more for beer and booze than before Prohibition, eventually buying it out of Chicago, as demand mounted. Still pretty green behind the ears as town marshal when the U. S. voted to go dry, Sweeney had to learn fast. Realizing distributors were staying abreast of his routines, he started keeping track of them. He took late evening drives to popular skid roads in the country-side. Once there, he'd back Baby, his Model T, into a farm field hidden from view along a grove of trees, switch off the headlights and engine, then commence to sit and wait. Not long after a seller would drive up and make repeated trips into the ditch with hootch, bathtub gin, or brick of wine in hand, and speed off. A short while later, the first customers would arrive to retrieve their orders. New buyers showed up from time to time, too. Sweeney still couldn't place the flash of red he'd recently seen in the moonlight. Looked strangely like Bierkoff's car.

He suspected a few area law officers took bribes to look the other way, which downgraded the reputation of all of them. Jails became revolving doors. According to newspapers, so many cases flooded courts nationwide, judges threw out pending cases by the truckload. The biggest bootleg-ging case to hit local newspapers involved two Haar brothers, Willie and Fred Jr., and their father, Fred Haar Sr., sentenced to the Atlanta Federal Penitentiary in '25. Twenty-four months later they made headlines yet again…the new indictment: coercion, for paying the prison chaplain and the warden for special privileges providing all the comfort of a good hotel accommodation. The judge increased their sentences, and the prison got a few new inmates. Sometimes the law prevailed.

Admittedly, Sweeney embraced a certain amount of celebrity worship of Capone, and anyone else with a rags to riches story, though that sure hadn't been his experience or his family's. His Irish grandfather, as was likely the case for the Italian Capones, immigrated to America around the middle of the nineteenth century. He told stories of how the Irish and

Italians, the last two immigrant groups to arrive, settled in the Five Points District of New York. The Irish were considered lowlifes, ranking socially lower than African slaves. His grandfather arrived on America's shores with only a few dollars in his pocket, enough to pay the first four-dollar-a-month rent and feed the family for a week. If men like his grandfather didn't have a skill, like barbering, where they might earn a nickel a haircut, they'd end up hauling bricks up ladders for gutter pay. Ultimately the only occupations Irishmen found to feed their families were dangerous jobs others didn't want: policeman and fireman.

Conversations with Captain Hughes in recent years had shed light on the situation in the biggest cities since Prohibition. He said young boys often joined a kid gang for protection and survival. Those who excelled eventually joined an adult gang, where guns replaced knives and petty thefts progressed to armed robberies. The most hard-knuckled and vulgar wormed their way into jobs at places like the Harvard Inn, hangout of mafia leaders, who'd organized the non-union bricklayers and the laundrymen into the Unione Siciliana.

There, young men added hijacking and bootlegging to their repertoire, along with the art of extortion and delivering votes at election time. If one was particularly given to malevolent tendencies, some big boss like Johnny Torrio invited him to Chicago and offered twenty-five percent of the action. Those who advanced to the top of America's Public Enemy list came from New York and Chicago. Alphonse Capone, now No. 1 on the list, claimed to have grown his fortune to an impressive thirty million dollars. Other lethal goons included Louis "Two Gun" Alterie, the Genna brothers, and John Scalise and Albert Anselmi. Still, city directories listed most as salesmen or cigar store employees. Capone's first enterprise had been a furniture store, even had the family Bible opened on the chest next to a bed in the display window, though his customers yearned for the illicit action in the back room and upper floors.

The face of Louie La Cava appeared like an apparition in Sweeney's mind. He imagined Louie likely ended up in the business following a route similar to Capone's. But at least Louie kept his nose clean when in Oxbow.

Sweeney checked the time. It was ten past three and he needed to start his second patrol to see all the doors of the town were safely locked for the night. He picked up his billy club and flashlight, a lit Chesterfield sagging in one corner of his mouth, and left the engine house. A coughing jag hit him as he locked the side door, and for the next couple minutes he crouched in the grass, hacking. Cigarettes are gonna stop me cold one day, he thought.

He also knew if a crook was in the vicinity, the commotion sounded the alarm he was beginning his final round of the night. He charged easterly toward the Telephone Exchange, first shining the beam of the flashlight through the front window where Agnes Triggers slumbered on the cot next to the switchboard. In the Brick Hotel lobby, a tabby cat's green eyes stared hypnotically into the light. No visible molestation had transpired at Chapman Lumber, Park Gas or the Wiltse Hotel. Next, he staggered down the shadowy, stinky alley behind the hotel, amidst washouts, thickets, boxes, garbage, rats and outhouses. All was quiet at the Bon Ton at the end of the block...the same for Curley's in the next block, at least until he managed to stumble into a cloud of flies swarming around boxes of carcass bones. For a minute he expelled those he'd managed to inhale. A block away, Dugger's mutt barked, the same dog that most mornings prevented him his sleep until Peters' truck left the neighborhood. *Judas Priest! What's making the dog yap at this hour?* he wondered.

In the narrow passageway between Curley's and Weibel's, Sweeney knew ne'er-do-wells could easily hide. He crouched behind the young trunk of a maple tree, waited and listened, immediately thinking he might have seen a shadow move. He froze in place. Then he heard a faint noise... someone was there! Suspending the billy club on the hook on his belt, he released his gun holster cover, gingerly lifted the revolver, and released the safety. Another quick glance around the tree and he realized the side window to Weibel's was open, and a half-filled gunny sack lay on the ground nearby. Sweeney raised his right hand to steady his left holding the .38. How many might be inside? Would he be able to shoot to kill if they resisted arrest? How long had it been since his last target practice at the limestone quarry north of town?

A few minutes later, a farmer boot emerged through the window, then the rest of a darkly-clad body unfolded through it, and two hands reached up and pulled the window shut. As the robber bent down to pick up his cache, Sweeney bounded from behind the tree, stumbling toward him, pointing the revolver and flashlight in the man's face.

"Stick 'em up, mister! You're under arrest! Just what do you think you're doing here? Who else is in there? Who are you?"

"Only me, only me!" the man said, raising his hands above his head.

"Okay, owl! You from around these parts? And what might you have in here?" Sweeney said, relieving the robber of his loot.

He scanned the contents. Bewildered, he closed it back up and tucked it under one arm.

"You been drinkin'? Walk this way. You're going to jail. In Chicago coppers shoot crooks in the balls. I can't promise that my aim is that good, but I can promise you won't be standing."

Pointing his gun at the robber's boy-sized chest, Sweeney felt its unfamiliar weight in his hand. He spun the crook around, redirected the gun to his back, and nudged him up the alley, crossing Main Street at the Telephone Exchange, where Sweeney pounded on the door with the fist holding the flashlight.

"Agnes, it's me, Sweeney! I need you to call the sheriff in Independence to send a car to haul this crook off to jail... Found a guy breaking into Weibel's Hardware."

Sweeney got no response. He pounded on the door once more.

"Agnes, wake up...call the sheriff in Independence!"

Agnes stirred from her slumber and squinted with one eye into the beam of his flashlight.

"Go away, Sweeney! I'm off duty, you know!"

Agnes could be difficult, Sweeney knew all too well. *No surprise to me why you're an old maid!* he thought.

He redirected his not-so-masterful-at-crime man-child in the direction of the cinderblock jail next to the city building. Still puzzled, he pondered: *and this man is going to jail for stealing—what? Some things don't make any sense.* He fished the skeleton key from his pocket, swung open the solid outer door followed by the inside steel-barred one, prodded the man inside the first cell, and closed and locked both doors.

"The bed is hard as a rock, but it's a bed," he hollered from outside the jail.

He holstered the revolver on his way to the engine house. There, he was able to raise Olivia on the ham radio. Agnes answered Olivia's phone call, and she soon reported back Sheriff Willey said he'd send a car first thing in the morning.

Well, that went well for my first time! Sweeney thought, as he placed the gunny sack, billy club and flashlight on the workbench, reached for a fresh Chesterfield in his shirt pocket and placed it loosely between his lips. *What was that all about—that's some sick mush! Who is this guy? I pretty much know everyone in these parts. And why Weibel's?* He'd call on Emil Weibel in the morning and inform him of the break-in.

He struck a match and lit the Chesterfield, anticipating the calming effect of nicotine in his body, and tried to figure out where he'd left off greasing the water pump earlier in the day. The workbench ran parallel to the fire-engine-red Model A truck, which the town council had purchased a year earlier. Then Oxbow built the new engine house. Next year, installation of a new water system would get underway. All fell under the scope of his purview.

He mounted a wooden stool beside the workbench, picked up a crescent wrench, placed it on a coupling and pulled down. It slipped off. He replaced the wrench—it slipped off again. *It's going to be one of those nights,* he thought. He could hear the rain start. The wind was picking up, too. He'd discovered it was noisy spending the night in the tin-roofed structure when it rained, deafening during thunder and lightning. It sounded like the side door was rattling, opening...though he was certain he'd turned the lock when he came inside. He twisted around on the stool... someone was coming through the door.

"Oh, Louie, you scared the hell out of me!" Sweeney said. "Come in out of the rain."

"Saw light...on way home," Louie said. "You busy? I come back."

"Just finished making rounds, that's all," Sweeney said. "Not having much luck with this coupling...need to grease this pump. Care to give it a lash?"

Louie hung up his overcoat and fedora. Rainwater pooled in the crease sprayed onto the floor. Sweeney waited for Louie to scale the stool next to his, then handed him a large wrench.

"Put it there and hold real tight while I put mine on the other side," Sweeney directed. "This coupling is really stuck."

Louie grabbed onto the wrench with his smooth olive-colored hands. Sweeney saw the manicured nails and noted for the first time how much his hands resembled those of a banker's.

Louie positioned the wrench at the place where Sweeney had directed, and Sweeney attached his wrench in a counter position. Both put their full weight into it. Nothing budged. They tried over and over. Sweeney finally released his wrench and gave the coupling a hard whack.

"It's banjaxed…I'll put some lubricant on it, let it sit overnight. Maybe tomorrow it'll budge. What 'ya been up to tonight, Louie?"

"Dance by Oran… Russell's Orchestra play."

"Big crowd?"

"*Si…* No alcohol serve, but everyone drink!"

"That's pretty much how bootlegging works, isn't it?" Sweeney said with a grin.

"*Imagino.* Met Mr. Allen, owner. Said has no idea where people get drink. Had 'twinkle in eye'—believe how you say it," Louie said.

"Lotta people trying to get rich since Prohibition," Sweeney said. "Law enforcement looks the other way for most of it. Not enough resources or time to arrest everybody making panther piss in a still out back of the barn. Really hard to tell a national ban on manufacture of intoxicating beverages is in effect. And real interesting what greed does to people, how it changes them. I think poverty is at the crux of the problem…if people grew up with enough to eat, a warm place to live, a loving family…

"Say, Louie, I've been readin' about Chicago. What's it like to spend time in the crime capital of the world? Heard bombings are really big these days. Over a hundred in the windy city already this year. How'd you ever end up workin' in such a stinky, sweaty, killin' place?"

Louie fidgeted in his chair, lowering his eyes as though searching the cuffs of his pants for words. With a finger, he flicked onto the floor a sliver of metal from the coupling that had landed on his pant leg, readjusted his coat, and slipped his right hand in the side pocket. Sweeney watched him closely as he took a long drag on his cigarette.

"Not good life for *famiglia* in Italy," Louie said. "Pappa and Mamma go America to make better life. I go school when I'mma young. Then find work in Chicago…where meet Jess. She and sister left da *casa*, go Chicago, too. Jess and I marry. She has *grande famiglia* here."

He paused, then added: "You hunt, Sweeney? I like hunt rabbit, pheasant, duck, deer…"

"What kind of guns do you own, Louie?"

"Have da right gun for killing animals. We should hunt…I show you my guns. Also, I wonder, does Vanessa enjoy da Opera House? Sweet girl, Vanessa…real beauty."

"She does. And I thank you for inviting her. Been meaning to ask, Louie, what do you do for a living? Don't think you ever told me."

"Salesman…cigar company, New York. Make cigar bands. Work takes me Chicago, other places."

Sweeney scrutinized Louie's demeanor, looking for just one involuntary flicker from just one honest muscle in his body: a quiver in a cheek, a tremor in a hand, a flinch from a foot. But he was steady, his eyes steely and cold, didn't blink an eyelid. His boss had risen to the top of the nation's Public Enemy list, a heartless brute who manipulated poor and rich alike, bribed, extorted, and murdered…and for what? The almighty dollar, that's what! Yet Louie was able to sit there, keeping company with a town marshal, with all the composure of a schoolmarm teaching arithmetic to her class of prodigies.

"Any talk in Chicago or New York on what's going on with the stock market? Don't really know what all the fluctuation means I read in the newspapers, but I understand the market affects jobs. Things have been pretty good for a long time, well, except for the farmers. They seem to have missed the last decade of prosperity. Still, most folks got used to eating three squares a day, plus socking away a few bucks in a bank account. You got any money in the stock market?"

"My money in bank, keep little under mattress for rainy day," Louie said. He eyed the gunny sack on the workbench and gave a sly grin.

"All you money tied up in dat sack, Sweeney?"

CHAPTER TEN

Hayward

Louie neared the end of the long drive to Capone's 400-acre site in northern Wisconsin. A week earlier he'd received word: "Don't bother to bring da books, Three Fingers, it's not dat kinda meetin'." An Italian phrase came to mind: *si sta facendo buio*, it is getting dark. He'd heard his mother speak those words every evening awaiting his father's return home after a day of hard work. At long last, his bent-over form emerged in the doorway, when dusk was *un nero viola*, a purple blackness, as his mother called it.

Louie checked his watch. Capone had called a meeting for seven p.m. He cranked the Lincoln off the gravel highway and onto a crooked road skulking for a quarter mile to a guard house. There, machine-gun toting foot soldiers swarmed like buzzards scouring for fall roadkill. He recognized Shorty carrying a Thompson typewriter loaded with .45 caliber dumdum bullets, his finger pulsing on the trigger. Shorty scrutinized the Lincoln's interior and waved him down the narrow tree-lined trail retreating into the shadowy forest. Ten minutes later the lights of the car illuminated an eight-foot stone guard house positioned at the approach of the main house. Louie pulled up next to a row of Cadillac town sedans, painted in green and black to match Chicago police cars, customized with back windows that dropped down and side windows with cavities so kinsmen could stick their guns out of the windows and shoot without hindrance.

He thought he recognized the flashy Rolls Royce Silver Ghost nearby.

From inside the Lincoln, he surveyed Capone's copious tract of land and stronghold he'd constructed which would repel even his worst enemies, including the Feds. The large lake next to the house was perfect for flying in shipments of bootleg liquor from Canada, Florida and New York, then loading onto trucks bound for Chicago and Detroit. And for landing a plane when Capone needed to go on the lam. A dozen men roamed the perimeter of the rustic two-story stone house.

Louie left the car and hiked across the lawn toward a large screened porch. A sallow-faced Capone bodyguard stood at the door, cigarette drooping from listless lips.

"Good see you, Three Fingers," said Frank Nitti, called "The Enforcer," because whenever the Don said, "Frankie, send dis punk's mother some flowers," it meant drive across the country and whack the bastard. Nitti also controlled whisky and alcohol operations and was real good at shakedowns. If some car passing by ever threw enough lead to bump off the Boss, Nitti could take over Chicago Outfit in a minute.

"Thanks, Frankie—you lookin' good today," Louie said, brushing by Nitti's skinny frame, close enough to sense the distinct butt of .38 Colt Police Positive in an inside coat pocket, and view the gat hugging the whitewashed wall at his side.

Louie had come to the meeting heavy himself.

"The Don's in da middle of some business," Nitti growled, as the two passed into the first room of the lodge. "Your bedroom is on right, end of hall, bathroom nearby," pointing up the double open staircase, a massive stone fireplace dividing them. "Dinner at seven. Fresh lobster flown in from Maine."

Louie started up the stairs, suitcase in hand, pausing momentarily to tip his hat to familiar faces staring up at him in an adjacent parlor: Capone's wife, Mae, a devout Irish Catholic woman, and Capone's son, Albert Francis, "Sonny," as he was called. Nearby were Capone's chief aides: Jake Guzik, financial genius and trusted consigliere; Ralph "Bottles" Capone, Al's older brother—best known for his Cotton Club in Chicago, featuring Negro chorus girls, and open to anyone except da Feds; and John Scalise and Albert Anselmi, Capone's most lethal torpedoes, occupying a small settee where they were playing cards.

Louie found his way to the knotty pine bedroom at the end of the hallway, placed his suitcase on the bed and opened it.

So here am I... da once exiled in center of Capone lair, he thought. *Capone will plan another job now...but way too soon!*

Just the thought brought about a nervous twitch, and his left hand began to shake irrepressibly. He clamped down on it with the other, waiting for the shaking to wane. The acid in his gut rose to the top of his throat, culminating in repetitive belches.

He laid out a fresh suit, shirt and tie from the suitcase, and stashed the remaining items in a bureau drawer. Gathering toiletries, he walked to the bathroom.

At a quarter of seven, he appeared in the center of the tall archway opening into the dining room. Alphonse Gabriel Capone pushed back his chair from the dining table, rose and graciously extended a hand to greet him. Louie stepped forward, noticing Capone's grasso carriage and wide forehead laced with perspiration, a wide drop snaking down one cheek and spilling onto the front of his custom purple silk suit from Marshall Field. Louie felt Capone's hand clamp onto his, squeezing hard, then he was pulled forward, nearly off balance. The Big Shot's diamond pinky ring gouged his hand, and Capone's intense cologne rapidly swallowed up his own witch hazel. Out of the corner of his eye, he caught a glimpse of Phillip D'Andrea, Capone's taut, no-nonsense body guard, scrutinizing his every move.

"My apologies for being absent at your arrival, Three Fingers. Come sit next to me," Capone said. "My chef has prepared a nice meal. He once worked at Jim Colosimo's Chicago restaurant...you probably heard of it. Did Nitti tell you we're having fresh lobster, or steak? Both, if you prefer... came in by plane first thing this morning."

"Thanks for da invitation, real beautiful place here." Louie said, pulling back the chair to Capone's right and taking the seat with its back to the arched doorway.

"I'll give you a tour after dinner," Capone continued. "Eight car garage, bunkhouse, more buildings out back. Feel free to survey the property— take Nitti with you."

The elongated table laid out with white linen, fine china, silver and crystal was set for ten. Before Louie had time to unfold the thick white napkin, the rest of the chairs began to fill in: Nitti, Scalise and Anselmi sitting to his right; Mae, Sonny, Bottles, and Guzik on the other side of the table. The place opposite Al at the end of the table remained unclaimed.

"We'll have an additional guest join us in time," Capone said.

White-aproned staff entered from the kitchen door with platters of meats, steaming bowls of soup and spaghetti, plates of fried eggplant and cheeses—steak and lobster—and bottles of red and white wine. D'Andrea departed the room as the meal commenced and Capone bore down on the conversation.

"I'm enjoying my new G.H.Q. at the Lexington Hotel…go by George Phillips now. And just purchased, for forty gran' attractive new property, Palm Island Estate, three miles from downtown Miami. Reminds me of sunny shores of family home in Salerno, though I've gotten chilly reception from my Miami neighbors so far. Go figure! I'm bringing a lotta business to da region. People should be grateful. Louie, I'll throw dinner party to introduce you to politicians, government officials, Hollywood stars, too, next time you're in town. Maybe we'll go a round in boxing match in my gym."

The meal persisted for two hours over talk of the Capone family's recent trip to Paris, commentary about important political races, and Al's tribulations with the ponies, the last chair at the table never occupied. In time, the Cuban super coronas distributed, Capone rose from his chair, signaling the move to the living room. Louie hung back to observe the boss lean over to give Mae and Sonny a tender kiss on each cheek, whispering, "Good night, my dears," then watched as they made their way up the stairs, lingering until the moment they vanished from his sight.

Louie joined the others in the living room, where Capone's driver, Paul, stood before a French cabinet along the north wall, its top laden with luxuriant looking corked bottles standing flat-footed at attention: synthetic bourbon, rye, Scotch, brandy, rum, gin and sweet cognac from Capone's alkycooking centers, alcohol with flavoring and coloring and an Al Capone label smeared across the fat face of each. The faux booze reminded him of Capone's disgust for the Chicago elite on the Gold Coast, the wealthy lake front area; those who preferred to ship in European booze rather than get their toot from Capone bootleg booze.

Paul poured him a drink before departing and started the Victrola to play a familiar march by Verdi just as Capone and D'Andrea entered through the double doors.

"Can't help but notice you're wearing the belt buckle I gave you, Three Fingers," Capone said.

"Wear often…and my brothers send greetings."

Capone nodded as he walked to the cabinet to pick up the glass of Templeton rye whiskey bottled in a northwest Iowa distillery left for him by Paul. Then, turning to face his guests, he extended his arm with glass raised high and offered a toast: "To members of my *borgata* here tonight—Salute!"

"Salute!" came the reply in unison from around the circle.

The moment was interrupted by a knock on the door.

Capone excused himself. Several minutes elapsed before he returned with an old nemesis, Jack Zuta.

"You remember Zuta, don't you, Three Fingers?" Capone said.

Unsurprised, Louie walked over to shake Jack's hand. "Thought might be you to join us, Jack. You miss real fine meal."

"And toast to members of the family, old and new…that includes you, Jack. Welcome to my Hayward estate," Capone said.

Guzik poured a brandy and handed it to Zuta, who in turn raised his glass and offered a "Salute!"

"Zuta's been occupied this evening, already working on new project for me," Capone said. "He and I go back to early '20s—like you, La Cava. Last thing he did for me was help with contributions to Mayor Thompson's reelection campaign. Sometime along the road he lost his way and defected to dat Irish bastard Bugs Moran…Zuta tells me he's seen the light and wants to come back to work for me.

"Scalise and Anselmi—you still carrying torch for Moran or Northsiders?"

"None whatsoever, Don! Our loyalty's to you!" said Scalise.

Capone paused, his fiery green-grey eyes seemingly entangled with those of the soldiers standing in formation before him.

"Now, let's get down to business," Capone continued.

Louie took notice of the flare in Capone's wide nose and four-inch scar across his cheek as he spoke. His every gesture to remind his hatchet men of their place.

"You know I got lot of pressure on me. Guess you probably saw the *Chicago Trib* article by that babbo Jake Lingle. Listed over two hundred of my gambling houses in Chicago. Said I generate daily business of two point five million dollars. Jesus Christ! Feds on my back for tax evasion.

"Jake's been on my fucking payroll for years. Kept me informed about police activities and fixing things. Owns a nice home on Michigan Lake. Living quarters at a plush hotel in Chicago. Winters in Florida. How you do that on salary of newspaper reporter? Point is, now he's crossed me… publishing my affairs in the goddamn newspaper."

Zuta poured a second hit of brandy for himself and calmly submitted, "I'll have nice talk with him. I'm certain he's a reasonable fella, and I can make case to omit statements concerning family business from the papers in future."

"The boy spends afternoons at da race track," Capone said. "La Cava, go with Zuta on that call. You two worked together before on similar matters. Clock him! If Lingle is wearing the belt, return it to me.

"Now, another discussion of importance. I've worked hard to build my business. Installed my own Chicago mayor. Added policemen and politicians to my payroll. Took over gambling houses. Built resorts, dog and horse thoroughbred race tracks. Point is, I made every facet of my outfit run with precision and efficiency. And you won't find any police record of any criminalities against me. Always had my alibi ready.

"And I've survived a lot of wars. Enemies trying to muscle in on my business. This year…already a dozen attempts on my life.

"Lost my brother Frank in a '24 election skirmish. *Anima buona,* God rest his soul." He paused before continuing. "This past September assassins took my dear friend Tony Lombardo, third president of the *Unione Siciliana.* Funeral procession two miles long. Laid to rest in Mount Carmel, without benefit of priest. Not right for the Catholic church to refuse to give a funeral mass for a great man like Tony Lombardo. He gave a lot money to the needy.

"It's time all dis killin' came to an end and we all live in harmony under the protection only I provide. I have an idea to eliminate my biggest competitor, the Northsiders. I'm fed up with them hijacking my trucks. Scalise, take the lead on this with Anselmi. Needs to be big, very well thought out, every detail analyzed by that brilliant brain of yours. Can't nothin' go wrong. Work with Nitti, Guzik...La Cava, too. Louie, you used to be one of my best collectors, snappin' your fingers in contempt of Federal Court, operating a saloon under the eyes of the police. You still got the nerve it takes to do a big job like this? Don't want no repeat of '24 when you was chased outta town. Or maybe you prefer just keepin' books."

"I got guts. Frankie Yale's a stiff, ain't he?" Louie boasted, just as he felt a rise in his chest and let out the Mount Vesuvius of belches. "*Scusa!* Have upset gut since morning."

"When the plan's put together, see me. But be careful what you say on the blower. Next meetin' will be at my G.H.Q.," Capone added.

Once more he scanned the faces of the button men in the room, waiting for any beefs to surface, and looking for any indication of who might be in need of a head shrinker. Eventually, business conducted, Capone pulled a handkerchief from a breast pocket and made two wide swipes across his brow, then down each cheek.

"Okay, boys, let's talk about more congenial subjects."

"Need to excuse myself and get back to business, Don," Zuta interjected. "We'll talk tomorrow." He left the room.

Capone redirected his attention to La Cava.

"Hope you enjoyed dinner, Three Fingers. We didn't get around to talking about your wife and family."

"Enjoyed dinner, boss. Lobster real fresh and tasty. My wife Jess is well. Tonight she stay with sister and husband in Oxbow. Nice town, simple folk...real welcoming. Town marshal is duck soup."

"I promised you a tour of the property," Louie.

Louie felt Capone's hand land on his shoulder as they headed toward the double doors, with D'Andrea swiftly joining them.

"Nitti, come join us, too, in case I'm called away," Capone said, leading the way to the stairs that would take them to his underground garrison.

"We'll start in the basement. All walls are 18-inch thick plus one-foot thick reinforced masonry walls. Then will show you the jail and walled fence my men use for training. Got to stay in shape like college athletes if they work for me. The escape tunnel leads to another fortified building in the woods and secret back road.

"Want to hear a fuckin' crazy story from earlier this evening? When I stepped outa the meetin', they told me someone, probably from out of the area—locals know well enough to stay away—showed up at the front guard house tonight. The fellas shoved a gat in his face and told the ossified fool to get the hell off da premises... This is private property, after all. Half hour later he wandered up the back road.

"Senseless things people do when they get smoked. It'll get you blipped."

CHAPTER ELEVEN

The Drowning

Olivia knew no one thinks when they first step into the river, *I'm going to drown today.* Since the 1900s, township annals logged several drownings on the Little Wapsie. It wasn't the depth of the water that took 'em; it was the turbulence from which they couldn't break free.

Mary Huegnot and her husband had gone to the Old Swimmin' Hole on the Wapsie to bathe one evening, knowing well enough to avoid the high churning water just below the old log dam. Mary, who never waded in very far from the water's edge, bent down and began to wash her lower body. Her husband strode out chest-high, as always, where the swift current quickly lifted his feet, carrying him to the river's center, where he would playfully call out to her and wave.

On this evening, the flow gently spun him 'round and hauled him upstream along the far bank. She squatted to wash her hair, looking up moments later to see him wave once more, seemingly unconcerned as he neared the outer edge of swirling, frothy brown water. Next time she raised her eyes, it was to witness him being pulled toward the deepest pool at the dam's bottom. Then he disappeared. Finally, he reappeared, coughing and sputtering—when she saw the first pang of concern sweep across his face.

She called out to him: "Swim! you can make it."

He thrust his energy into freeing himself from the treacherous undertow. Guardedly she ventured out farther with an outstretched arm, frantically urging him to come toward her, all the while screaming in the direction of town, hoping someone would hear her call for help. He disappeared a second time in the roiling water. More seconds passed before he resurfaced.

Feverishly she now ran from the water's edge toward town, only to turn and plunge back into the river, hoping her beloved had found a way out of the churning river. After a while, old man Lou Miller, the blacksmith, heard her shrieks and came running. "What's wrong?" he asked.

"My husband disappeared. He's drowning, I fear. I can't reach him, can you save him? I saw him over there!" pointing to the turbulent water some forty feet away. Dropping his apron and shoes on the riverbank, Lou waded in, diving repeatedly near the murky, agitating water. But Mary never saw her beloved alive again. The next morning the sheriff recovered his body a half-mile down river.

In the days after the funeral, Mary voiced concern about how she'd now provide for herself. A man of good stature in the community reminded her of her talent for styling hair, and offered her a loan to take a course at a beauty shop in Oelwein. A half dozen years later, Mary found she needed extra help from time to time. Olivia offered to give it a try, and thereafter, the two worked side by side several afternoons and evenings a month in Mary's shop.

Olivia soon found herself immersed in the art and science of caring for hair, and a whole lot more knowledgeable about the heart and soul of the women of the community. Washing, waving and shingling the tresses of her clients, she learned about the goings-on in their homes, of their churches and faith, the trials and travails of family and friends, and of

She heard stories that buckled her knees from laughter, like the day Lydia, a rock-solid woman of faith and a leader of the Free Will Baptist Church, who believed it her calling to boldly proselytize in whatever situation she found herself, asked anyone in the shop if they knew the answer to the question she wished to pose to them:

"Do you know why Baptists don't believe in relations before marriage?"

The room fell into a prickly silence. Not hearing any responses, Lydia said, "It's because it might lead to dancing—of course!"

The proselytizer had a sense of humor after all. Who knew? She'd caught everyone off guard. Olivia viewed Lydia differently after that day.

Then there was Alice, a staunch member of the Methodist church, who'd gotten a letter from a Pentecostal relative in Indiana, a letter which sent her sense of indignation through the roof. Alice read a few lines from the note, "I'm deeply concerned that perhaps you aren't going to heaven when you die, Alice. Going to church and reading the Bible isn't enough—you have to have a personal relationship with God. I don't wish to offend you, I just want to make sure you end up in your choice of destination."

Alice said the letter made her so angry she wanted to throw the note on the floor. "I didn't, because I consider myself a good Christian woman and will try to overlook her actions. Here's the real crux of the matter: she thinks because I don't speak in tongues, I'm not a Christian, or going to heaven!" Alice added.

And Olivia caught glimpses of untold stories that made her heart ache, women who came in with bruises on their faces, necks or arms. "A clumsy fall; silly me for not looking where I was going," Olivia would be told outright. Nureen, who worked as a cook at the school, was married to a man," she said, "who didn't come back home the same person after the Great War." Three or four nights a week he and other vets got together to drink, which frequently ended up in fights in the alley behind Curley's store. Olivia knew about those fights; Sweeney got calls to break 'em up, usually right after he'd sat down for supper with the family.

Other customers, very private women, preferred to keep discourse to a minimum. When Olivia learned to beautify in silence. She learned early on that Josephine La Cava was one who didn't care to talk much. Whenever she and her husband Louie were in town, she made appointments at the shop. They stayed at her sister's house, the cute little two-story yellow bungalow with a wide porch on East Main Street. Most of Josephine's siblings still lived in the area. They were a close-knit Catholic family.

Olivia recalled the day she told of Sweeney's propensity to fight whenever an umpire made a call in a baseball game he didn't agree with. It happened more than once and was the reason he gave up baseball. By the end of her account, she detected Josephine fidgeting in her chair, her lips tightly pursed. Both she and her sister, Mary O'Malley, seemed uncomfortable when others were too familiar.

Olivia finally finished washing and rinsing Josephine's long brunette locks in the kitchen sink, wrung out her hair, swaddling her head in a towel, and directed her to the vacant swivel chair.

"Long hair takes a lot of care, ever think about getting a bob? Mary took a class on the latest bob styles in Des Moines—they're apparently all the rage in New York. And permanents, though you should plan a full day for those," Olivia said.

"Lou likes my hair long…doesn't want me to look like a boy. Besides, I hear bobs give headaches," Josephine said, pleasantly but bluntly, then sorted through the meager offering of reading material on the small wooden table at her side. She quickly chose an out-of-date news magazine, instead of a gossip rag or *Radio Listeners Guide & Call Book*, and began to immerse herself in the publication.

Olivia retrieved the large flat tray of assorted metal hairpins, wavers and clips and began to comb through Josephine's thin strands with a comb, parting the hair into sections, maneuvering from the crown to the nape, wrapping and clipping each curl in place. Periodically she glanced over Josephine's shoulder to glimpse a photo or headline in the magazine.

Josephine flipped the page, exposing a stark black and white photo spread across its top half showing a police officer standing over several suited bodies lying along a whitewashed wall in a Chicago warehouse.

Oliva gently tilted Josephine's head to one side to reach the section above her left ear, and to be able to read the first paragraphs. She felt Josephine's neck tighten.

Seven of Bugs Moran's Gang Gunned
Down on St. Valentine's Day

February 15, 1929—"In only ten seconds it was all over," said Frank Gusenberg, who was riddled with 14 bullets, one of seven to survive the massacre. When asked by police: "Who shot you?" he responded, "Nobody shot me!"

It's believed seven members of the George "Bugs" Moran operation at the northside garage were awaiting a delivery of bootleg spirits, when several men walked into the place, a few wearing police uniforms, and asked those present to line up along the wall.

Anticipating it was yet another police raid, which would result in charges dropped and all equipment returned, the men complied.

Then Tommy guns came out, capable of 850 rounds a minute. Six men were quickly gunned down. Moran, believed to be heir to the North Side Gang after Dion O'Banion's assassination in 1924, was on his way to the garage that morning, and escaped the shooting.

Al Capone, longtime archenemy of Moran over control of beer and booze smuggling and trafficking operations, was questioned about the murders, and offered his view:

"You ought to question Bugs Moran... he's the only man who slays like that!"

Josephine looked up as the open magazine tumbled onto her lap. Olivia noticed a pallor in Josephine's face and fresh beads of moisture on her brow.

"Are you all right, Josephine? Can I get you a glass of water? It is a bit close in here this morning," Olivia said.

She waited for Josephine to speak.

"Yes, I believe I could use a drink...I am suddenly feeling a bit light-headed," she said at last.

Olivia set the comb and clips aside, hurried to the kitchen sink and pumped water from the cistern into a small glass, and handed it to her.

"Here, drink this. I'll try to finish up quickly," Olivia said.

Josephine took the glass and sipped the water. The other hand lay limply draped across the magazine.

"That's quite a ghastly picture...haven't read the article myself, but it's surely enough to take the wind out of one's sail. Is Louie in town? Wasn't sure who dropped you off at the shop this morning," Olivia said.

"Lou is in Chicago on business," Josephine said. "My brother-in-law Lawrence will pick me up when you're finished."

Olivia wondered what thoughts might be threading through Josephine's mind…*was she trying to retrace Louie's whereabouts during the month of February?* Sweeney kept track of Louie. So did a few others, like Delbert Haberkamp, who'd accompanied Louie on a trip or two to Chicago. The day Delbert read about the St. Valentine's Day massacre in the paper, he paid Sweeney a visit. *"Wasn't it an odd coincidence that Louie abruptly showed up in town the morning after all those men in Chicago were gunned down?"* Delbert had asked Sweeney. Then Louie remained in town for over a month, when normally his extended stays only happened in the summer months. Olivia speculated whether Josephine, the next time she talked to Louie, might ask him about the magazine article. Probably he'd tell her not to concern herself with what she read in newspapers.

Josephine would likely acquiesce, and that would be that.

She set the glass on the table and raised the magazine from her lap once more, flipping to a story about President Coolidge. He'd announced to the nation in '27 he'd not seek a second term. "Silent Cal," as he was called, couldn't make a decision if his life depended on it, the caption under his photo read. Some speculated the country would probably end up in a dump down the road because he and the other great men refused to put the brakes on the stock market.

"It's ten cents for a shampoo and twenty cents for a set," Olivia said. "Perhaps it's best today if you finish drying and combing out your hair at home. You can return the clips next time you're nearby. I'll call the switchboard and ask Agnes to phone your brother-in-law to come get you."

Josephine retrieved her purse from the side table and pulled out a small coin purse, selected a few coins, and counted them out into Olivia's palm.

"Thank you for your extra kindness today, dear Olivia. I don't know what came over me. I felt just then as though I couldn't breathe, like I was drowning," Josephine said softly.

Olivia dropped the coins in a nearby bowl marked "Receipts."

Josephine's words transported Olivia's mind to a year earlier, when a male fetus was pulled from the Wapsie. Seemed like a heartless way to dispose of an innocent baby. She often found herself scrutinizing the women who came into the shop, wondering if that child might have belonged to one of them.

In the next instant, she sensed her own breathing becoming lumbered. *No matter how long it's been, it can still become hard to breathe,* she thought.

The next minute she found herself racing to the pump where she reached for a fresh tumbler, anxiously pumped the long red handle, and waited for water to rise from its throat. At last, the clear, clean liquid gushed forth and overflowed the brim. She stared at her hand, feeling the coolness penetrate through the glass. Her eyes rose to the mirror above the sink, where she stared at her reflection, then watched as she drank the water. Every last drop.

She remembered Josephine was waiting for her ride.

"I'll make your call now, Josephine, it'll just take a moment."

Unsteadily, she walked to the coffin phone on the wall by the front door, lifted the receiver to her ear, and listened for Agnes' voice.

"What number, Olivia?"

"Call the O'Malleys."

I could have helped that woman, she thought. *If only I'd known—I could have helped her through her grief.*

CHAPTER TWELVE

Kill The Sonofabitch

Sweeney stoked the black pot-bellied stove along the north wall of Fats' Barber Shop, then lifted a chunk of coal from the tin bucket on the floor and placed it on the crackling fire. The flames reminded him of a quote by Irish novelist James Joyce. Ironically, Joyce had written, "I fear big words, as they can make one so unhappy." Sweeney thought it true about a depression. And the Wall Street Crash in October had forever changed the way he'd view winter.

"Morning, *Bürgermeister!*" Fats said, as Mayor Gardner stepped through the front door of the shop. "Bet these hard times give you pause about running for another term as mayor about right now."

"*Gott im Himmel!*" Mayor Gardner said. "Farmers bank close, and A. H. Nieman take over presisen of State Bank. Ze people of Oxbow need zehr money."

"Don't mind at all I read water meters and put drunks in jail for a living—at least it's a job," Sweeney interjected, as he closed the stove door and claimed the chair closest to the heat.

The mayor nodded as he hung his old wool winter coat and hat smelling of mothballs on the tree by the door. Gardner was 70-ish, from the Old County, among the Lutheran Germans who'd emigrated to America in their youth, initially settling in Bremer and Fayette counties.

Fats lifted the cotton cape from the steel chair back and waited for the mayor to mount the seat.

Sweeney looked over at Louie seated in Fat's personal leather armchair in the rear corner. Louie lowered the newspaper in his hands long enough for his eyes to briefly connect with the mayor's, then resumed reading.

"You can use the ashtray in the arm for your ciggy," Fats reminded, as he wrapped a narrow strip of white paper around the mayor's neck, draped the cape over his shoulders and cinched it tight around his neck. Lastly, he pumped the hydraulic lever to elevate the chair to its highest position.

Sweeney grinned, seeing the cape cover the mayor's body down to his calves with his tiny black-shoed feet dangling mid-air above the footrest.

"Shave this morning?" Fats said.

"Shave and haircut, ja," Mayor Gardner said. "Short 'round da ears. Meine Frau likes der mustache." He passed his index finger across the thin strip of hair lining his upper lip. "Jus' a liddle trim for der *Schnurrbart*. She says it make me *sehr männlich*, real handsam."

"Oh boy, there he goes!" Sweeney shook his head. "Sure wish yer missus was here...wonder if she'd agree with any of that talk?"

Fats let go of gut-busting laughter that reverberated in the room as he swung the barber chair around until the mayor faced the mirror.

Still smirking, Sweeney released a whopping smoke ring from his corpulent lips, and watched it lazily merge into the thin layer of fumes along the ceiling.

"I'm already hearing of a couple farms up for quick sale," Fats added. "Corn prices sinkin' through the basement, cost of everything else expected to rise. People told not to report for work. Expect it'll only get worse. Helluva worse for those who can't get any work at all."

Sweeney chimed in: "Olivia's working with the Phythian Sisters, churches and businesses to raise money to feed people. But where they gonna live? A few families have a little extra space and money, but the need will quickly get out of hand."

"Come to de council meet tonight...Talk more about this." Mayor Gardner said. "Charles Grantham says de *Oxbow View* to fold...de Oper, too. Und Robert Bentley and Bill Crook take over de gristmill Everybody goes to big city, and der stock market drop mehr."

The conversation paused as Walter entered the shop and crossed the floor to the stove to warm himself.

"Morning, Walter," Fats said, "Everyone here know Walter Bierkoff? " Louie eyed Walter up and down. Eventually he folded the paper, tucked it under one arm, rose from the armchair and walked toward Walter.

"Louie La Cava, not sure we met."

"Nice to meet you," Walter said, as the two initiated a limp handshake.

Sweeney watched as Walter made a quick scan of the well-dressed gangster, first time he'd probably seen the man up close. On more than one occasion, Walter had expressed contempt for Louie, for what he'd done to the innocent Josephine, a young girl who couldn't possibly know what she was getting herself into marrying a thug, and for how Louie had involved her family in the business. Plus, he'd paraded the town's innocent children up and down Main Street, using them for protection—only a depraved man does that to children, to an entire town. And he kills and robs so he can dress and live like a congressman, senator, or president of the United States.

He figured about now Walter's blood was probably boiling…might even wish he owned a pistol so he could grab the dirty thug by the throat and pistol whip him until he was senseless. Sweeney subtly redirected the holstered pistol on his hip away from Walter, uncertain if he might yet propel himself toward Sweeney, try to pull the pistol from his holster, and go after Louie. He knew a part of Walter wanted to kill the sonofabitch. But Sweeney was bettin' Walter's better judgement would prevail. Perhaps there'd be no justice in this world for Louie's sins, but justice was in God's hands, not Walter's.

Walter finally managed to look away, his emotions laid bare, guilt washing over him. Sweeney wondered if perhaps Walter's strong emotions weren't only about Louie.

Louie's eyes remained trained on Walter's as he gradually retracted his hand.

Sweeney's voice cut through the tension: "How's Emma doing, Walter? Did you get her down to the sanatorium? How are the boys holding up—okay?"

Walter slowly pivoted toward Sweeney in search of a vacant chair.

"Doc Ward wanted her to go to Waverly Hills in Kentucky… but we agreed on Oakdale Sanatorium. It's over by Iowa City."

Walter's first words sounded like pops from the Winchester pump action .22 he used to kill wild rabbits, and an occasional coyote.

"It's hard on the boys to see her go. My brother John and his wife Onnalee are helping with the boys, Noritta and Ed Schumer, too."

Bill Biggs passed by the front window. A second later he thrust open the front door and poked the top half of his broad torso into the shop.

Sweeney noticed the small brown bag tied with string under one arm.

"Surprised to see you stop by this morning, Bill…things must be quiet at the Bon Ton," Sweeney said.

"Morning, gents! Just ran to pick up more flour at King's. Thought I'd stop and see if I could learn any gossip. Anyone here go the dance on Saturday night? Musta been quite a sight, all those cars up on blocks of wood when folks were ready to go home. A lot of no one going anywhere, Hear it was pretty hilarious. Sure do wonder who'd ever do such a thing."

Sweeney listened with keen interest. "I heard about it, all right. Some jokester, I presume. No idea who that might be, Bill?"

"No confessions here. Say, Fats… I could stop by later in the day with leftovers from the bakery. I sure hate to see them go to waste."

"Sounds mighty good. I'm open 'til the last customer tonight, just like every other night," Fats said.

Bill turned and left the shop. The walls shuddered as he jerked the door closed behind him.

Louie walked to the coat tree and lifted his elegant black wool coat, scarf and hat.

"Must go, run errand—then back to work. See you next time in town. You give real close shave, Fats…good straight edge," he said as he finished dressing.

"Uh—see you, Louie," Sweeney said, curious about Louie's pressing need to return to a place where the most bottom-dwellers of the nation call home. *What's so urgent?* he thought, though certain he'd never hear it from Louie's lips.

Everyone watched Louie's exodus from the shop in a cloud of burnt tobacco, talcum powder, Murray's Superior Pomade, and witch hazel.

He passed by the bay window, red and white barber pole hanging from the facade, then got into his Lincoln parked by the front door and drove off.

"Did I ever tell you about the time I pitched a game between Oxbow and Quasqueton?" Sweeney bellowed as soon as Louie was out of sight. "I warmed up, took a step forward on the mound and pitched the ball. Batter wasn't watching, and I beaned him. Thought I'd killed the guy! Coach pulled me from the game. I was the best pitcher for miles around. Coulda happened to anyone. I was mad as hell."

"You were really something back in the day, Sweeney. No one better than you!" Fats said, echoing Sweeney's undisputed reputation. "Things like that happen in baseball."

"Hear you vere hotshot!" the mayor chided. "Hard believe you grab sweet Olivia. Bet you grow a mustache to pull zat off!"

"Not one facial hair, mayor, not one! She fell for me just as I was. Completely head-over-heels—still is! It's my natural boyish good looks."

The chimes atop the phone box sounded. Fats walked to the wall and lifted the receiver.

"Hello…yes, Agnes, he's here. Just give him a couple minutes."

Fats replaced the receiver and eyed Sweeney. "Guess you heard…Miss Triggers says she's got an urgent call for you."

"Thanks, Fats," Sweeney said, grabbing his coat and attempting to stuff his long arms into the sleeves before departing the shop.

Quivering phone bells greeted him as he pushed through his office door. Raising the receiver to one ear, Agnes announced, "I have a call from Captain Hughes in Chicago, Sweeney."

"Morning, Captain Hughes."

"Got a few updates for you, Sweeney. First, the St. Valentine's Day massacre remains unsolved. Capone did it, no doubt; though proving it will take time. Second, a few weeks ago, Jack Zuta, once vice lord with the North Side Moran-Aiello gang, was found shot to death in a roadhouse in Delafield, Wisconsin. Feds found Zuta kept a meticulous journal of all his business affairs. Mentions one payment of twenty-seven grand to your mystery guy."

"You don't say!"

"Feds also believe Zuta is tied somehow to the murder of Jake Lingle, a reporter for the *Chicago Trib*, assassinated a couple months before Zuta's death, though no one's been able to figure out why the mob put a hit on Lingle. Took a single shot to the back of his head with a .38. Capone's Outfit is involved, mark my words, which means your guy's implicated. You get any of this news in the newspapers back there, Sweeney?"

"We get the major stories in the Waterloo and Des Moines newspapers, which I manage to read on Sundays," Sweeney said.

"Plus, your guy's still thought to be involved in the '26 triple murders that included Assistant State's Attorney McSwiggin...first time police brought him in for questioning was June of that year.

"The final part of my call is to inform you the Feds recently found your guy's name listed on a Pinkert State Bank deposit box—alongside Capone's. Feds plan to serve your guy with a grand jury subpoena as a star witness for the prosecution on Capone's tax evasion trial. No guarantee your guy will talk, of course—most don't when thugs glare at 'em a few feet away in the courtroom."

"Sure would shut up a fella real quick!" Sweeney said.

"Did I tell you the Feds have developed a way of tapping telephone lines? That'll come in handy in bringing an indictment against Capone," Captain Hughes continued. "Big problem though, your guy's come up missin'. Only a couple sightings of him in New York and Cleveland. Any chance he's there with you?"

"I can confirm he's been back a day or so. First time I knew he was here was when he came in for a shave this morning at the barber shop. Strangest thing... He never lets the barber turn his chair away from facing the front door. And another, he always makes a small hole in middle of the newspaper he's reading, both probably for the same reason. Told me about a half hour ago he's headin' back to work, though can't promise he's drivin' your way."

"Wish I could tell you to just go and arrest him, but the Feds will catch up with him eventually. Meanwhile, if you hear of any changes to your guy's travel plans, let me know. Over and out!"

Sweeney heard the disconnect of the captain's phone and hung on a few extra seconds to listen for a second click from the Telephone Exchange next door. But all was silent. He replaced the receiver and walked toward the front door, passing by the mugshots on the wall. He slid his fingers across Capone's scar. "The Feds will be knockin' on your door soon, my man—very soon!" he said.

He headed back toward the barber shop, hoping to catch up with Walter to finish their conversation. He saw Bierkoff on the street, crank in hand, standing next to Maggie's front fender.

"Hold up there, Walter!" Sweeney said, loping toward him. "Didn't get a chance to ask you earlier. Olivia and I were wondering what we could do to help in Emma's absence. Olivia can arrange for meals to be brought out to the farm, help with laundry, anything else you might need."

Walter struggled to contain his emotions. "I appreciate that, Sweeney. Have Olivia call Noritta or Onnalee. I'm real worried about the boys. They cry themselves to sleep at night, and their school work likely will suffer. Father Halpin and Sister Keith are being most helpful."

"Bank closings gonna cause you any problems? Hearing rumors of some farms in jeopardy," Sweeney said.

"Doc Wilson came to the farm again to test my milk herd for TB. Everybody can soon read in the paper how many cattle I'll have to put down. But we're okay, for now."

"And how are you holding up, Walter? Pretty rough stretch of road ahead, a lot on your shoulders. Remember, you've got a lot of friends in this community."

"Thanks for asking, Sweeney. It means more than I can tell you. Come to think of it, there is something that you could do, well, for my son, really. If you have the time, would you teach Leonard some of your baseball pitches? A lesson once in a while, when you can find the time. He admires you, wants to be a pitcher. It would mean everything to him, especially right now."

"Will do, Walter! I'll start right away."

Walter climbed aboard Maggie. As the car pulled from the boardwalk, Sweeney reached down and twisted off lengths of field ragweed hung up on the bumper. And he couldn't help but notice the red funeral ribbon still hanging from the driver's door, stoically fluttering in the icy air.

He watched until Maggie's approach to the steel bridge. As she crossed over the Wapsie, he fully expected by then the floodgates had opened.

CHAPTER THIRTEEN

Winters Without Mercy

The clammy face of Al Capone came to mind as Louie turned the Lincoln onto the new dirt road along the Catholic church's south side. The Don didn't fear any priest or day of reckoning before God. The only name that made him sweat was the name Henry Earl J. Wojciechowski, better known as the Northsider Earl "Hymie" Weiss. The inventor of car ride therapy. Any back dirt road or street would do. His brutality induced a fear one took to the grave.

Louie backed the sedan into his spot under the oak tree, the leaves still the color of mature red Cubanelle peppers. He got out, stood up, glanced into the side mirror to adjust his coat and tie, then pushed the heavy car door shut. The blast of bitter wind smacked him in the face, enough to make him take a step backward. It was first of the season, yet familiar. *Winter is part of God's eternal promise to send complications to da people He loves*, he thought. And was there any worse place than spending winter next to large body of water? His domicile for the foreseeable future: the shores of Lake Erie. He'd come to refer to November through May, with every passing year, as winters without mercy. For a moment he visualized climbing back into his sanctuary and speeding off.

He fed the top button through the buttonhole of his wool coat and made his way across the dirt parking lot and up the concrete steps leading to the double front doors of the church. A damp coldness greeted him as he stepped into the vestibule. In the dimly lit nave, he searched for the confessional.

"That you, Louie?" Father Halpin called out.

Louie ambled in the direction of the voice, quickly seeing the priest's hand extended from a partially opened door of the ornate compartment.

"Yes, Father! Good you make special appoint for me," he said, taking extravagant time to unbutton his coat before inserting his body into the tiny space opposite the priest. He pulled the door closed behind him and situated himself on the narrow wooden kneeler facing the window, a thick black velvet curtain the only thing between them.

An old memory of stale air inside the stall rushed over him, one reminiscent of a time he couldn't place. He loosened his tie and unbuttoned the top button of his white shirt and pushed down yet another strong impulse to leave now, escape.

"I like new south road, easy to reach church from da west now."

"It's been long in coming. May be one of my last accomplishments at this parish," Father Halpin said, his speech muffled by the cloth.

"You go, Father?"

"I've been here thirteen years already. Wouldn't surprise me at all if the diocese made a change within the year. Have you examined your conscience, and are you ready to make your confession?" Father Halpin said, readjusting himself on his bench.

Louie could hear the priest's movement, including what he interpreted as a deep sigh, which made him wonder if Father Halpin felt the same uneasiness in doing this as did he. More thoughts followed: *Did priest have knowledge of his depravities? Perhaps this was scam, trap—a way to trick him. Did Feds listen from next room?*

"Si, I ready make my confess." His words sounded as though scraped from the floor of a parched desert. He plunged his hands deep into the side pockets of his coat, the right one holding tightly to the only god in whom he'd trusted for a very long time.

"What mortal sins have you to confess?"

Convoluted apparitions began parading through Louie's mind: *First mortal sin: steal candy from store as boy, then lie to Pappa and Mamma 'bout theft, followed by lie to priest, the man who confer threat of Hell, penalty for rejecting God's Law and Love.*

This was followed by memory of family's beginnings, story told by Pappa and Mamma, how they flee from Civil War in Italy to promise of a new country: *one day leave old life behind, take boat 'cross endless ocean, stand together along rail above treacherous sea in stench of death; da smell of emigrés in long lines at Ellis Island. Papers. Waiting and waiting. Finally, home in New Country—but not welcome! Brothers grow up on streets with bandi, offer friendship and safety: in guns we trust! Then, first time! Confusion. Tortured soul. Renew vow to God...*

Suddenly an overwhelming sense of claustrophobia hit him, like taking a .38 Special to the chest while wearing a bulletproof vest. His heart raced. Breathing, burdened. Blotches arose on his forehead and upper lip. Words that had escorted him to safety a hundred times screamed in his head: *Run! Flee! Escape!*

"Not easy speak of things I wish to say, Father," he managed to utter. "Jess urge me come see you. Good for my soul, she say."

"The Sacrament of Confession is good, Louie. It confers grace that helps us to live a Christian life. I urge you to continue, to make your full confession to God."

"I raise Catholic, too. Never miss Mass. Altar boy for priest, like you, Father. I trust God and priest. Go church for Mamma. She wish me be good Catholic."

He was aware his voice had now dropped to a bare whisper.

"Jess wonder...I wonder...if commit...perhaps grave sin, but if die before have time to ask forgiveness, will Inna go heaven or hell?"

Father Halpin repositioned himself on the bench once more, brushing up against the curtain, perhaps with a shoulder, Louie thought, to better hear the timid words from other side.

"What grave sin do you speak of? Perhaps I can give advice on how to better your life and overcome these things."

Louie paused to thoughtfully consider his next words. *Taking a crucial hiatus was part of his learned craft, extending it as long as needed. Many times he sat in car waitin' for some stronzo to appear in doorway before lifting a sawed-off Chicago chopper from his lap and blasting away.* The voice inside his head cautioned: *Be careful, be very careful. Better to push open door, leave now!*

"Sometimes I take advantage of poor, not always give as I should, when need is great." His voice now gave way to a quiver, something he never before allowed. "This mortal sin, I know. If give to poor fifty times, but omit fifty others, how does God measure grace?"

Louie eyed the tranquil curtain awaiting the priest's response. He thought, *perhaps priest take time to reflect, like when I must tell Pappa and Mamma a family member in terrible jeopardy—dying.*

He heard Father Halpin take a deep breath as he began to speak.

"We all incur the daily struggle in the interior life and must heroically fulfill our duty right through to the end. Each day we must be conscious of our duty to be saints. And fully embrace God's law and love."

An instant later, Louie felt a familial grit coursing through his veins. He knew it was time to end his confessional obligation to the priest. He slid off the kneeler, withdrew a white handkerchief from a breast pocket and wiped his brow and upper lip.

"*Scusi*, Father," he said. "Must go now…have appointment must keep. Hope return soon."

He heard Father Halpin jostle in his seat, which was followed by another sigh, then silence.

"Then let us pray before you depart, Louie," the priest offered, though more protracted seconds ticked by before he uttered a word.

"Oh, Jesus, forgive Louie his sins. Save him from the fires of hell. Lead his soul and all souls to heaven, especially all those who have most need of your mercy. Amen."

Louie quickly withdrew from the confessional, adjusted his tie, rebuttoned his coat, and gently closed the confessional door.

"Thank for hear my confess," he said, waiting for Father Halpin to emerge from the chamber.

Louie made fleeting eye contact with the priest as he stood.

Father Halpin faced-off with Louie, grasped his hand and locked eyes with him.

"Say five Hail Marys, two Our Fathers, and pray the Act of Contrition. Pray the rosary every morning and evening, and you will find the strength you need."

Together they walked to the front doors of the church in silence. Outside, the priest remained behind on the concrete steps as Louie continued on to the sedan. He could feel Father Halpin's eyes on his back. Reaching for the door handle, he wondered if the Archdiocese of Dubuque had issued the same order as had Cardinal Mudelein in Chicago: Priests must refuse to hold a funeral Mass for gangsters.

Probably not heard of dat order, he surmised.

Louie started the sedan, revved the engine, and floored the accelerator pedal. The rear wheels of the Lincoln slewed back and forth on the fallen oak leaves as he slipped away.

Odio il cazzo dell'inverno—I hate da fucking winter! he said as he drove off.

CHAPTER FOURTEEN

Landing A Sailfish

In late December 1930, General Al Capone scoured the landscape through the triple bay windows on the second floor of the Lexington Hotel from his two-room parlor suite and command center overlooking Chicago's most prominent corner on Michigan Boulevard. Barney was late for his appointment. The fresh foot of snow overnight had likely held him up.

Al's remedy for a Chicago winter: Miami.

He took a seat at his mammoth mahogany desk, sensing the gaze of esteemed generals on the wall over his shoulder. He rotated his leather chair around for a better look at the portraits. The first was President George Washington, commander in chief of the Continental Army during the American Revolutionary War and a Founding Father of the United States. Second was Chicago Mayor William Hale Thompson, Capone's guy in City Hall, who'd brilliantly led the charge and brought Al's sundry plans to fruition, even a gambling establishment a block from City Hall. "Big Bill" understood Chicagoans wanted their alcohol, so did a lot of other good citizens on the east coast, Canada, Bahamas and Midwest, and have it they should. How he admired the trifecta of Generals in the room, each formidable in his own right.

The row of carved ivory elephants aligned on the desk caught his attention, each with its trunk in the highest position, a sign of good luck, he'd believed for a very long time. Only recently had he realized the stance warned of aggressive intent. Once more he felt the sting of the loss of his eldest brother Ralph Capone, indicted in October '29, and sentenced to a three-spot. The following March brought the indictment and trial of longtime trusted friend, Jake Guzik. Jake went down the river in only thirty days, faster than anyone in judicial history. He got five years. The third blow in December befell Frank Nitti, who'd been at his side and done his bidding since his rise to power in Chicago, no questions asked. Frank pled guilty, spilled his guts, and got eighteen months. Al pulled every lever in his machinery to try to save the three, now cellmates in Leavenworth on income tax evasion.

A familiar quiver traveled down his spinal cord to the nerves in the tips of his hands and feet. He pulled open the top drawer of the desk and reached for his wooden tray of religious medals, lifting the first precious St. Christopher's medal he'd received as a young Catholic boy. He read its engraving: "Be My Guide."

The chain of rosary beads from his mother, Theresa, lay nearby. He lifted and gently pressed the cross dangling at its center to his lips. He contemplated the other great influence in his life: Johnny "The Immune" Torrio, the man who'd seen in him intelligence, the ability to understand men, his shrewd sense for business and courage. He'd taught him the rackets and dicey ways of the underworld. And to curb his tendency for violence. To cool off, negotiate.

The medals, beads and Torrio, each its own remedy in quashing waves of despair.

He heard a sharp rap on the suite door. Phillip D'Andrea's face appeared, and behind him was Barney. The informant had come up to the floor through the secret stair passageway used only by Al, his bodyguards, and mistresses. Barney was the guy who for years reliably alerted him of impending police raids on his places of gambling and prostitution. He could find out in five minutes the gang behind every hijacking and booze running, the bomber behind every bombing, the killer behind every murder. The bulk of his information these days came through personal visits from Barney, and a few others. Months ago, he realized the shiny brass candlestick phone on his desk had been bugged.

He learned that fact the hard way. Several times.

"Whattya got for me, Barney? Where's La Cava?" he said, signaling for Barney to sit on the sofa.

"Sorry, Don, nothing new to report. Three Fingers last seen over year ago; spotted among those in and out of D.A.'s office pretty much daily back then. Since, da rat's disappeared off da face of da earth."

Al took a seat on the leather wingback chair by the fireplace. "La Cava always said he'd rather take the rap than get in the middle, so for Christ's sake, why's he gone on lam?"

"You got good Washington lawyer and you know da Feds been tryin' to build a case against you for long time. My guess is government agents want to slap La Cava with subpoena, seeing he worked as secretary for you and Torrio. Hard to say where Three Fingers is holed up."

"I've had my share of friendly visits from government agents. Told 'em through my lawyer to write down I'm a gambler, and tax me on my actual earnings of two thousand a month, then tell me what I owe in taxes, and I'll pay whatever they ask. But I refused to turn over records of my fucking earnings. None of their goddamn business how I make my living. Never heard nothing back."

"You asked for a report on Fred Ries, too. Not one sign of Ries since day he didn't show up for work at da Smoke Shop. Word is Feds sent him to South America, and they only bring him back to testify."

Capone lowered his eyes.

"Feds tapped my phone months ago, overheard my conversation with Pete Penovich. We discussed his plans to leave next morning for Canada. Feds handed him a subpoena before he could board the plane. Didn't know my phone was bugged, or I'd have sure as hell kept my mouth shut."

"Anything else you wanna know, Don? Else I should leave. The Feds got cars parked outside. They saw me come here this morning. If I get picked up, I'll say I came in for a shoeshine."

"Nothing more you can tell me, well, then that's it. I'm probably headin' to Florida. Not sure when I'll be back. You know how to reach me. This'll all blow over, wait and see. All Feds have on me is chaff. Might have evidence of money I earned, but that doesn't prove gross income. Could get two to three, at most."

Barney stood and walked to the suite door. Outside, D'Andrea directed a bodyguard to escort Barney back down the passageway.

"Send word to Mae. We leave for Florida in an hour!" Al called out to D'Andrea.

"Right, boss. Will you be removing Sonny from prep school?"

"No, leave him up there in St. Cloud. Mid-term break is coming up. He'll be back home then."

As the door closed, Al turned his gaze toward the flickering light in the fireplace made possible by light bulbs under stacked fake wood. The counterfeit light reminded him of his days in sleazy bars and bordellos in the Five Points District. His disease came from one of those scantily clothed, high-heeled broads, and there wasn't anything he could do to turn back the clock. Not one fucking goddamn thing.

He checked his watch again. How he looked forward to getting back into the Miami sun. January was the start of sailfish season in South Florida. Sailfish would bite on all kinds of bait. The trick wasn't so much hooking one, as getting it into the boat. The majority of them twist themselves off the hook and flip back into the ocean.

With renewed lightness, he proceeded to the closet where he plucked his hat and overcoat. He struggled for a few moments to get the coat on over the body armor under his clothes, then pulled the nickel-plated .38 Special from the left inside pocket, spun the cylinder and returned it to the pocket. He did the same with the Colt revolver in the holster under his arm. *I believe I've still got one or two tricks up my sleeve,* he thought.

He opened the suite door, and D'Andrea and a phalanx of bodyguards snapped into formation, Capone at the center. The unit moved toward the passageway and down the back staircase. At the bottom, D'Andrea escorted Al through the pulpy snow toward the waiting armored Cadillac, a scout car in front and a touring one behind. Al inserted his pudgy body inside the car. D'Andrea tucked in behind him.

The entourage pushed through tunneled streets of snow piled three foot-high, stopping in front of the two-flat brick house at 7244 Prairie Avenue, Al's home. He took note of the single black car parked a half block down the street, engine running. A minute later, Mae made her way from the house to the rear door of the Cadillac, two bodyguards at her side.

"I'm a little early. We're making one stop before we catch the plane to Miami," Al said, as his buxom blonde wife seated herself next to him and greeted him with an affectionate kiss on the lips.

"That's fine, Al," she said.

He caught a whiff of her rosewater perfume and ogled her svelte figure. She dressed fashionably, low heels on her small feet, perfectly painted lips and fingernails. He'd married her when she was twenty-one, a good Irish Catholic woman hand-picked by his mother as the girl best suited to marry her Al, and to raise Sonny. After his father Gabriele died of a heart attack and the barber shop closed, his mother came to live at the Cicero house he'd bought in '23. Theresa and Mae's home-cooked Sunday dinners became renown, with family and friends, politicians, Hollywood stars and trouble boys all sitting around the Italian table enjoying the bounty Al provided.

"Take care of business, Al. Then we'll go off for some rest and relaxation," Mae said. "I think you're right, we should shake off the dust of Chicago and live permanently in Florida. Who knows when we'll be back, if ever. Police blame you for everything here."

The vehicles slogged to a second address on Cicero's south side. After twenty minutes, the first of the cars veered onto a freshly plowed alley, halting in a half block behind a faded blue bungalow.

D'Andrea departed into the blustery wind which lifted snow from drifts and blew it back into the car's roomy interior. More henchmen joined D'Andrea, who soon gave the all-clear for the Don to leave his armored fort. Al squeezed Mae's hand as he moved through the open door. The squad, Capone in its middle, revolvers drawn, three bruisers with Tommy guns, hurriedly made its way up the narrowly shoveled pathway leading to the rear of the house. One soldier remained behind to guard the Caddy and pushed the car door shut.

Mae pulled her full-length fox fur coat tightly around her body. She found the frigid winter air refreshing after last summer's sweltering heat: a record nine days above one hundred. Al said he bought the place in Miami, so she and Sonny could live away from Chicago's heat.

Through the dark-tinted glass car window, her eyes caught sight of a scrawny yellow Labrador retriever pup barking at the end of a chain across the alley. A scruffy man came out of a house, presumably the dog's owner, clothed only in a white cotton undershirt, dark pants and tall black boots. He hollered at the dog: "Shut up, or I swear I'll kill you, you S.O.B!" The dog clamored inside a dilapidated doghouse buried in a vast snowdrift.

Periodically Mae glanced back at the shivering mutt, now with only its head and front feet visible in the open doorway. The dog monitored the car, too, seemingly curious about the action in the alley.

Inside the house, Al took a seat among four chairs around a small kitchen table. D'Andrea stood at his side. The rest of the bodyguards occupied positions at entrance points at the front and rear of the house. Al unfolded a scrap of paper with a New York phone number scrawled on it and handed it to the resident. The man moved to the wall phone and placed the call. When the connection was made, Al rose from the table, grabbed the receiver and whispered into the mouthpiece. "Five guys… thirty G's… Call this number when the job's done." He hung up the phone and indicated his readiness to depart.

"Thanks for your help, my friend," Al said, shaking the resident's hand. "Got to be real careful these days. Feds got my phones tapped. All my establishments under surveillance. I feel like a goddamn animal on end of a short chain."

"No problem, Don," the resident said. "Use my phone any time."

The crew prepared for the return to the Cadillac.

"That didn't take long," Mae said, as the car door opened and Al again took his place next to her.

"Just a little business, all taken care of now."

D'Andrea joined them momentarily, jerking the door closed behind him.

The cars crept forward. The renewed activity in the alley reinvigorated the dog's barking. Mae, peering through the car's side window, observed the scruffy man had reappeared, holding a bone in one hand, and what seemed to be a clawed club in the other behind his back. She lost sight of the scene as the Cadillac left the alley, then heard what sounded like a dog's yelp, followed by silence.

Al noticed Mae's body recoil into the fur coat. "What's wrong...are you cold?"

"That dog, back there, in the alley. We should go back and check."

"I didn't see a dog. What dog?" Al said, placing an arm around her shoulders, and tugging the fox-trimmed collar high under her chin.

"You're probably right, Al. Will you take me to Miami now? I could use a breather from Chicago. Can't wait to see all the new things you've ordered for the house. Let's have a swimming party as soon as we get there. I want to show off that marble bathing pool."

—

During the fifty days of winter in 1930-1931, in a dumpy apartment along Lake Erie, Louie waited for word of Capone's indictment. Nearly two years had passed. His Godfather Johnny "Papa" Torrio had risen to No. 2 on New York's Public Enemy list and cartel organizer of bootleggers along the Eastern Seaboard. In May 1929, Torrio presided over an Atlantic City assembly of the Big Seven mafia from across the country, though Charles Luciana, New York head of the *Union Siciliano*, was considered the Big Boss. The meeting was to talk about recent events in Chicago: the St. Valentine's Day massacre, followed by the baseball bat beating deaths of Albert Anselmi and John Scalise. Louie heard that Capone, in trouble with the Feds, sat next to Luciana at the head table, along with Genovese and Gambino family representatives, all waiting for the chance to take over the Chicago Outfit.

The *borgata* had also formed a national syndicate to share in revenues of narcotics, loan-sharking, and rackets when Prohibition ended. Torrio provided a few words of wisdom to the boys: "Generate tax returns and include some lawful business in 'em." The following year Torrio himself purchased a legitimate wholesale liquor concern, the Prendergast-Davies company, the largest liquor import business in New York. Preferring to keep his name out of the business for tax purposes, he named as president William Stockblower, Torrio's brother-in-law, and Louie as a third stockholder.

Through Torrio and newspapers, he kept abreast of the indictments and sentencing of Capone's chiefs. He knew the Feds considered himself the missing link, as a lieutenant for Al's organization in the chain of evidence in the attempt to build its case against Capone on tax evasion.

In March 1931, during a trip to Pittsburgh, Federal Agent Clarence Converse served him with a subpoena to testify as a star witness at Capone's trial.

A month later, Louie noticed a mystifying front-page article in the *Chicago Trib*...a complete account of a murder plot by Al Capone of four government men, including U.S. Attorney Johnson, information fed to the newspaper by a representative of the Cook County State's Attorney.

.

April 21, 1931—The Feds learned of the plot from phone taps of associates, cronies and lieutenants of the Capone Outfit across the country. Five New York thugs were seen days later cruising in a blue sedan bearing a New York license tag. Another phone conversation with Capone laid out the date and time for the meeting in a house with himself and a few of his henchmen. Detectives from the State's Attorney of Cook County made plans to raid the house. An informant alerted Capone of the impending raid, and upon arrival, they found the house empty.

Capone has not been seen in the Chicago area since. His office suite in the Lexington Hotel in the heart of Chicago's fashionable near South Side is all but abandoned.

Capone is also under investigation for the murder of Jake Lingle, a reporter for the Chicago Tribune, in June 1930.

Lingle was a personal friend of Al Capone, who knew a great deal about his illegal activities.

President Hoover has received daily updates on the case the Treasury Department is building to charge Capone with defrauding the government by not paying income tax. His edict to Federal agents: "Put Capone out of business—for good!"

It appears the end is near for Al Capone.

Louie's hand began to tremble, a daily occurrence now, any time he contemplated the tight spot in which he found himself.

Frankie Yale is responsible for dis whole fucking fiasco! he thought. Frankie and Al went back to the days when they were kids in the Five Points gang. Frankie was in his early twenties when he became Big Boss of the Italian colonies in Brooklyn and New York's east side, then director of the Black Hand gang. He organized the non-union bricklayers and laundrymen. And as boss of the Harvard Inn, he hired Al as bouncer. They were still friends in '25, when Al, fighting to become No. 1 bootlegger in Chicago, reached out to Frankie for help in recruiting his eighteen-man bodyguard. Officially, Frankie's business card stated he was owner of a New York cigar factory, Frankie Yale Cigars. Unofficially, Frankie was in Chicago in '24 when torpedo killers bagged Dion O'Banion. Capone hired Frankie for that kill. Frankie's power grew, and he got greedy. Then Capone's booze shipments began to disappear. If Frankie had not double-crossed the boss, he would not have been cut down, nor would police have found the guns linked to the boss in Frankie's car. Capone had been on the run ever since. *Si—this all Frankie's fault!*

"Imma sittin' duck," Louie had told Jess the last time he saw her. "I getta subpoena...but if break da code and squeal to Feds, I getta bumpoff. Gotta go on da lam—maybe for a long time."

Now, spring just around the corner, he felt as testy as a black bear dozing in a murky den in the Allegheny Mountains of Ohio. Though the winter had been mild, only dumping two feet of snow instead of the normal sixty inches, he was hungry for emancipation. And he yearned for the companionship of his mate.

Finally, he saw the notice of Capone's indictment splashed on the front page of a Cleveland newspaper:

Capone Indicted on Tax Evasion Charges

June 5, 1931—The indictment in Chicago this week of 'Scarface' Al Capone, the country's most notorious gangster, was brought about after two years of secret service work by the U.S. Intelligence Unit of the Bureau of the Internal Revenue.

Capone, who defied law and order in Chicago for about 10 years, owes his plight to little bits of incriminating evidence, documentary and otherwise, left here and there at various times throughout his career.

Early last year a book of record showing distribution of profits from the Hawthorne Smoke Shop, a gambling house in Cicero, suburb of Chicago, was seized in the raid of another house in Cicero. The smoke shop raid provided the needed evidence to show Capone's connection to it.

In the past year, grand juries heard evidence against Capone. Witnesses testified, government agents, hoodlums, Capone's ex-followers. Reports are that one of the government's star witnesses against Capone is Louis La Cava, former gambling house guard and gunman for Capone. In March he was served with a subpoena to testify as one of the star witnesses at Capone's trial, ending a two-year search for La Cava.

Louie picked up the phone and called his wife.

"You see da newspaper, Jess? Capone…he's inna jail! Imma in witness protect, but I gotta come to Oxbow an' see you—soon!"

CHAPTER FIFTEEN

Christmas —1931

If being a hero means hanging on one minute longer, then the Wall Street crash of 1929 created a lot of them. An awful lot of people were holding on by a thread.

A few weeks before Christmas, Walter stood at the eastern kitchen window of his farmhouse, staring across the frozen yard as the distant, cold sun rose above the horizon. In its foreground: the speckled-white barn housing a dairy herd of twenty-seven, minus the two that had to be put down, infected with bovine tuberculosis; plus, last spring's crop of calves, a half-dozen draft horses, a haymow full of hay and silo full of silage. For centuries the barn stood at the center of farm life, its churchlike architecture evidence of the family's heritage and future. There, Walter learned the confidence that comes from hard physical labor: feeding and caring for livestock, mucking out animal stalls, repairing broken equipment, patching a broken roof. Now, barns blatantly advertised to passers-by, if almost deserted of animals and machinery, to watch for a rapid farm sale.

Two older structures abutted the house: a well house, and round smokehouse with its tin roof and chimney, where he'd helped his father and grandfather smoke sides of beef, pork and wild turkeys. Nearby, Emma's small flower garden followed along the cement walkway leading to the porch where dainty lavender flowers bloomed prolifically all summer. On this morning, only the blue-mantled head of the three-foot Madonna statue penetrated the snow cap, and a polar wind skipped haphazardly across the landscape, kicking up thin white squalls to the top of the stately forty-foot evergreen nearby, though the tree's thick core and branches hardly shifted from the force. Who'd planted the tree? He did not know, but for nearly a century it had withstood, with fierce tenacity, whatever Mother Nature could dish out.

The scene stirred deeply rooted memories from a childhood long ago. Pleasant reminiscences, though overshadowed from time to time by the darkest ones, which Walter referred to as the trials of Job, when the God of his religion didn't show up. Over the years, he'd tried to read every book, poem and writings of sages from the ages he could lay his hands on. The wily, searing truths of Mark Twain spoke to him like none other. Twain lost several family members to common diseases, then his father to pneumonia, which contributed to the family's fiscal instability, forcing them to sell property, even the very furniture they sat and slept upon.

Twain wrote in 1879: "Religion consists in a set of things which the average man thinks he believes, and wishes he was certain of."

Thus, with the arrival of each new season and every pass across the fields—plowing, planting, and harvesting—a cultivated ideology emerged to make better sense of the vagaries of life. Keeping one foot in the church, the other he kept out.

Now he wondered what his sons Leonard and Samuel would take from this time of strain on their family, which hadn't yet seen its end. He parlayed his wisdom most recently when he told the boys of their mother's need to go to a sanatorium, for perhaps a very long time:

"Pray for your mother as though nothing else will help, but work as hard at school and home as though no prayer can help."

The tears he'd been able to hold back now trickled down his cheeks as he stared at Emma's most recent letter in his hand, though it warmed his heart that she'd found such an imaginative way to lighten the news of her months at the Oakdale Sanatorium.

She wrote large portions of the text in circles on the pages.

Dear Walter, Leonard and Samuel—

How hard it is to be separated from you, approaching my second Christmas at the sanatorium. I do hope by now you have gone to the grove and cut the most resplendent Christmas tree, put it up in the living room, and adorned it, top to bottom, with white candles. Do this to remember our Christmases past, and those we will share together in the future, God willing. I say the rosary several times a day for you and ask God and the Blessed Virgin Mary to keep all of us in His care.

I am still in the admissions wing, next door to the nurses' room and told I shall remain here, according to Dr. Sparrow, the super-intendent of the hospital, for likely my entire stay. I continue to recover from my surgery where Dr. Oskar, the surgeon, collapsed my right lung for a period of time. I am still very weak, but am told I'm progressing as well as hoped. Dr. Oskar says fresh air, good food, and rest are the best weapons now to fight the disease. Great care is given to boiling bedding and handkerchiefs, and containing coughs and destroying spittle.

As I told you, the admissions wing is a glassed-in porch where our beds are lined up side by side, and many mornings we awaken to fresh snow drifts that have settled on top of the blankets. The nurses place warmed rocks amongst the bedding to keep us from freezing. We have a pleasant view of the countryside, a few snow-covered meadows, a herd of cows—so it is very much like looking outside a window of our house on the farm.

I'm told the sanatorium has reached its peak of about 700 lungers. I've made friends with several women in the beds nearby. Myrtle Jamison, whom I wrote about in my last letter, sadly, died two days ago. Her family will arrive today to claim her body. I've lost many other new friends to consumption, but most are like me, sur-viving the disease day by day. I'm told by Dr. Oskar that research is underway on a new tuberculosis treatment that hopefully will greatly revolutionize treatment of the disease. For now, there are plans to add a wing here, including a new surgical center.

I spend many hours reading each day. The sanatorium receives a Roman Catholic periodical, <u>The Witness</u>. I just finished a lengthy article on Pope Pius XI, speaking out against the ecumenical movement that promotes cooperation and better understanding among different religious denominations. He says: "Certainly such attempts can nowise be approved by Catholics, founded as they are on that false opinion which considers all religions to be more or less good and praiseworthy." He also says, "Those who hold this opinion are in error and deceived." What do you make of this, Walter? You are better read than I. On one hand, I understand the Pope wishes to preserve Roman Catholic purity; on the other hand, it seems we would all be better served with a universal Christian unity. The anti-Catholic attitude in this country has not come about without reason—the Pope, even labeled the Antichrist. I do look forward to hearing your wisdom on the subject.

And I read an article about Vatican City, the world's smallest country, which was recently made an enclave of Rome. Do we really need our own country? Who will pay for it? Which reminds me that we are still behind in our giving to the I.C. Church. Remember, Walter: member annual giving is put in the December church bulletin—please do not let the boys see that we've not put in our share.

On a lighter side, several radios have been donated to the sanatorium, and they turn them up real loud in the evenings so as many as possible can listen to the "Amos & Andy" and "Little Orphan Annie" programs. And a new one: "Lone Ranger" out of WXYZ in Detroit. Such wonderful stories they tell! A radio would be a nice Christmas present for the boys—perhaps it will be possible another year.

I look forward to hearing about the progress the boys are making in school. Leonard, be sure and take your religion studies seriously—only two more years until your confirmation. And Samuel, how proud I am of your arithmetic grades. Mommy loves both of you so much. I hope to be home soon. What a reunion it will be!

Walter—please express our gratitude to Father Halpin and Sister Keith for their extra kindnesses to our family during our hardship. Rev. Striechman, too, was kind to stop by before my departure, and I look forward to meeting your new pastor when he arrives. Lean on him and others from your church who've offered their help. They'll be a blessing to you if you'll but reach out to them. Most importantly, we are called to cheerfully love and serve one another—and we must also be grateful recipients of these graces.

Every day when the post arrives, everyone stops everything to see if there might be a letter or package from home. I've received parcels from the ladies at I.C. Church: rosaries, books, cards they all signed, along with assorted cookies and cakes. Also, from the Pythian Sisters, and the Esther Circle from your church. Noritta writes every day, of course. All have greatly lifted my spirits.

Finally, I understand that Father Halpin has recently transferred to Dubuque, and I so look forward to meeting the new priest, Father Torpey, soon.

My deepest love, Emma.

Walter looked up as Leonard bounded down the stairs for breakfast, outfitted in an ill-fitted scratchy wool sweater, last year's dark dress pants reaching just above his ankle bones, and outgrown bedroom slippers on stocking feet. The St. Christopher medal on a silver chain in his hand soon fell around his neck. The site brought to mind the medal he'd received as a boy, with the engraving on the front of the saint carrying a child, an icon of God's promise to help its owner live a life pleasing to Him and to hear whenever a young boy beckoned for help.

Samuel, dressed in Leonard's hand-me-downs, shadowed him into the kitchen, and the boys soon were racing toward the same chair, the one at the table closest to the stove. Samuel arrived second, as usual.

"Good morning, boys! Yesterday Onnallee prepared pancake batter… hope that's okay with you?"

Walter turned his back to the boys to cork the brown bottle he'd been hugging in one hand before returning it to the cupboard. On his way to the kerosene stove, he dropped the letter on the table's center.

"Did we get a new letter from Mommy?" Leonard asked excitedly, eying the envelope, and recognizing Emma's beautiful handwriting:

To: Mr. Walter Bierkoff
And Masters Leonard & Samuel Bierkoff
R.F.D., Oxbow, Iowa

"Yes, we got another letter. We'll read it this afternoon after school. Her doctor says she has a strong disposition and is progressing well in her treatment," Walter said, dropping a spoonful of bacon grease on the surface of the searing hot steel grill, followed by two large dollops of batter.

"I miss Mommy… I cry at school sometimes," Samuel said. "The sisters told me to say this prayer for Mommy while she's away. Maybe we can say it before bed at night: 'Remember, O most gracious Virgin Mary, never was it known that anyone who fled to your protection, implored your help or sought your intercession, was left unaided.'"

"Of course, that's exactly what we'll do," Walter said.

"It looks like we'll get more snow today," Leonard said, "I should probably stay home from school."

"I was hoping for a fresh coating of snow in time for Christmas, better than having a dingy-white Christmas," Walter said, responding to his son's inexplicable anxiety over every dark cloud that appeared in the sky. Since a very young boy, he'd kept track of *Almanac* weather forecasts.

His Great-grandfather Johann, whom Leonard had never met, experienced the same fear of falling precipitation.

"Why did God make Mommy sick?" Samuel said, fingering the silver fork next to the plate before him.

Walter studied the expression on his second-born's face. Such an articulate child...so much like Emma. An old soul, who spoke of things, asked questions, far beyond his years. Most recently, Samuel talked of one day building a machine that would carefully lift people in and out of bed without hurting their sick bodies.

"Remember, Mommy said in her letters not to worry. Her doctor has her on bed rest on the porch in the sun. This means she's getting better every day—right, Father?" said Leonard.

"That's right, boys," Walter said, as Samuel began to sob, with Leonard quickly following.

"Let's write another letter to Mommy tonight right after we read her letter to us," Walter said, firmly grasping each boy by a shoulder with one hand. "We can tell her about Christmas Eve Mass. Sister Mary Margaret tells me, Leonard, you'll be reading part of the Christmas story from the book of Luke? She says you need to practice every day."

Wiping both eyes then his nose with a sweatered forearm, Leonard sputtered: "I got a ruler to my hand yesterday from Sister Mary Margaret because I couldn't stop stuttering. I get nervous when I read...then I stutter.

"And Sister Mary Margaret is trying to make Gina Bundy write with her right hand. Gina says nuns at her old school used to tie her left arm behind her back every day until she was in third grade...it made her arm hurt! They promised holy cards, rosaries and medals of the Blessed Virgin and Jesus if she'd stop using her left hand. What's wrong with writing with your left hand, Father? It's just like me, and stuttering, I can't help it." Leonard said.

"I'll help you practice your reading so you won't stutter at all when it comes time to read your part," Walter said.

"And I'm going to be a donkey," Samuel said, with a wide smile, fat tears still clinging to his cheeks. "Noritta is measuring me for my donkey costume. She's going to make me enormous ears too...and a donkey tail. I don't have any lines, 'cause everyone knows donkeys can't talk."

"Then we'll practice being a donkey, too, Samuel, so you'll be the best donkey standing next to the baby Jesus there ever was."

"And Gina says her father didn't come to the funeral when her mother died because he wasn't Catholic," Leonard said. "That made her sad. She and her brothers are living with their grandmother in Oran. Her father lives at their old house in Oelwein."

"Tell me more about Sister Keith, Leonard. She's been at the school for a couple years now... I imagine the kids have really grown to love her."

"Sister Keith told Sister Mary Margaret never to hit me again with a ruler! Father Halpin came to the home room later, and said he wanted to talk with Sister Keith in private. But I can tell Victor really likes Sister Keith, so Sister Mary Margaret can hit me with the ruler or chalkboard pointer as much as she wants, as long as Sister Keith makes Victor happy. Sister Keith says Victor doesn't hear too well, but he's really good at arithmetic—might even be a genius!"

"You need to mind the Sisters...they mean well," Walter said. "And hopefully, Mommy will be home soon. She reminds us in her letter to get ready for Christmas! Next Saturday morning we'll take the wagon and team of horses and go to the grove and cut down a tree. We'll pick out a real tall one."

Walter stopped himself before adding: "...and we'll have the most merry, joyous, blessed Christmas ever"...words that seemed woefully hollow since Emma's departure, the wife, mother, and center of their family. And theirs would be another bleak Christmas this year, with only an apple or orange and a few pieces of candy for the boys from Santa left under the tree.

"Eat your pancakes now... John and Onnallee will be here soon to take you to country school, Samuel. You too, Leonard—eat!"

Walter retrieved a layer of newspapers from a box in the corner of the room and sat next to the boys at the table. He noted the photo on the front page of the top paper, showing a hundred people lined up outside the Salvation Army soup kitchen in Waterloo. Its headline: **"No Sign of Depression's End in Sight"** The first paragraph quoted a child in a family of five: "We only eat bread most days. Father says we can sprinkle it with either a little bit of sugar—slice of onion, or over-ripe banana that we get from a grocery store before it gets thrown out. We come to the soup kitchen for a little meat in our diet."

The painful recollection of the recent funeral of a neighbor came to mind. He'd been found by his wife hanging from a rafter in his barn. Two other suicides had happened in as many months, each man taking a bullet to the head in a cornfield....forever banned from entering heaven's gates, according to the Christian Church. Nor were they allowed burial in a cemetery. Finally, a farmer offered a small corner of his field for a final resting place for suicides.

Walter lifted a second paper from the box, intending to note portions in his Capone journal. The article laid out La Cava's history with Capone.

Gambler, Banished from Chicago by King Capone, Returns to Aid in Move to Put Al Behind Bars

June 17, 1931—For more than two years the case against Al Capone, the king of the Prohibition Era, has been mounting. Documentary evidence collected. Myriad witnesses testified—from government agents to hoodlums.

By accident, Frank Wilson, the IRS's Special Intelligence Unit assigned to focus on Capone, found a cash receipts ledger, confiscated years earlier during a raid of a Capone gambling establishment by Chicago police, which not only showed the operation's net profits for a gambling house, but contained Capone's name—a record of Capone's income.

In 1924 alone his income was estimated at over $300,000. Capone never filed an income tax return, owned nothing in his own name, and never made a declaration of assets or income.

Among Capone's henchmen was Louis La Cava, now of Cleveland, who was discovered to have shared a safety deposit box with Capone. In March La Cava was served with a subpoena to testify as one of the star witnesses at Capone's trial, ending a two-year search for La Cava.

La Cava left Chicago in the early 1920s obeying Capone's dictum: Go or be killed! In a letter written to Jack Zuta, slain vice lord, La Cava sought permission to join the ranks of the Moran-Aiello crowd, a crowd hostile to Capone. La Cava hated Capone, but never so much as now. And government agents knew it. Prosecutors believed he could tell the grand jury much about Capone.

La Cava is also being questioned regarding his relationship with Johnny Torrio, for whom he once served as secretary.

La Cava's testimony, the man once banished from Chicago by Capone, is expected to make the case for Federal authorities and send Capone to the Federal penitentiary at Leavenworth, Kanas.

Walter looked across the table at the boys taking their last bites of food. "Go wash up now, Samuel. Your ride will be here in ten minutes."

He grabbed another newspaper that spelled out Capone's conviction and sentencing, and those of his henchmen.

Man who topped the Public Enemy list, convicted at the Federal courthouse in downtown Chicago

October 17, 1931—Capone is currently being confined at the Cook County Jail until arrangements can be made for his transfer to Atlanta, the toughest of the Federal prisons. The trial concluded two years of secret service work by the U.S. Intelligence Unit of the Bureau of the Internal Revenue. Capone had defied law and order for 10 years—but left bits of evidence.

The Feds weren't able to bring him to justice on charges of murder, extortion, or bootlegging—but rather for failing to pay his income tax for the years 1924-1929. He was sentenced to 11 years in prison, and assessed a fine of $50,000, court costs of $30,000, and $215,000 plus interest for back taxes.

At age 33 Capone's career as crime boss is finally over.

One statement in particular caught Walter's attention:

Capone told reporters after his sentencing: "I've been made an issue throughout America, but I wonder why they don't go after all those bankers who took the savings of thousands of poor people who lost them in bank failures?"

He read on:

The conviction of two public officials, three of Capone's chiefs, and indictments of several of his minor henchmen, preceded Capone's indictment and conviction.

Ralph Capone, Al's brother, who was brought home from South America, was the first to be indicted in October 1929, and sentenced to three years in a penitentiary on failure to pay taxes on income of one million dollars between 1924-1926. As he watched others at the top of his organization go down the river, Capone knew the end was near.

Among Capone's other henchmen was Louis La Cava— who is also being questioned regarding his relationship with Johnny Torrio, whom the Feds believed may have conspired to defraud the government in evasion of payment of income tax on Torrio's income. La Cava has also been interrogated regarding several gangland murders, but no arrest has been made.

Hearing a passing motorist, Walter set the papers aside and stood up to look out the window.

"Time to go, boys. Hurry!"

Samuel rose, put on his coat, cap and galoshes, and grabbed his book bag and lunch pail. From the kitchen window, Walter watched him trudge through the deep snow toward his brother John's car parked at the top of the driveway.

"I'll get Maggie and pull her out front, Leonard. Wouldn't it be nice if the school could afford one of those new Endgate school buses? Sure would make life easier if country kids got picked up by a bus."

Walter put on his winter attire and plodded out the front door to the double corn bin that doubled as a garage for Maggie. Earlier that morning he'd set cobs afire in a shallow pan and pushed it under her engine. Now he pulled out the pan with a wooden rake, carried it to a snowbank, and doused the coals with several shovelfuls of snow.

Maggie's engine quickly turned over. Rounding the bin corner, he spied Barney Finkle's Model T turning onto the driveway. Walter stopped the car by the front of the house, left the engine running, got out and made his way to Barney.

"Are ya headin' out?" Walter said, as Barney cranked down the car window. "Looks like everything you own in this world is packed inside or tied to the roof of the car."

"I've sent my wife and children on ahead to Detroit… We'll plan to stay with my brother and family. He says there are logger jobs there. You gonna be okay on your farm, Walter?" Barney said, glancing around at the buildings. "I tell ya…it's real tough to let it all go. No money to pay taxes or my mortgage. Lost everything I worked for my entire life."

Barney dug for a handkerchief in his coat pocket as tears spewed from his eyes. Finally, he buried his entire face in the red bandanna and wept uncontrollably.

Walter reached inside the car and placed his hand on his friend's shoulder.

"The countryside will never be the same. It kills me to see you go, Barney. You and so many others I might never see again. Let us know how you're getting along from time to time."

Walter withdrew his hand, reached for a few dollars in his overall breast pocket and handed the bills to Barney.

"This isn't much…Emma, the boys and I wish it was more. I hear the government is offering a little help, too. You should check in with 'em when you get settled. Hope you can bring yourself to accept the extra help 'til you get back on your feet."

"Thank you, Walter. Thank you very much," Barney said, gratefully accepting the gift. The two tightly clasped hands for what Walter believed might be the last time.

"Keep the faith… Those who keep the faith survive. And try not to let yourself worry too much," Walter said, realizing his words were meant for his own benefit as much as Barney's.

Leonard emerged from the house, placed his school things inside the sputtering Maggie, and made his way to Walter's side. Together they watched Barney back the Model T onto the road and drive off.

"I don't want to be late for school. We need to go now, Father," Leonard said.

"I'm ready," Walter said, his eyes still welled up with tears.

For the first miles, the only sound Walter heard was the lamentation of Maggie's engine as her balloon tires bounced in and out of icy ruts in the road.

He remembered last summer's infestation of grasshoppers, which had probably killed off Barney's last chance of survival on the farm. It was all so unfair. Only decades earlier, farmers like him represented the flourishing seed planted by their immigrant ancestors. Those who came to America, initially working as farmhands and living frugally for years, were finally able to buy a plot of land, a milestone guaranteeing the promise of a better life for future generations. That promise had now vanished like a snowflake on a dog's warm nose. Whole families had been torn apart, with children going to live with relatives or friends. Tens of thousands ended up in orphanages, and on orphan trains that crisscrossed the country where they hoped to find a family willing to adopt them at a stop along the way.

Iowans had taken an additional hit. They'd placed enthusiastic faith in Hoover as the 31st President of the United States. But after his third year in office, their "Iowa-boy-made-good" and self-made millionaire had clearly lost the mandate of the people by failing to leverage the power of the Federal government to address the depression.

Nonetheless, Walter found he empathized with Hoover. It must be difficult for him to be viewed as callous and insensitive toward the suffering of millions of desperate Americans, as he himself had been orphaned at a young age and sent to live with a relative. Still, it was doubtful Hoover would be re-elected.

"When will we see Barney again, Father?" Leonard asked.

Walter looked across the seat and smiled at the boy. "I don't know, but I'm sure gonna miss Barney and his family. You're probably feeling the same way."

The rest of the trip Walter could fixate only on Maggie's shadow in the rays of the cold and distant morning sun.

—

The people of Oxbow went about preparing for the arrival of Christmas as best they could, depression or not. Store owners along Main Street strung the previous years' decorations in their windows. Between the electric poles in the center of town, city council members looped a few lengths of fresh pine garland and wreaths with red-ribboned bows. And Sweeney rehung the old gas lanterns on poles, removed when the town got electricity over a decade earlier. He lit them each evening at sunset and extinguished their fire around midnight to save on fuel. The warm glow of the lamps was his attempt to remind people of good times past, and of even better times which surely lay ahead. But Main Street this holiday season largely seemed devoid of much cheerfulness, save for the red bows and a little glitter.

Sweeney always made it a point to visit business owners to wish them a Merry Christmas. Today he'd stop by Bill Rechkemmer's new Ford showroom in the former Opera House. As he locked the office door, behind him he could hear the drone of the town's Wehr road grader snowplow.

He twisted around to wave at Walt Polege, a local hired as full-time street commissioner soon after owners of the first Model Ts began to demand better road maintenance. Polege's slight build somehow seemed larger than life in the grader's tall open cab. Typically, he wore a flannel shirt underneath striped bib overalls, with red union suit peeking out from beneath. Sweeney believed that underwear came off Walt's body but once a week, only on wash day. Walt was a hard worker though, and just keeping open the town's main thoroughfare during the winter months was a full-time job.

Sweeney watched the Wehr belch heavy black smoke from the smoke-stack as it pushed the deep snow from the street's center up against the boardwalk. A magazine advertisement from years earlier claimed the plow was a "one man operation with the power to make all roads good roads, and capable of clearing rural highways of six-to-eight-foot snow drifts". The machine completely failed the test in the countryside, as it generally got buried a couple times a day, when Polege would have to summon help from some nearby farmer with draft horses to pull it from its snowy grave.

Melting snow would transform the dirt Main Street into a boulevard of slippery, gooey mud, which was when Walt would lay a raised plank sidewalk across the width of the street, beginning in front of Miller Hardware, so men, women, children and dogs could cleanly cross over to the other side. But no planks would be necessary in the days before Christmas this year, as the forecast called for another heavy snowfall before turning frigid cold.

Sweeney hollered at Polege: "Where you gonna put all the snow yet to fall this winter?" though he couldn't be sure Walt heard him above the engine's whine.

Opening the showroom door, he found himself next to a 1928 Jewitt Six parked beside a brand-spanking-new Ford Model A, both built in Detroit, Michigan. *Bill had done pretty well for himself,* he thought, *considering he'd lost a leg during the war.*

"I hoped to be able to continue to sell Jewitts, along with Fords," Bill said. "The last in production was this beauty. The Jewitt company was sold in '29. Too bad…they're really a fine-looking car."

"I like Fords myself," Sweeney said, recalling the day in the mid-twenties when he purchased his Ford. "Olivia was opposed to buying our first car, she said we couldn't afford one. Then I built a garage to house it."

Absolutely nothing made Sweeney grin more than winning an argument, and just the thought of even an old victory made him fish for a celebratory cigarette.

"Olivia will have no problem achieving sainthood, Sweeney, I can promise you that." Bill said, rolling his eyes as he spoke.

"By the way," he added, "Olivia stopped by for a collection for the poor fund a few weeks ago. Said the Pythian Sisters needed donations for families at Christmas—a few pieces of fruit, candy, and a little smoked ham or turkey to the most destitute. Gave her every nickel I could spare. Maybe the impoverished in large cities can be relegated to the slums and put out of sight, but in a small town the poverty stares you in the face every day."

"I know Olivia was grateful for your donation. Now I must get going… only wanted to stop by and wish you a Merry Christmas. Wouldn't it be great if this economy turned around in the new year?"

Outside, Sweeney waited on the boardwalk for the Wehr to make another pass. Bill's comment about the Pythian Sisters gave him pause, remembering he still needed to speak with Agnes Triggers. Olivia told him after the December Pythian Sisters meeting Agnes had surprised the group during roll call. When members were asked to state something for which each was grateful, Agnes said, "I'm grateful that the evil Al Capone has been put in a Federal penitentiary, but I do wonder why Louie La Cava isn't in the jail cell right next to him, after all, Louie did everything Capone did, in addition to hiding Capone's income in that little cloth book."

"All I could do was stare at Agnes in disbelief," Olivia had said. "People just don't speak ill of Louie La Cava. What if he heard about what Agnes said?"

Sweeney's beef with Agnes, however, was official. While most people acknowledged she listened in on phone conversations, sometimes even interrupting with: "So-and-so isn't home right now, she's gone to visit a relative in such-and-such a place," Agnes' comment confirmed she'd listened in on Sweeney's calls. How else would she have known about the little cloth book?

Sweeney made a mental note: Some serious sparks are gonna fly over this, sister!

—

Sweeney usually took in at least one Christmas program among the dozen or so country schools, always an occasion of great excitement. Desks were pushed to one side of the schoolroom, replaced with rows of wooden folding chairs to seat parents, grandpas and grandmas, aunts, uncles, siblings, friends and neighbors. The teacher's desk area became a stage, a six-foot tall piece of cardboard painted with a manger scene its backdrop. And children dressed in home-sewn costumes enacted the roles of Mary and Joseph, the Christ Child, wise men, angels and animals—all who mysteriously found themselves congregated in a lowly stable one evening beneath a brilliant star in the sky that had pointed them to the manger.

This year, he and Oliva and the girls sat with Walter and Leonard. Sweeney counted a dozen mice as part of the unofficial pageantry. Afterwards Leonard congratulated Samuel, saying: "Your ears were pretty believable for a donkey!"

And the public school's Christmas pageant had its largest attendance on record, according to Sweeney, the current school board president.

Thereafter, day and night, mill pond became the popular hangout, with Sweeney among them. Folks collected old tires from filling stations and started them afire to keep warm while ice skating. On this evening, he noticed Tuffy Adams warming himself next to the fire. He and his wife recently took in one of the orphaned Brandt children, whose family had lived in the house across from the Baptist church. Both parents had been killed in a car mishap on icy roads several weeks earlier. Taking in a child was something people did in the township without thinking twice about it.

Sweeney skated over to talk to Tuffy.

"You and Evelyn are heroes!" Sweeney said, nodding in the direction of the young boy across the way. "You've helped that lad hang on when all footing had given out beneath him. I heard the grandparents in Fayette County took in the other boy. Too bad they had to be split up."

"At least the boys will see each other often. Evelyn and I always felt we were meant to have more children. But these boys are the real heroes. None of us knows what it'll take for them to survive this, they're just beginning that journey. Their mother wrote for the *Oxbow View*...and our Brandt boy likes to write, too. We'll probably read about all of us in a book some day."

"It's times like this when I appreciate what Hoover did before leaving office...creating the 'Children's Bill of Rights'," Sweeney said. "We still boast that Iowa is the best place in the country to raise a child, but you only have to look around to see kids in general have become malnourished during this depression."

"Not to change the subject," Tuffy said, "but I saw Louie La Cava's car parked out front of the O'Malley house a few days ago. He's been gone a long time. Hate to see him back in the area... I'm afraid for my family."

"How much do you know about the guy?" Sweeney said.

"Read about him in newspapers...so do a lot of others. He's a killer, a thug. Saw him and his wife at the Mealey Hotel for dinner some time back. Told my kids not to even look in his direction. Don't want anything to do with that man."

—

The churches advertised their Christmas Eve service in local news-papers and on marquees out front, when angelic children would recite Scripture and sing the age-old songs announcing the birth of the Christ Child and entrance of the Savior into the world. And each congregation diligently equipped for over-flow crowds, anticipating every seat in the house would be filled.

Two days before Christmas a soundless, steady wet snowfall began that dropped a thick, white coating onto frozen roads, barren trees and steeped rooftops, turning the landscape into a brumous wonderland. Then, on Christmas Eve day, the temperature plummeted into the low teens.

Undeterred, townsfolk made plans for the trek to church for the midnight service by car or on foot. Several families in the countryside though, like ancestors of old, harnessed horses to a wooden sleigh or wagon, and climbed aboard, bundled in heavy coats, boots, scarves, hats and gloves, with heated bricks at their feet, and covered over by a thick horse blanket, to sing carols mile after mile to the rhythmic accompaniment of sleigh bells dangling from leather horse harnesses, the ringing intermingled with the crunch of horse hooves and wheels traversing snow-packed roads; the light from a crisp moon illumining their way, enough that sightings of Santa could be called out.

In town, the old gas lamps lit the way, and sweet-toned bells resonated from church bell towers, inviting one and all: "Come! Come! Come!"

One by one worshippers reached the front doors of the Lutheran, Methodist and Baptist churches, where frozen faces, fingers and toes received proper attention by the membership. The Methodists had the biggest draw for any unchurched, as Dr. George Eickelberg, the town's dentist, and a big man known for his booming bass voice, sang in the choir.

The nuns at the Catholic church cared for shivering arrivals for midnight Mass, which this year included Walter and his sons. Shoulder to shoulder sat the parishioners, an ocean of Roman Catholics huddled in candlelit pews in the frosty cathedral-like nave.

"Excuse me," Josephine La Cava whispered, standing next to Walter in the wide center aisle. "Can you fit two more into this row?"

Walter and the boys stepped out into the aisle while worshippers in the pew bumped together, enough so the La Cavas could be seated. Finally, the three sat back down, with Louie's shoulder smashed up against Walter's, the smell of evergreen boughs in the windows now intermingled with Louie's witch hazel.

"We're late getting to church," Walter overheard Josephine say to the woman next to her. "Lou has just recently come back to town. It is so good to have him home...one of God's miracles on an evening of miracles."

Walter finished reading the bulletin announcements, covertly folded the notation about member giving, and inserted it in an inside a coat pocket.

Suddenly, everyone rose to their feet, except Walter, as the procession and entrance song began. Down the center aisle came the censer bearer, followed by the cross bearers, the readers, and deacon who carried the Book of the Gospels, slightly elevated, then the other concelebrants, and finally, the priest celebrant, the new priest: Father Torpey.

Nearing the reading of the passage from the Gospel of Luke, Leonard went forward to read from the Lectionary for Mass, where he spoke slowly, hardly stuttering at all.

Walter whispered, "Good job, son!" as Leonard returned to his seat.

The homily from the priest was about the unspeakable joy that comes from belief in God, delivered in its fulfillment at Christmas. And about the response of believers: living lives of gratitude for sending Jesus Christ to reconcile all in the world.

"Jesus Christ is the voice of the poor," the priest declared. "God is merciful and calls us to obedience. Ours is a covenant of kinship. With God and neighbors, we must live in love. It is our calling, in this time of shared sorrow with so many."

After Holy Communion, the priest began the litany of prayers: Prayers for the Saints. Prayers of Thanksgiving. Prayers of Supplication. And Prayers of the Faithful, naming them one by one, and finally...

"We pray for Emma Bierkoff. May God give her the strength to endure her illness, bring her once more to full health, and return her home to Walter and the boys, Leonard and Samuel."

Walter didn't know how much of what the Christian Church had preached throughout the ages was true about the Creator God, or which parts were hope disguised as truth. He still had questions. What he knew for certain was the feeling of warmth that came over him during the prayer for Emma. And he felt swaddled in the love and kindness of these people.

Even if they were Catholics.

CHAPTER SIXTEEN

Lucy Ann Dean Wiltse Minton

The storms of life undeniably alter us. Some things we only learn in a storm. Embrace every storm—embrace them one and all, was Olivia's motto.

Sweeney came home earlier than usual that morning in early March 1933 to report that Olivia's dear friend Lucy Minton had died, the woman for whom she'd worked since girlhood. Within the hour, Olivia went to the Wiltse Hotel, and found Jacob on the settee in the living room, a box of Lucy's papers beside him.

"I'm so sorry for your loss, Jacob," she said. "Lucy's passing leaves a void in the whole community. You had a dozen really good years together, and I know she loved you a great deal."

"I couldn't awaken her in bed at sunrise," he said tearfully. "I'm going through her papers... I must put a notice in the newspaper. She never said much about her early life, nor about the years she was married to Dr. Wiltse... I don't know where to begin."

Olivia took a seat next to Jacob. "I probably know more about Lucy than anyone else. I can help you. She told me her mother was a hotel keeper in Vermont. I'm not sure how Lucy ended up in Iowa, but I know she was raised by an aunt here from a young age."

Olivia paused, trying to remember. "Did you know she had a dressmaking business? She showed me her card once. It said: 'Miss Lucy Ann Dean, Dressmaker, from Iowa.' She met Edwin Wiltse when she was just 18. He was from Strawberry Point, a college man. She and Edwin went off to Chicago after they married. He attended Bennet Medical College, then he began his medical practice. They built the Wiltse in Oxbow before the railroad came to town, around 1877. Edwin had his office in the hotel. They eventually divorced. Folks have their opinions on what went wrong... but Lucy never said. Some things are private, I guess. He moved back to Canada around 1914, and that was when the Wiltse was sold. When the new owners wanted out, Lucy persuaded Clarence Everett at the Oxbow State Bank to give her a loan for six thousand dollars, and she ran the Wiltse alone—."

"Until 1920," Jacob said smiling, evidently remembering the year he and Lucy had married.

"I only wish we'd wed sooner, but for a long time I never dared hope a fine woman like Lucy would ever marry a man like me."

"The wedding was no surprise. What astonished everyone was how long it took before you proposed, Jacob," Olivia said, a broad, warm grin washing over her face. "She probably wouldn't have been able to manage if you hadn't been her handyman during that time. It was clear to everyone that the two of you were a good match."

It was true. There'd been no whirlwind romance between Jacob Minton Jr. and Lucy. Theirs was more a meeting of minds. Within a year they'd added the Minton Sinclair garage and filling station next door to the Wiltse, run by Jacob.

Olivia pulled a few items from the box before returning it to Jacob. "I can write up what I know about Lucy, and bring it by later," she said.

As Lucy died on the first Saturday in March, her obituary appeared in local papers the next day, and her funeral was held on the third day.

Lucy Ann Minton was born in Yorkshire, New York, March 29, 1854, and died March 4, 1933, at the age of 78 years, 11 months, and 25 days at Oxbow, Iowa. Her funeral will be held at 11 am on Tuesday, March 7 at the M. E. Church in Oxbow.

As a very small girl, she came to Iowa, where she lived the rest of her life, spending over fifty years in Oxbow. She was indeed a real pioneer of Oxbow, opening her hotel before the railroad was built through the town, and conducting the affairs of the hotel for over 40 years.

She was married to Dr. Edwin Wiltse, resident physician of Oxbow. Following his death, she was married to Jacob Minton of Oxbow. She leaves behind to mourn her death, her husband, Jacob Minton, an aunt, Sarah Ann Leffingwell, of Coon Rapids, Iowa, who is 92 years old, and four cousins, besides a host of other relatives and friends. One sister, Hattie Kendall Dean, preceded her in death in 1927.

She was noted for her charity, having sheltered and partially reared several homeless children. During the World War, she was the directing spirit of the community in kitting for the soldiers. For this work she was recognized by the wife of President Wilson, who sent her a letter of gratitude and a gift handkerchief. Her hotel was an unofficial headquarters for the community workman's work in wartime. She was a member until quite recently of the Women's Relief Corps. At the Methodist Episcopal Church, she was especially active in the work of the Ladies Aid Society.

On the day of her funeral, Lucy was laid out in the plain coffin in the living room of the Wiltse. Bogart, the caged parrot, was strangely silent as the bereaved passed by the coffin. The viewing line, which curved out the front door and down Main Street for blocks, alternated between clusters of Protestants and Catholics.

At the appointed hour, eight townsmen carried Lucy from the hotel to Youngman's horse drawn black hearse-wagon, which delivered her to the Methodist church, where Rev. Oelfke delivered a short, yet powerful sermon, entitled: "I Know There Is a Heaven!"

As people filed by Lucy to say their final goodbyes, Olivia overheard a comment, one she figured probably echoed the thoughts of the other mourners: "Would Jacob be able to keep the hotel and filling station going, now that Lucy was gone?"

Olivia already knew the answer. No one could ever fill the shoes of Lucy Ann Dean Wiltse Minton.

And she knew something else… Sometimes the storms of life envelop a whole community.

Olivia bent down to help Youngman move flowers to the gravesite. Her eyes caught sight of a spray in an enormous white basket. She looked for a card. *Strange*, she thought. *No card. Wonder who this is from?*

—

Agnes Triggers meticulously recorded her absences from the Telephone Exchange on her home wall calendar. On the day of Lucy Minton's funeral, she noted being away from the office for two hours. Six months passed before she made another notation, due to illness, which, as it turned out, would later serve as a reminder to tell Sweeney of a rather odd event that happened late that evening.

Admittedly, Agnes was a woman who'd come into this world with an insatiable interest in people. Now in her sixties, she yet wangled a way to know every childish, silly and vulgar detail of the populace for miles around. She said she could change anytime she wanted...as long as she remembered to bring along an extra set of clothing.

And she thought she'd struck gold living directly across the street from the O'Malley house, where it wasn't unusual to see Louie La Cava arrive in town in the middle of the night.

Feeling sick that day in October 1933, she'd left work early. Late in the night her sickness became so severe that she'd subsequently say she could lay claim to every celestial happening as seen through the cut-out halfmoon in the two-seater in the back yard. Around three a.m., returning to her house through the back door once more, she heard a car bumping along on the cratered dirt road of Main Street, the trunk lid banging as it slunk to a stop.

Peering through the white lace curtains of a living room window facing the street, her insides still gurgling, she immediately recognized Louie La Cava's black Lincoln. He got out the driver's door and walked to the trunk, where he seemed to enfold long bulky items in a blanket, then carried the bundle to the side door of the house and disappeared inside.

A light in the house went on.

He revisited the car again, this time to retrieve a small suitcase, which he also took inside.

Resisting yet another urge to return to the outhouse, Agnes, her shadow looming at the window's corner, observed Louie and Josephine's short embrace through the bay window.

Then she saw what appeared to be renewed activity in the car. Something had moved—there was a flutter in the back seat! she was certain. Difficult to see in the dim glow of the street light... perhaps it was a foot or limb flailing against the window.

Finally, her rumbling gut again demanding, the curtain fell, and she retreated to the little brown shack one more time.

CHAPTER SEVENTEEN

A Nickel An Ante

The very day Lucy Minton died, Franklin D. Roosevelt became the country's thirty-second U.S. President. Once and for all, the heartless Hoover was gone! *When God closes a door, he opens a window,* Sweeney thought.

During President Roosevelt's first 100 days in office, he began addressing the American people through weekly radio "fireside chats" on the bank crisis. This was followed by his New Deal proposal to the U.S. Congress, outlining a series of fiscal programs: relief for the unemployed and poor; recovery of the economy to normal levels; and reform of the financial system to prevent a repeat depression. Through Works Progress Association projects, millions of Americans went back to work. That was how Oxbow got funding for a footbridge, its design by Charles Grantham.

Finally, Charles would be able to promote and hold boxing matches on the Island Park once more.

Along with Hoover, gone was the racket on Main Street. For months town folk had endured the clamor of men hammering rivets in the construction of a new 100-foot water tower with a 50,000-gallon tank. Now the only sounds came from a dozen shovels gently clanking against layers of limestone mixed with clay as men dug in the new water mains, along with echoes of hooting children and barking dogs who followed the workers street to street, one or two of them often tottering too closely to the narrow trench for a peek into the abyss, when a worker would call out: "Stand back, or you'll fall in—along with a wall of dirt behind you!"

How Sweeney preferred the sounds of blissful youngsters, even clinking shovels, to that of pounding rivets.

He tried hard not to think about the tank with all that water hovering high above the engine house, particularly on Friday nights when a few of the guys came for a little poker. But he did find himself wondering, on occasion, what weighty things had hung over the head of the first town marshal, John Walgamot. The earliest township election was held in the basement of the Methodist Church in 1891. Sweeney conjectured those first elected officials probably got together for some cards from time to time, covertly though, as clergy would have frowned on such merriment.

That part hadn't changed.

Since 1916, he'd overseen the 10:30 poker game, which entailed rolling out the round wooden table from a corner and setting a few chairs around its perimeter. He put out a deck of cards and fresh box of Corona cigars, plus a large communal red metal ashtray. A year ago he began bringing Olivia's new electric coffee pot. A clean kitchen cloth, also from home, was for wiping out the spiders and anything else over the last seven days that had crept inside the chipped porcelain cups from his great-grand-mother's tea set. The covered floral sugar bowl contained a few cubes for those prissy men who said they didn't enjoy a black cup of coffee any more without a little sugar. Later, the cups would be repurposed, when George Weiland brought out the booze. Lastly, he set out a pretty plate of sweet bread that Olivia had made earlier in the day.

He glanced up at the classy heavy Tiffany fixture with green glass shades overhead, which, he believed, cast the perfect hue over a smoke-laden table for an evening of high stakes gambling, a nickel an ante, a maximum raise of a quarter.

And for tonight's game, he dropped the front page of yesterday's news-paper on top of the workbench. One story he believed might be of interest to Louie, if he showed up.

Iowa Hunts Bandits After Attempted Bank Holdup at Oelwein

September 30, 1933—Police are on the trail of six bandits after two persons were shot in an attempted holdup of the First National Bank in Oelwein today.

The six men traveling in a large automobile were traced to Center Grove, IA, but eluded four squads of police armed with machine guns. A short time later the trail was picked up south of Dubuque and police sped on the Dubuque-Davenport highway in pursuit.

City and county authorities were notified, and stationed forces along the route. Reports from Maquoketa, Clinton and Davenport, however, failed to reveal the whereabouts of the missing gunmen.

The search for the bandits was still in progress late into the night.

Sweeney checked the time and walked out the side door to the well shed under the water tower. He reached inside the door and flipped the switch to start the pump to raise the water table in the tank, something he did several times a day, the last time, around midnight.

George Weiland met up with him on the lawn as he returned to the engine house.

"Sure makes it easier to get booze since Prohibition ended," George said, waving the obvious brown-bagged bottle in Sweeney's face. "And it sure didn't take much time for Rechkemmer to turn his Ford dealership into a beer tavern!"

"Prohibition will go down in history as one of the strangest eras in our country's history," Sweeney said. "And apparently, though the liquor wars are over, that's not the case for bank robberies."

The two passed through the side door. Sweeney picked up the newspaper from the workbench and handed it to George.

"Saw the article. Word on the street is the two who were shot will likely recover," George said, setting the brown bag next to the coffee cups on the bench before taking a seat at the table and spreading the newspaper in front of him.

"Most excitement we've had in years... I was part of the manhunt—up all night," said Sweeney. "Thought we had 'em cornered for a while, but they seemed to know every backroad in the state. Sheriff Willey thinks the robbers may be part of the Black Hand gang out of New York and Chicago. They've been trying to extort money from Oelwein businesses for years, but owners said they weren't going to pay for protection. Apparently, the Black Hand gang is still around. Lotta strangers hang out at the 190 Club south of Oelwein, some say the club is owned by the mafia. Wouldn't surprise me at all if someday I learned that building caught fire."

Sweeney wondered what, if anything, Louie had to do with the robbery. When in the area, he seemed to spend a fair amount of time in Oelwein with its fifty-plus Italian families. The new county road between the two towns made travel a lot easier, too.

"These are desperate times…for even the average Joe. We're still in a deep depression, people fighting over money, land, status. Iowa's experienced nine times more murders than a year ago. Police finally solved one of the most appalling crimes. Do you remember the murder of the two elderly Keefer sisters over by Knoxville a couple of years ago?"

"I read about it at the time," George said, "but forgot all about the case. How'd it turn out?"

"The farmhand was convicted. Police found shells from his .22 at the scene. The bank said he'd been behind on payments for his Model T, and suddenly found the cash to pay it off. They say it's one for the record books…first conviction in the nation based on ballistic evidence."

Coach Gayle Peick emerged through the side door.

"Good evening, gentlemen. Looking forward to playing some poker. Ready to go long into the night."

"We've been talkin' about this depression, Coach," Sweeney said. "A kinda slow creepin' fear is settin' in, the kind that makes desperate people do desperate things. Didya hear about the man in bib overalls who put a mask over his face, Colt .45 in his hip pocket, waltzed into the Oran bank and held it up? Sheriff Willey thinks he's a local."

"I've heard a few pretty scary stories myself," Coach Peick said. "Two area families were recently robbed while sitting down for the evening meal. Heard a knock on the farmhouse door. Robbed at gun point…cash, jewelry, anything of value. Plus, a number of farmers have reported thefts of livestock…a truck load of pigs. Missing cows. Probably taken by a neighbor who drove onto a farm when no one was at home. One farmer lost almost a thousand chickens… but you probably heard about these cases and a lot more, huh, Sweeney?"

Francis Durham and Bill Lehmkuhl entered through the side door—Louie, behind them. They joined Coach Peick at the workbench to pick up coffee.

Sweeney added a sixth chair around the table before taking his seat at the table's head, where he picked up a cigar, took a moment to savor its aroma, then struck a match, rotated its end 'til it glowed evenly, and took the first puffs. The table filled in around him, each man lighting up, except for Louie, who'd again brought his own brand of premium cigar between his lips.

"I wish to sit there," Louie said, standing next to the chair occupied by George, who looked up at Louie, shook his head in disgust and moved to the vacant chair. Louie unapologetically occupied the seat.

"What's that all about," Bill said. "One chair's as good as another, isn't it?"

Sweeney knew, as did everyone else in the place, about Louie's preference for the chair facing the side and front doors. Still they put him through the same ribbing every time.

Louie saw the newspaper spread before him, picked it up, folded it in half and tossed it on top of the workbench.

"Olivia made us a nice treat for later, and George brought us his usual beverage… I think you know where to find everything," Sweeney said.

Sweeney handed the deck to Coach Peick to his right, who shuffled the cards, then placed the stack on the table in front of Sweeney, who cut it and pushed it back toward the coach. The coach dealt five cards off the top to the players as each threw in the ante to the center of the table.

"I begin tonight, gents!" Sweeney said, scrutinizing his cards of three aces, the queen of hearts and a ten of spades. "I'll open with a quarter." He tossed another coin and thumped the table with his knuckles to indicate the bid had been passed.

Sweeney looked over at Louie. Grey smoke from his cigar curled up into his wide nostrils and deep-set eyes squinted from shadowed sockets at the cards he held in his hands.

"See you quarter and raise quarter…fifty cents, Bill," Louie finally said.

"I'm folding," Bill said. "Too rich for me already, haven't got the cards."

"Me, too… You gave me garbage," said Frank. "Hope this isn't the way it's gonna go for me the whole night."

"I'm still in," George said. "I'll see your fifty cents and raise ya a quarter."

Coach Peick took a moment to slow the game, as he liked to do, giving him more time to ponder the cards in his hand.

"Big day coming up for you and Olivia, Sweeney," he said. "Vanessa will be graduating high school next year. Talented young lady. You two should be proud. I think there's a young man p-r-e-t-t-y sweet on her, though not sure she's given him the time of day."

"She's got plenty of time for that, coach…plenty of time. Now, are you going to bid or just yap all night?" Sweeney bellowed, grinning ear to ear with pride.

"You know what? I think I'm going to pass…and leave this battle between the three of you," Coach Peick said.

Sweeney laid his hand face down on the table and picked up the deck. "Whattya want for cards, Louie?"

"Uno!" Louie said, discarding a single card from his hand, as Sweeney passed him another from the top of the deck.

"Give me two," George said, dropping a pair from his hand. Sweeney dealt him two fresh cards.

"And I'll take one," Sweeney said, tossing away one card then taking the next card from the deck. "I'll raise a quarter," he quickly added.

"See quarter, and raise quarter," Louie said.

"Well, I'm out, too!" George said, throwing in his hand.

"I call," said Sweeney, who promptly spread his cards face up on the table. "Full house…three aces, two queens."

Louie's eyes narrowed as he gaped at Sweeney's cards. "Guess you take first hand," he said, spreading his two kings and three eights on the table.

Sweeney raked in the small pile of coins to a spot on his left, then picked up his smoking cigar from the ashtray and puffed away, watching as the white-grey billows rose up, up, and up to the green lamp overhead. He reached up and touched the edge of the lamp, which soon began to sway, and he grinned with satisfaction.

Louie collected the discarded cards, added them to the pile, and reshuffled the deck.

"Done any hunting lately, Louie?" Sweeney said. "We should go again some morning after I get off work. Whitetail deer are scarce, but plenty of ring neck pheasants, Canadian geese and mallard ducks. Gonna be in town for a while?"

"Care split deck?" Louie said, pushing the deck in front of Bill, who split it into three stacks, reordered the pile and pushed it back to Louie.

"Late fall, maybe," Louie said, distributing five cards, one at a time, to the players.

Sweeney picked up his cards and instantly employed his best poker face to hide the winning hand he believed he'd just been dealt.

Coach Peick said: "I'm open to some fishing this Saturday, Sweeney. Tell Olivia again how much I enjoyed eating roe at your home this spring. No one fixes fish eggs better than your wife...dredging them in flour with a little salt and pepper...and frying them up in butter."

Sweeney nodded, before continuing.

"All of us are hunters around the table... I was reading an article in last month's *Time* magazine on the new science of guns. Seems every gun has its peculiarities...the grooves and lands of the bore put distinctive striations on the bullets. Also, breech block and firing pin imprint their telltale hieroglyphics on shells and primers. No two guns produce identical markings."

"You first bid, Bill," Louie said.

"Nice cards, Louie—thanks! Everyone throw in the ante? I'll raise a quarter. Your bid, Francis."

"Makes it easy to identify weapons used in other crimes," Sweeney added. "A man is killed in a restaurant in Cleveland. Hundreds of miles away and months later in an obscure garage, seven men are killed. A year passes, and a gangster shoots a patrolman. The scientist now peering through the microscope can connect all three. Same thing applies to hunting animals. If there are those who don't follow the law, it's now possible to link a bullet in a dead deer to someone's gun."

"Whattya got, Francis?" Louie said.

"I'm folding again," Frank said, throwing down his cards in disgust.

"As a law man, I found the article of great interest. Anyone else care to read it, you can borrow it from me anytime."

"I'd like to take a look at it, Sweeney. Bring it along on Saturday," Coach Peick said, spreading his cards on the table, face up, revealing four of a kind.

Sweeney felt his face flush, his early hot streak broken.

Throughout the evening, each took their turn at winning hands. George held off until midnight to crack open his bottle of rum, first collecting the coffee cups and rinsing them, before returning each to its owner with a generous portion of heavenly hooch.

"It'll cure what're ails ya!" George said, before guzzling his first cup and pouring himself a second.

"Prohibition is over, but that sure hasn't ended the craving for booze, has it?" Sweeney said. "Still get my share of desperate phone calls when someone's husband has been drinking, hasn't come home and he's out there somewhere walking the streets. Their womenfolk ask me if I'll go search for 'em. Sometimes she says she wants him found before the Catholics start going to church, or before he's seen passed out under the tree in front of the Wiltse or sleeping on the river bank by the bridge."

Louie picked up the pile of cards and ordered them in one hand.

"Dey make legal…da problem go away," he muttered in a low growl.

Sweeney jerked his head around to eyeball Louie, staring in disbelief at the man who'd just spewed insight into society's moral decay.

Wondering how much the booze might have loosened the gangster's tongue, Sweeney probed.

"That reminds me, Louie…don't think you were in town for your friend Lucy Minton's funeral. A real nice gal, a saint if there ever was one. Went through tough times in her life…Rev. Oelfke called them spiritual deserts. But she pulled up 'er britches and got on with life. Ended up doing a whole lot of good in this world."

"She not friend, really—only rent room a few time," Louie said.

"Think the reverend is right? Are we all going to stand before the Almighty in the hereafter and be held accountable for our sins?"

"Datsa da Catholic belief, where I attend," Louie said.

George, who had taken doubles for everyone's singles since the booze came out, which typically converted him to a cynical philosopher, suddenly pushed his chair back and stood up, the signal he was about to pontificate.

"I believe God does not expect us to be perfect, and I'm definitely not without my faults. But I believe I'll be accepted into heaven. If such a place really exists. If a God really exists. I think we're all gonna be very surprised about our Creator, and any afterlife...after all, who knew that President Roosevelt was a cripple when we elected him. Now we find out he lives every day in a wheelchair!" Then he fell back into his chair with a thud.

Sweeney glanced at Louie, watching as he calmly withdrew the cigar from his mouth with three fingers. He thought he caught the slight quiver of his lower lip as though trying to hold back words as substantial as a body of water collected behind a dam.

"Seem who write da history is how history get remember...usually who has upper hand at da time. History, da Bible—no different," he finally said, without so much as raising an eyebrow.

"What do you think about the saying: 'When God closes a door, he opens a window?'" Sweeney redirected.

Louie's face broke into a wide grin, seeing Sweeney's smirking face staring back at him through the smoky fog.

"You know dat not in da Bible—right, Sweeney? I like better: 'God help dem who help demself.'"

Sweeney, suddenly feeling drunker than a monkey from his own four back-to-back hits of rum, no doubt, reached over and placed his cup on the workbench.

"I think that's enough hooch for me for one evening. A pint of beer is all I'm really used to any more... I believe I'll check to see if there's a spot of coffee left."

He got up, poured himself a cup, sat back down and took several substantial sips as the next hand was being dealt. Still feeling soused, he settled for a conversation about a more congenial poker topic: town gossip.

"Bill, I hear you're reopening Lehmkuhl Hardware in the old post office building, and the post office is moving to the M. J. Collins building."

He lifted his cup toward Bill, saying: "Here's hoping the family business is around for a long time to come." The others joined him in lifting their cups to Bill, followed by a swig of rum.

"And I hear Dr. Eickelberg is retiring, setting up a Dr. Plass to take over," Sweeney continued. "A fella I know went to Eickelberg. Told me 'he spit jaw bone for a week', so I've put off seeing the dentist about the ache in my jaw. Guess I'll wait and have it tended to when Plass takes over."

The card game persisted unabated until around two a.m. then a discharge of rain, heavy as a cow pissing on a flat rock, began to spill down the side windows and those in the double doors.

Sweeney jumped up to peer outside, skeptical of the sudden deluge dropping from the harvest sky.

About a half-hour later, the flow unrelenting, Mayor Gardner emerged through the side door of the engine house, his hat, clothing and shoes drenched.

The little man hopped up and down. "For Christ's sake, Sweeney! You haf forgot to turn off die pumpe in de vell shed...der wasserturm overflows. You flood alle Main Street!" the mayor said. "You tink es ist ein regensturm? Das ist *verrückt*—crazy!"

CHAPTER EIGHTEEN

Even The Sparrows

September 12, 1933—My dearest Walter, Leonard and Samuel,

I am writing with such wonderful news—I am coming home! Though plans have yet to be finalized. I will write again in a few days to let you when you should arrive at the sanatorium to collect me. Isn't it all so wonderful? I am well—finally well enough to come home!

This news comes after a most remarkable event. Several months ago, when I desperately wondered if this day would ever arrive, I got on my knees and prayed, prayed more fervently than any time before in my life, and I asked God for a sign—a sign that confirmed He was real; that He knew I existed; and that He was hearing my pleas to rejoin you and be back in my home caring for you in the way I have done in the past.

I reminded God of His promise in Matthew 10:29-31: "Are not two sparrows sold for a farthing? and one of them shall not fall on the ground without your Father. But the very hairs of your head are all numbered. Fear ye not therefore, ye are of more value than many sparrows." I asked God to give me proof: I didn't need beautiful doves—just send me lowly sparrows, I pleaded. Then feeling bolder, I asked Him to send me a whole flock! Almost before the last words had passed from my lips, outside the window next to my bed, a single sparrow soon appeared, landing on the sill, and turned its head to seemingly stare into my eyes.

I did not write of this before because I feared what I had experienced might have been a delusion. I waited to see if the promise would come to fruition—and just yesterday, Dr. Sparrow pronounced me well enough to return home. So it is true, once and for all: God is real, my beloveds! God hears our prayers! We are not alone!

And—isn't it strange that my doctor is Dr. Sparrow?

How I long to be reunited with you, and may God be so gracious as to never let us be separated again in this world to come. With all my deepest love, Emma.

After nearly three long years, their dark night was over. Walter clutched Emma's letter in one hand, his hip flask in the other. Seated on the riverbank next to the mill pond, tears pooled in his eyes, his cheeks their spillway. How Emma loved this place. He'd made a habit of visiting his wife's favorite spot since her departure. It had become his sanctuary, a special place to feel near to her. To cry. To scream. To call out to the Universe. To sit for a time and listen.

Eventually, a comforting friend joined him.

"Is that you, Walter?" Sweeney called out, appearing out of the shadows of the old grist mill. "Making my first rounds this fall evening... I think I've seen you here before. Pretty quiet here this time of night."

Walter tucked the flask inside his coat and wiped his cheeks with his denim coat sleeve before responding.

"Oh, Sweeney, yes—I come here often. Emma loves this spot, you know."

"I believe I did know that... whattya hearing from her? Olivia and I have been praying for you and the boys every day since she left."

"Just got a letter!" Walter said, displaying the single sheet of paper in one hand. "She writes much of her text in circles on the page. She sends good news... Expects to soon be released from the sanatorium. Gonna let me know when to collect her."

"That's great, Walter. As soon as you know the date, you must let Father Torpey know...he'll surely want to make an announcement at Mass. Too bad Emma didn't get to say goodbye to Father Halpin, or Sister Keith before leaving."

"I'll contact Father Torpey when I hear from Emma again. The church has done a great deal for us. I'm very appreciative."

"Has Leonard reported back to you on our pitching practices? He's grown into quite a young man, Walter. He has the natural talent to become a pretty good pitcher. Got a big game against Oelwein's Sacred Heart next week. I think the I.C. boys have a good chance of winning. Hope Emma is back by then. I know it would mean everything to Leonard if his entire family could be there."

Walter nodded, choking back the tears. "I'm not planning to tell Leonard and Samuel about Emma's letter just yet, just in case there should be a delay. I want her return to be a pleasant surprise to them."

"Well, if you need my assistance in any way, I can put you in touch with the right help. You're not alone, my friend—you are not alone. There's a saying, and I believe I heard it from you, Walter: As long as we have breath, we have to keep learning how to live," Sweeney said.

—

Marshal Delaney and Leonard stood next to the ramshackle wooden home team bleachers along the third base line of the baseball diamond northeast of the public school. Each held a well-worn leather glove on one hand. Leonard's left-hander was on loan from Coach Peick.

"Let's go toss a few," Sweeney said, motioning for Leonard to take the mound as he made his way toward home plate.

Throwing the ball to Leonard, he called out: "Are you ready?"

Leonard caught the ball and tossed it back. "Practiced the way you taught me. First of the week I started throwing twenty to thirty pitches with my dad most evenings after school, then a few more each day. Yesterday I took the day off."

Sweeney threw the ball back. "How's your curveball?"

"Doing it just like you taught. It might be my strongest pitch now."

"Let's see it then."

Leonard hurled a half dozen curveballs. Sweeney eyed each closely. "Attaboy...keep them dropping in this area," he said, pointing to the front side of the strike zone. "Now throw five or six more."

Sweeney looked across the way at the cars arriving for the five o'clock game. The Sacred Heart team had arrived, wearing nice new red uniforms and caps.

"There'll be a lot of commotion and noise today," Sweeney continued. "You'll have to block it all out and concentrate on what you're doing."

They passed the ball back and forth several more times. Leonard's pitches picked up velocity with each effort.

"I watched a recent game at Sacred Heart—it got rained out," Sweeney added, "but I was there long enough to know their pitcher, Dave Spankey, has a pretty good arm... Struck out a lot of players. You two are pretty evenly matched as pitchers go...don't need to tell you, as the older kid, Spankey is gonna try to dominate the game. Don't let him take this win from you. You can do this, Leonard. Just stay focused. Stick to your best ball, the fastball. And throw a curve from time to time to keep 'em guessing.

"And you know Father Torpey may take you out of the game at some point, if he thinks your arm is done. Now don't be a jerk about it like I was as a young man and take it personally. You're the best pitcher we have— the team needs you. Listen to your coach."

"I will, Marshal Delaney, I promise," Leonard said. He glanced up at a few grey clouds in the distance. "But it's possible we could get a rainout, don't you think?"

Sweeney motioned for Jason McCuniff, the I.C. catcher standing on the sidelines, to come and replace him at the plate.

"No rain in the forecast today, Leonard, guaranteed sunshine all day long," Sweeney said.

Jason arrived, his chest protector, straps and pads flapping with each step.

"I need to check on parking... Keep the warm-up going with Jason. Not too hard, Leonard, and only a dozen more. I'll be watching the game from the bleachers. Good luck!"

As Sweeney left the ball diamond, he listened for the sound of Leonard's pitches landing in Jason's glove. *Pop! Pop! Pop!*

Sweeney detoured to the weedy outfield where Father Torpey had been drilling the I.C. baseball team in calisthenics, and now had the boys facing each other in two parallel lines, throwing balls back and forth.

"Take a dozen or so easy tosses, then gradually start to throw the ball like your life depends on it. Those Sacred Heart boys want to win this game as badly as you do," Father Torpey said. "And I have a bet going with the Sacred Heart priest—wouldn't want me to have to pay up, would you?"

Seeing Sweeney's approach, the priest ambled toward him.

"Should be a pretty equally matched game today. What's up with the new red uniforms for the Sacred Heart team? I thought we were in a depression!" Sweeney said.

"From an area benefactor, I believe. Probably boosted the team's morale quite a bit," Father Torpey said.

"Getting uniforms for the I.C. boys could be a good first project for Emma Bierkoff, once she returns. But Sacred Heart is going to need a lot more than new uniforms to beat our boys this afternoon. I've got Leonard pretty fired up."

"Real nice talking to you, Sweeney," Father Torpey said, subtly releasing him from any further obligations relating to the I.C. team.

Sweeney took the hint. "Talk to you after the game, Father." He headed to the grassy parking area where two public high school kids guided arriving vehicles. Noticing they had everything under control, he walked toward the grade school boys raking the ball diamond.

"It's a quarter of five now. Just whisk off the bases, and that should do it," Sweeney said.

Out of the corner of an eye, Sweeney saw Walter Bierkoff's vehicle enter the parking area. He waved and caught Walter's attention in time to point him toward an open space next to the bleachers.

"You made it! Great to have you back with us, Emma—Leonard is going to be so pleased. Why don't you stay here in the shade… you'll be able to see the game from here, and I'll come and get you to sit with me on the bleachers later. Wouldn't want you to get all worn out your first day back with us. Does that sound okay to you, Emma?"

"Yes, that will be fine," she said, her voice sounding as frail as her transformed demeanor: the soft grey-green eyes seemed further sunken above sharp cheekbones in her once-vital face; her long brunette hair was now thin strands streaked with grey.

"Both my boys have grown up so much without me...can you believe Leonard is pitching? And Walter tells me we have you to thank for that."

"I'll be back for you before the final innings, I promise," Sweeney said.

Leonard had difficulty getting started in the first inning, and the first two Sacred Heart batters got base hits. He struck out the third, and the fourth hit a high pop-up which was caught by Jason. The last batter managed to snag a ball that went high to the shortstop, who threw it to first for an easy out. The teams changed places.

By the bottom of the fifth inning, the score was six to five—I.C.

Sweeney left the bleachers and headed for the home bench to confer with Father Torpey about his pitcher. He put his hand on Leonard's shoulder.

"How's the arm holding up?"

Father Torpey interrupted: "I'm thinking of putting in Danny Little to pitch the last innings. How does that sound to you, Leonard?"

"I'm a little tired, but I think my arm is still solid. I promise to let you know the minute my arm feels sore," Leonard pleaded with the priest.

"What do you say, Father? You can always continue to evaluate the situation by inning. He's still looking pretty good from where I've been sitting," Sweeney said.

"Okay, Leonard, let's see what you've still got," Farther Torpey said.

"Batter up!" Umpire Bill Biggs shouted.

Father Torpey caught hold of Sweeney's arm. "I think I'm seeing signs Spankey's arm is waning and expect Sacred Heart will put in a new pitcher next inning. I would like to keep Leonard in there to get the win. You've got the pitching expertise, Sweeney—motion to me when you think I should make a change."

"Will do!" Sweeney said.

Tommy Thunker, Sacred Heart's best hitter, strolled up to home plate. From the mound, Leonard signaled Thunker back from the plate to allow him to throw a couple practice pitches. En route to the bleachers, Sweeney listened for the thud of Leonard's balls hitting the sweet spot of Jason's glove. *Pop!... Pop!... Pop!*

Thunker moved up to the plate. Sweeney watched Leonard's windup and delivery of his first pitch of the inning. His technique was good; perhaps even better than Sweeney's at that age, and the ball was cruising to home plate at a speed that seemed new territory for Leonard.

"Strike!" said Umpire Biggs.

Thunker, with the bat still perched above his right shoulder, grimaced at the call.

Leonard wound up again and delivered another fastball to the lower left corner of the plate. Thunker swung and missed.

"Strike two!" said Umpire Biggs.

From the bleachers, Sweeney saw something new afoot as Jason zinged the ball across the plate into Leonard's glove. The two were working in tandem, one force, exactly what he'd hoped would happen, each helping the other to improve.

Leonard soundly put his next pitch right of the plate, waist-high to the batter, pushing Thunker back from the box.

Umpire Biggs called, "Out!"

Thunker threw his bat and kicked at the ground as he headed toward the visitors' bench.

By the top of the seventh, both teams had scored another run. As Leonard took the mound at the bottom of the inning, he motioned Jason to his side. "My arm is getting pretty sore, Jason. You think I should tell Father Torpey?"

"Look what you've done already today, Leonard. Who knew you could pitch like this. My Pop tells me going beyond what we can be is just as bad as falling short. Has to be your call, that's all I can tell you. Good luck!"

Jason walked back to home plate.

Out of the corner of his eye, Leonard saw the priest pacing along the sidelines as Danny Little warmed up nearby. Sweeney was nowhere to be seen in the bleachers.

Leonard went into the windup and sent another ball ripping across the far-right side of the plate. The batter swung, but sorely missed.

"Strike!" Umpire Biggs said.

Jason mouthed "Two to go," holding up two fingers as he returned the ball to Leonard.

Leonard prepared for the next windup, first glancing again at the bleachers to find Sweeney's face in the small crowd. He saw the marshal helping his mother to a seat on the bottom row. Confounded, Leonard dropped the ball and scrambled to retrieve it. He looked back at the bleachers. His mother was waving at him, a white handkerchief in her hand, seemingly trying to say something to him.

He thought he heard the word "sparrow," though that made no sense to him. None at all.

Out of the blue, Leonard suddenly found the noise and chatter of the small crowd overwhelming. He recalled Sweeney's words: "There'll be a lot of commotion today. You'll have to block it all out and concentrate on what you're doing." He reconnected his eyes with Jason's. Leonard looked away, then back. Was he really seeing what he thought he saw: Jason—grinning?

The ball in his glove felt the weight of a cannonball as he sent the next pitch high over the catcher's head.

"Ball!" Umpire Biggs said.

Jason caught up with the gyrating ball on the ground, picked it up and confidently tossed it back to Leonard.

Leonard again gaped at Jason. This time there was no mistaking the expansive grin across the catcher's face.

The next pitch resulted in a solid hit toward second. The runner was thrown out, only inches before his foot stepped on first base.

"Out!" Umpire Biggs said.

The rest of the game seemed to happen as if in slow motion...

He could feel his body beginning the rotation of the
wind-up, fingers clasping ball, middle and index
fingers conjoined at the widest part between seams,
then nimbly extending pitching arm, and projectile gets
released, as an upward draft of southwesterly breeze
helps bowdlerize the homeward released, where batter
eyes approaching rotating orb, with gripped bat, one hand
cupped over the other, barrel raised high over a shoulder;
the tricky ball soon upon him, now in severe gravitational
descent, plummets toward earth, the batter yet swinging,
downward and through, as the white orb sails by.

"Out!" Leonard heard the umpire say. But that was all he heard.

He dropped the ball and glove on the mound,
as the home team ran toward him, Father Torpey
in their midst, Leonard's feet though carrying him
along the white third baseline, toward the bleachers,
through the home crowd jumping up and down in euphoria,
finally coming to a standstill before the
woman who had waved to him from the bleachers.

"When did you return, Mother?" was all he could mutter before he fell
into her waiting arms, head buried in her bosom, his own chest heaving.

"I wanted my return to be a surprise today," she said, her voice barely
audible. "You've grown from a boy into a young man while I was away...
I'm sorry I was gone for so long." She lifted his head and cupped it in her
hands. "Now I am pronounced well, and my first request was to see you
pitch today. And you pitched so wonderfully, my son."

Leonard studied her lovely, weary face, only turning away only when
the shadow of a familiar tall, long-legged figure closed in beside him.

"Congratulations on your win today, Leonard!" Sweeney said. "We're
all really proud of you."

"Thank you, Marshal Delaney! I'll never forget what you've done for me," Leonard said, rising to extend his hand to Sweeney, one man to another.

Samuel darted up and spun Leonard around, exclaiming: "You're a champion, Leonard...just like Hack Wilson with the Cubs in '30!"

Emma took both boys into her arms.

"You understand, don't you, Sweeney? We really must be on our way... We are most anxious to go home now. I've tired here today. But won't you, Olivia and Vanessa stop by the farm very soon?"

CHAPTER NINETEEN

The Duck Blind

Ice fragments in the pre-dawn November 1933 air sparred with Sweeney's face as he took inventory of the supplies he'd packed in the trunk of "Baby," his Ford sedan: his Browning A-5 twelve-gauge shotgun, several boxes of shells, and a bevy of decoys. The never-fail wood duck caller got tucked into the pocket of his coat before he ever left the house.

Earlier that morning he began the process of starting Baby: lighting a fire in a bucket of cobs soaked in kerosene, setting it on fire and pushing it under the crankcase; after the engine had time to thaw, he poured warm water into the radiator, then cranked like hell. Eventually she let loose with her first pop of the day.

Now he and the two-year-old black Labrador retriever, Bailey, on loan from Coach Peick, awaited Louie's arrival.

The damp and frigid morning air taxed his gangly body. He jerked his coat zipper to its highest point under his chin, tugged down at the sides of his wool cap, and lit up his third-of-the-morning Chesterfield. The shotgun in the trunk again caught his eye. He reached for it once more to examine the barrel and magazine; both were clean as a whistle. He leaned against the rear of the car and took an exceptionally long drag on the cigarette, then stared mesmerizingly at the smoky vapor emerging from his nose and mouth. *Uncanny*, he thought, *how long the smoke holds together before dissipating in the heavy air.* A flock of plain brown sparrows finally broke the spell as they swooped down and landed in leafless bushes a few feet away, birds he normally completely overlooked.

Finally, Louie's Lincoln turned south onto Residence Street, with its headlights off, just as the first rays of sun pierced the orange horizon. After a few minutes, he nudged the car into a spot adjacent to Sweeney's garage.

Sweeney watched Louie's exodus, cautiously eyeing his surroundings, side-by-side sawed-off shotgun held deftly in one hand. In due course, he reached back inside the car to load his coat pockets with shells, then kicked the door closed and moseyed toward Sweeney, shotgun pointed toward the sky, a stump of a lit Cuban cigar clamped between his teeth.

"You gonna be warm enough in that short coat?" Sweeney said. "I've got another longer one hangin' in the garage."

"My coat and hat are wool like yours. If get cold, I come back town."

Sweeney nodded. He understood his words sometimes sounded fatherly, though he had Louie only by a decade in age.

"Olivia sent a thermos of hot coffee and made us a couple fried egg sandwiches to enjoy along the way," he said, waiting for Louie to put his shotgun inside the trunk before closing the top-hinged lid.

Bailey squirmed on the ground next to the driver's door. Sweeney opened the door, and the Lab bounded into the back seat and spun around until sitting face forward like a child on a pew at Sunday morning church. Louie got himself situated on the cold bench seat opposite Sweeney, and soon the Ford jolted northward toward Main Street.

"I left a note for Olivia to put a pail of water on the stove and have it piping hot upon my return in a couple hours. When I walk in with our brace of birds, she'll have the kitchen floor lined with newspapers, ready for the cleaning to begin. Thought we'd keep only what we can use and sell the rest to the meat shops in town… The Coffin Café might get a couple, too, if that's okay with you. We can't be sure what we'll get today. After the drought last summer, don't know how much the ducks were affected. Congress is talking about passing a new hunting license to prevent overkill of migratory fowl."

"Fine, Sweeney. You decide—okay to handle ducks like last time," Louie said, blowing smoky warm air onto his gloved hands.

A half mile out of town Louie passed out the sandwiches and poured a round of hot coffee. They traveled in silence. Sweeney felt the distant sun's rays penetrate the windows, aware of the sun's inability this time of year to add much warmth to the car's frosty interior. He pointed the Ford southwesterly toward the wetland about seven miles away where he kept a blind next to the Wapsie.

Sweeney drained his cup and handed it back to Louie just before turning the Ford onto a furrowed cow path choked with weeds and thickets, where she bumped along for another half-mile before arriving at a small clearing next to the timberline, about ten yards from the river.

He wrenched the car to a stop and the two disembarked. The Lab sprung from the back seat and looped dizzyingly at Sweeney's heels, ready to go to work. Sweeney's long strides quickly took him through the brittle knee-high grass to the car's rear, where he swung open the trunk and began to load up.

Louie took his sweet time scanning the area before grabbing his shotgun and armload of hand-carved basswood duck decoys.

Struck once more by the icy air and dampness of the morning air, Sweeney took a moment to pull down the felt flaps from inside his cap and cup them over his sizable ears. Louie headed for the blind, seemingly impatient with Sweeney's dawdling. Sweeney finished sinking a box of ammo into each coat pocket, picked up his Browning and remaining decoys and followed after Louie. In no time, he and the dog overtook the lead.

"Kind of wish I'd made it just a bit bigger," Sweeney said, as he entered the blind camouflaged with plywood, tree branches and natural vegetation. Its opening faced the river and a portion of the sky. "But I've gotten as many as four of us in here, so we should have plenty of room to reload."

"Heater be nice, too, Sweeney," Louie said, slapping Sweeney on the back as he propped his gun against an inside wall, then the two walked to the backwater while Bailey bounded back and forth in the weeds in front of them.

Sweeney waded out past the willows and cattails into the icy brown river in his waders, positioning the decoys several feet apart. Then, returning to shore, he studied the position of the decoys bobbing up and down in the waves he had just created. The last step was to reach into the side pocket of his overalls, pull out a small bag of shelled field corn, and toss large handfuls onto the water near the decoys.

They returned to the blind to load up, inserting brass shells into their magazines, a final one in each barrel.

"Safety is on!" Sweeney said, glancing at Louie, who was about to flip his safety switch. Finally, Sweeney pulled the duck call lanyard from his pocket and placed it around his neck, leaving the caller dangling chest-high.

"Blow a call well, my father taught me," Sweeney said, "and you'll bring ducks in close enough to identify individual birds and make clean kills. That's key to a good day of duck hunting." Then he stuck the caller between his lips, where it would hardly move the rest of the morning. All the while Bailey sat restlessly at his feet.

Sweeney caught the first flock of birds circling downwind. He cupped his fingers around the caller and began to sound rounds of five-to-seven note greeting calls to draw in the ducks, with the last notes diminishing. Then, remembering on still, cloudy days feeding calls had worked best for him, he began a kind of low rapid chatter. The flock swung 'round headed toward the blind. He watched for signs indicating some wary Julie or Patty was thinking something seemed amiss. If the birds started to move their heads and necks considerably from side to side or when their wing rhythm changed, indicating their flight path was wavering, he would need to blow the greeting call another time. But the birds headed solidly toward the decoys.

As the first soft sound of wings in the air hit his ears, he increased the speed and urgency of the calling. The last hundred yards, he sounded the call one last time. He glanced over at Louie and saw he was in position, stock resting on his shoulder, barrel pointed toward the gaggle, an eye steadied on the sighting plane, and finger pressed against one of the triggers. He heard Louie whisper: "Safety—off!"

As the birds flew overhead, the two emptied their guns of ammo. By the time the shooting ended, Sweeney had counted four ducks dropping from the sky.

"Get 'em, Bailey!" Sweeney commanded as he and the dog sprinted toward the river. Bailey plunged into the water, hastily returning to Sweeney's side, bird between her teeth, steam lifting from her thick black coat.

"Release!" Sweeney commanded and collected the fowl from the dog's mouth. Then he sent Bailey out three more times.

"And that's how it's done!" Sweeney said, four greenheads at his feet, "Good time, Sweeney! You know how to bring 'em real close."

"I couldn't help noticing... You're pretty handy with that piece."

"Ready to go again, Sweeney," Louie said, breaking open his shotgun and reaching for more shells in his pocket.

Sweeney took a step forward and firmly grabbed hold of Louie's arm holding the shotgun.

Louie flinched in reaction to the aggression, cocked his head, and glowered into Sweeney's eyes.

"What goin' on, Sweeney?"

"For a lot of years you've come and gone in Oxbow. I know you don't bring the business with you. And we appreciate what you've done for the youngsters, taking them to the movies and all. But just want you to be clear... If the Feds ever show up or call to request my help in any way, the tin star on my shirt means I'm sworn to uphold the law. That's how it'll all come down, if it comes to that. Wouldn't want there to be any misunderstanding between us."

Sweeney held firm to Louie's arm, the two men locked eyeball to eyeball. Louie's dark eyes provided no hint what his next move might be.

When Sweeney finally released him, Louie jerked away and took a step back. Several seconds ticked by before Sweeney carefully moved one hand to a shirt pocket to retrieve a cigarette, then lit up, holding the smoke in his lungs for a long time before exhaling.

Louie, too, released a plume of smoke from his cigar that drifted into Sweeney's.

Suddenly, Louie yanked the SXS toward his chest, forced a shell into the barrel, snapped the gun shut, and pointed it at Sweeney.

"Think you can put da screws to me... I oughta fillya fulla lead, here and now. No one talk to me that way."

"Whoa, whoa... Hold up, hardchaw," Sweeney said, raising his hands out in front of his chest.

"Who you talk to... Whatta you say?" Louie said.

It was then that Sweeney noticed the slight tremor in Louie's right hand.

"Whattya gonna do, Louie—shoot me out here in the woods?" Sweeney then took a step toward Louie, grabbed the barrel of his gun with both hands, and forced it up and away from his chest. "Guess the law wouldn't have too far to look at who done the killin' out here, now would they?"

"Not good mess with me! Better watcha you back, Sweeney!"

"And all this time I kinda thought you liked me, and the privacy our small town afforded. It's all been workin' out so well for you."

Louie maintained a deadly glare at Sweeney.

Bailey edged closer at Sweeney's feet and whined, anxious to resume the hunt.

"I think it's time you leveled with me, and don't try to feed me any of your arkymalarkey... I'm just not in the mood for bullshit today."

Louie gradually relaxed his arms and Sweeney's hands fell from the barrel, just as a squall of mixed rain and sleet commenced to swirl around and between them.

Finally, Louie's lips slid into a slow grin. "Whattya know? Small-town marshal much, much smarter than he looks. You telling me we can't be friends no more, Sweeney?"

The tension finally broken, Sweeney reached for the second box of shells from his coat pocket and set it on the blind, opened the magazine of his Browning and proceeded to load up.

"By the way, Louie, any idea where Capone hid his twenty million? Rumors are it's stashed someplace for the day he gets released from the Big House... gonna need a lot of start over money, I guess. Heard it might even be hidden in the township."

Louie took his time loading up, finally spewing: "We gonna do more huntin' today, or not?"

"You bet! Let's see how many we can get in the next hour or so. I'm finding this cold dampness really intolerable this morning. My joints ache like I might be comin' down with somethin'.

A few minutes later, Sweeney pointed out thirty Canadian geese flying in formation about an eighth of a mile away.

Balancing the smoking Chesterfield on the blind, he raised the caller to his lips, and began to call once more with fingers and breath to the wild winged creatures in the distance.

A few seconds later, he stopped—remembering he'd wanted to put forth one additional question to Louie.

"By the way, what's your version of a story I was told about some half-dead person trying to kick his way out the back of your car late one evening a while back?"

Louie looked puzzled at first, then twigged it.

"Somebody see me bringin' a gunny sacka live chickens from da Lincoln, right? Musta gotta dat story from my nosy neighbor—huh, Sweeney?"

CHAPTER TWENTY

Morning Train

Charlie Daniels, Oxbow's depot agent, lifted the watch from a pocket of his smart prescribed CGW uniform, including badge, and gazed westerly in anticipation of the arrival of the Dinky on that May 1936 morning.

Since becoming agent in the early 1900s, news of a derailment or waves of arriving émigrés from the east coast had been what got his shiny pants all in a bundle. In later years, he'd secretly hoped Al Capone and his entourage might step from a train at his depot, a story he'd have liked to tell his grandchildren one day. He'd heard of sightings of Capone, La Cava, and other finely dressed men fishing side by side along the Wapise. Plus, two or three dapper men frequently waited next to La Cava's Lincoln when Mass let out on Sunday mornings…causing locals to speculate whether Capone might be in the area.

His hopes were dashed in '31 when he learned in a news reel that Capone had been sentenced to the Atlanta penitentiary; then in '34, a newspaper article stated Capone took his first train ride in the middle of the night to Alcatraz.

Other gangsters renowned to have roamed through these parts were all dead…killed by FBI agents: Tommy Carroll, John Dillinger, Charles Arthur "Pretty Boy" Floyd, Baby Face Nelson, and the Barker–Karpis gang. They had all sped around the Midwest in fast black cars, too.

La Cava still came to Oxbow as often as ever. And mysterious strangers from the train often inquired about his whereabouts.

But largely, the arrival of a sizeable group of Amish from Kansas was the most excitement Charlie could hope for these days.

In railroad terms, Oxbow was a jerkwater, a town too small to register but a couple stops a day, just long enough to transfer water from the small tower to the steam-powered hog. The Dinky—pulled by a kettle with six to eight red passenger cars and trailing caboose—made two daily scheduled stops. The morning train arrived at eleven and returned late in the afternoon. Locals caught the Dinky to Oelwein for a day of shopping and business, or to the city of Waterloo, some twenty-five miles to the southwest. Most of the ridership were on a first-name basis with hoggers, conductors, and porters.

The 9:20 mail train, called the redball, also zipped by daily, traveling eighty-five to one hundred miles an hour. The mail clerk aboard the train tossed a bag of incoming mail onto the depot's platform, just as a steel catcher arm on the train grabbed a canvas bag of outgoing mail from a special hook outside the school-house-size structure.

The town also got its share of freight trains—rattlers—whizzing by, each with a doubleheader, towing about a hundred rats: reefers, coal cars, and trailers piggybacked onto flatcars.

Charlie turned to watch the horse-drawn wagon driven by Darrel, a Brick Hotel employee, pull up next to the depot, presumably to transport the arriving Amish to the hotel for lunch. While the Amish all seemed the same—dressed in plain dark clothing, the hallmark dress of these Protestants who believed God wanted them to live peacefully and simply—Charlie knew first-hand there was more to their story.

Years earlier, an Amish elder had tutored him on Amish beliefs and practices after Brother Eli stopped by the depot one day to inquire about the cost of a round trip train ticket to Waterloo. Then he asked if Charlie might be willing to transport him by car instead. Charlie, largely able to find his way through Eli's thick Pennsylvania German accent, learned why some Amish men wore single or double suspenders, or no suspenders at all; black hats versus white hats; carriages, open or topped, the top color an additional variant. Which groups believed in shunning if a member married outside their order, and which were more liberal. Most recently, he'd learned the Yoder colony, due on today's train, was progressive when it came to technology, even using tractors for farm work and travel. Charlie wondered how well the Yoders would mix with Oxbow's Old Order Amish, and whether there might be a derailment of another sort in the making here.

Out of the corner of one eye, he noticed Mayor Gardner drawing near. He also owned the stockyards since 1914. Twice a day he crossed over from the other side of the tracks, he said, to monitor the comings and goings of folks, though not for much longer, as he'd already announced this would be his last two-year mayoral term.

"Sweeney say area grow wieder again," Mayor Gardner said, as he stepped onto the platform next to Charlie.

"True! it's a sizeable group arriving today from Kansas... Caught a train in Kansas City, which took them to Des Moines to Marshalltown to Waterloo, and finally, Oxbow."

Mayor Gardner nodded. "Why kommst du hier?"

"Probably because we already have one Amish colony. Plus, there isn't anything that won't grow in Iowa's black dirt—well, at least before the drought hit, that is. But dust storms in the Central Plains have put an extra economic strain on those farmers," Charlie said. "They likely are coming to Iowa thinking life will be better here."

The two caught sight of Francis Durham approaching from Emerson Grain east of the stockyards. Besides a corn and soybean granary and grain-loading elevator, the business included a John Deere implement dealership, plus coal...lump-, furnace-, and egg-size.

"Not the most excitin' thing to happen since the railroad came to town in '87, but I think our citizens will remember this day," Francis shouted while still ten yards away.

All conversation ceased when the first shrill blast of air whistle echoed through the canyon along the Wapsie a half mile away, where the train was passing over the railroad bridge. A few minutes later the wide black snout of the locomotive materialized, heading full throttle toward the depot, a thick black cloud streaming from its dome. Additional whistles followed, warning of the train's approach to the Fourth Street crossing, then the crossing a half block from the station.

At last, the iron horse and coal wagon stole past the depot platform with its noisy chuffing sound arising from coupled-wheels rolling across steel tracks. Hogger Cecil Stratler waved to Charlie; also, Delbert Johnson, the brakeman, who held fast to the brake that sent compounded steam to large shoes, and quickly flooded the train's lower cavity. The bakehead, Clifford Oliver, nodded, too, and smiled, his white teeth stark against a coal blackened face.

The train pulling a half dozen red wagons soon ground to a stop, and one by one the doors opened. Porter Daniel Washington dropped a wooden step stool on the ground in front of the first descending passengers. Conductor John Haskins also stepped from a car. "Watch your step!" he called out, as he eyed rooftops and steel truss rods beneath, looking for rintails, the indigent who rode the rails, going town to town hoping for work or a handout, though most had jumped the train long before reaching the depot. Freight trains, in particular, with their open-door boxcars, sometimes had so many people in them it looked like black crows descending. The railroad regularly hired bulls to arrest them, and beatings were commonplace.

Oxbow got its share of hobos. Fresh from the train, they wove between businesses and homes, bindle on a stick over a shoulder, hoping to find a kind-hearted soul who would respond to a knock at a back door, and plea: "Can you spare a little food, or a few coins?" Most offered to do a little work in return for a handout. Locals made them a simple baloney sandwich on thick homemade white bread, if they could, along with a small jug of milk or cup of water—the sandwich alone cost a nickel in a cafe. Occasionally someone reported to Sweeney the theft of a pair of pants and shirt from a clothesline; a couple of missing chickens from a backyard; or vegetables gone from a garden row. Then Sweeney followed up, sometimes throwing a bum on the next outgoing train with a warning not to come back.

The Brick employee dismounted the wagon and approached the Amish, motioning for them to come in his direction. Only the men followed, each dressed in a black cotton suit without lapel, white collarless shirt, wide-brimmed black hat, and black high-top laced leather boots. The women and children grouped on the weeded ground near the depot. Females wore long-sleeved black or blue solid-colored dresses and head covering, black stockings and black shoes.

Charlie shook his head. It was impossible to detect any difference between the old Amish colony and the new Yoders.

"Lunch is waiting for you at the Brick Hotel," Darrel said, as the Amish men boarded the wagon. "What about your womenfolk and children... won't they want a hot meal, too?"

A thickly-bearded elder male motioned with his hands to indicate the women and children would remain behind, and the crowded wagon of standing Amish men departed.

The conductor finished going wagon to wagon to verify remaining passengers held tickets to continue on down the line. As he approached the last wagon, the door opened and two hatted men in tweed suits stepped out onto the rear landing.

"Which way to downtown?" one of the men said.

The conductor pointed toward Main Street. "Follow that wagon if you're interested in a hot meal."

Mayor Gardner studied the two men, each with small keister in hand, as they hurried after the wagon.

"Mann on recht has bulge poke at coat seam," Mayor Gardner pointed out to the Charlie and Francis.

The conductor called out, "All aboard!" then stepped onto the bottom rung of the caboose and signaled to the engineer the 'all-clear' by swinging a lantern in a back and forth motion with one hand. Seconds later, the long arm of the water tower rose above the hog, which let out a long blast of steam that soared above the heads of the Amish women and children seated in weeds next to the depot, with their open baskets of bread and cheese nearby. Black sooty smoke once more poured from the locomotive's smoke stack as it began to chug forward, jerking at the wagons behind.

Charlie picked up the morning bag of mail from the platform and headed toward his car parked on the back side of the depot.

Francis shouted a reminder to him before he left: "The two o'clock needs to collect my wagons with last fall's grain to take to Piper in Cedar Rapids, plus, the mayor has beef and hogs headed to Chicago... Don't forget to switch the rattler to the other track so they get picked up."

Charlie waved to indicate he'd heard and drove off.

Downtown, Olivia watched as a wagon load of Amish men flooded the hotel cafe. A pair of men in tweed suits took the last open table.

"Just landed in town from da mornin' train, doll," one of the men said. "We're lookin' to find old friend…perhaps you know da guy…drives fancy car. Heard he married a girl in dis parts. Thought we look him up."

Olivia gave his question some consideration. "No, can't say I know the guy you describe. You might drop by Marshal Delaney's office in the city building in the next block…try later this afternoon."

"We pass car dealership—think we stop by there after da meal," said the other man.

"Earl Bentley or Claire Rechkemmer are the guys to talk to if you're in need of a car. I hear they might have sold one Chevy since the depression began, or maybe there were six cars sold in the whole county; I can't recall just now. If you're gonna be in town for a while, Earl will probably try to recruit you into joinin' the fire department… He's real civic minded," Olivia said.

After the meal, one by one the Amish filed outside and waited on the boardwalk. In a short time, a caravan of horse-drawn wagons and buggies showed up—open, and black topped—driven by local Amish menfolk. The women and children from the depot already on board, the new colony of Amish left town.

Noticing the two suited men had finished their meals, Olivia tore the check from her pad and placed it on their table. One immediately reached into a pocket, pulled out a thick wad of bills and paid her, including a twenty-five-cent tip.

"Thank you for the tip!" she said, pleasantly surprised, as they rose to leave the café.

From the window, she watched them cross Main Street in the direction of B & R. There, they'd probably find out about the big Mazziotti wedding happening the next day in Oelwein. The La Cavas, good friends of the Mazziottis, were likely staying at their favorite room on the top floor of

Hotel Mealey. A recent newspaper engagement announcement noted the reception would be held at the 190 Club.

Later that evening Olivia told Sweeney about the new large Amish colony that had come into the café earlier that morning:

"It's not unusual for threshing crews and the like to come to town for noon meals so their womenfolk don't have to cook for them, but never did I have so many Amish descend on the café all at once."

Several days passed before Aunt Gert found a newspaper article and showed it to Olivia, which explained the new colony's arrival:

> *Oxbow, Iowa, May 21, 1936—Because oil was discovered on their farmlands in Kansas, 39 Amish Mennonites have moved here. Although the Mennonites had an opportunity to reap a rich harvest when oil sprouted on their Kansas farms, they refused to extract full advantage of the situation, selling their farms for only $100 an acre.*

Which reminded Olivia she'd completely forgotten to tell Sweeney about the two men from the morning train, whom she believed might have been looking for Louie.

Sweeney told her Mayor Gardner had already alerted him, and he was far from thrilled to have two new mystery men in town, even if they didn't appear to stay long.

Olivia contemplated the village of Oxbow...a community of townsfolk and farmers; hobos, Amish and gangsters.

CHAPTER TWENTY ONE

Storm On The Horizon

Walter parked Maggie two blocks from the modest white Lutheran church building on the north end of Fourth Street. Above, its forty-foot steeple tower and cross pierced the town's eastern skyline. He stopped for a moment to listen to the sonorous vibration of clappers hitting the swinging cast bronze bells in the tower... *Bim-bam, bam-bam... bim-bam, bam-bam.*

Inside the front doors, Ham Moeller, a wealthy farmer, serving that day as usher, handed him a bulletin dated Sunday, May 24, 1939.

Walter found a seat in a back pew of the nave and listened to the last strikes of the bells. He was reminded of a day a few years earlier when Rev. Heilmann invited him to climb the steeple steps to see the unsurpassed aerial view of the township. The two had ascended the circular stairway that grew steeper and narrower with each step. At the top, he found the belfry walls open midway on all sides and strong gusts of wind pushed against his body, forcing him to hold tightly to the framework. There, he first gazed southerly at the panorama of storefronts lining Main Street. Easterly, small homes speckled the landscape, and north lay the expansive Protestant cemetery. The Island Park to the west appeared as a deep green paradise in the middle of the brown Wapsie. Just beyond that to the southwest was the dam, then I.C. church bell tower that soared above its surroundings: homes and barns, outhouses, and immense vegetable gardens lined both sides of the river.

That day he'd also seen La Cava's unmistakable Lincoln skirting a back street. The car stopped outside a small home next to the old mansion just west of the steel bridge. A man had gotten out of the car and walked inside the hovel before Louie drove off. La Cava's old boss, Al Capone was in prison, but Louie was still up to his old tricks. *Repugnant, how he worked his veiled plans behind a mask of normality, in plain sight,* he thought.

Walter remembered it had been a long time since he'd last seen La Cava around town, then recalled reading about the Johnny Torrio trial, soon to be underway. Probably the Feds had him under house arrest somewhere out east awaiting his trial.

Most recently, he'd begun paying attention to another gangster, this one, on the world stage: Chancellor Adolph Hitler in Germany. Creating the Third Reich and rearmament of the country meant breaking the Treaty of Versailles established at the end of the Great War. But for what purpose? What did Hitler have in mind?

The organist began to play "A Mighty Fortress is Our God," a hymn written by Martin Luther. He reached for a hymn book in the pew. The congregation rose as the robed choir, hymnal in hand, processed down the center aisle two by two. Rev. Heilmann, clothed in long flowing black robe, followed the procession, ultimately taking his place on an ornate chair next to the white altar that consumed the chancel area top to bottom. At the hymn's ending, he rose and walked to a short wooden stand to read the Old Testament Scripture, the first creation story in Genesis from the King James Bible. Finally, he climbed the steps to the pulpit that extended high above the congregation for the sermon.

"A second creation story follows a few verses later in Genesis," he began, and read the account from the Bible.

"In the first version, we're told man was created because God was lonely. In the second, God is not lonely but creates man out of mud to do the work of caring for His creation. He forms the creatures of the earth from the same mud. Man has no dominion over the land, or of God's creatures. They're all made of the same stuff—each belonging to the other. Together man and woman are the stewards of God's creation.

"It's easy to find a timely message in these words…the severe drought and dust storms we are experiencing come to mind. Some have asked me: 'Why did God cause such a calamity?' I tell you God did not bring this upon us, but, as is often the case, we've brought it upon ourselves. The calamity encompassing much of the Midwest follows decades of extensive farming without crop rotation, fallow fields, cover crops or other techniques to prevent wind erosion. Our topsoil will all blow away unless we change our ways of farming. There are consequences, individually and for society, when we don't do the right things. God is speaking, if we will but hear.

"But there is a more persistent message that tugs at the heart in these Scriptures. I remind you the Old Testament is shared by Christians—and Jews. And that as people of God, we're all made of the same stuff. We need to remember this as we're again hearing rumblings of war in Germany, and of the ill-treatment of the Jews. Surely, I need not remind you that our Savior, Jesus of Nazareth, was a Jew.

"Some of you may have heard on a recent Lutheran Hour radio broadcast about the Bethel Confession, co-authored by Protestant pastor and theologian Dietrich Bonhoeffer. No man has spoken more powerfully on behalf of the civil liberties of Christian Jews than Bonhoeffer. He ultimately refused to sign The Bethel Confession because it had been watered down to appease the Nazis. I urge you to listen to what Rev. Bonhoeffer has to say about the rise of nationalism in Germany. The rebroadcast dates and times of this program are in this morning's bulletin.

"These are most troubling times... I ask you to pray for the church in Germany, for its people, and for the persecution they're enduring. And pray for our nation and what our nation's response should be to this growing threat, which all too soon has possible worldwide implications. In the name of the Father, Son, and Holy Ghost. Amen."

At the close of the service, the membership rose and filed into the center aisle to shake Rev. Heilmann's hand. Walter overheard one parishioner express appreciation for the update on the suffering of Germany's people. Another said, "This is all pretty hard stuff to follow, Reverend. How are we supposed to do anything about the goings-on in Germany?"

In good time Walter, too, stood before his pastor.

"Good morning, Rev. Heilmann... So it appears we could find ourselves involved in another war. I would be opposed to America's involvement in another war—with Germany, or any other nation."

"I think everyone in this church probably agrees with you, Walter. Bonhoeffer says the issue is really Germanism or Christianity. And the sooner the conflict comes out in the open, the better. I tend to agree with Bonhoeffer."

"But how's this situation come about? I thought Germany embraced Jews… It's been the homeland for millions of them for a long time," Walter said.

"Hitler apparently needs someone to blame for Germany's problems. The country's economy has been in the dumps since the end of the Great War, which was followed by a worldwide depression. The German people are starving and praying for God to send a leader to turn their economy around. Hitler is making grand promises. Unfortunately, he's been able to coerce crucial support from the German Lutheran Church, the Reich Church, by quoting from pamphlets written by Martin Luther.

"How's it possible that Luther's involved?"

"Luther's pamphlets said the Jews blasphemed against Jesus for receiving him only as a prophet and teacher. Hitler has now used those words to gain support of the German Church to round up Jews to put 'em in jails or on trains for deportation. A few reports are saying whole neighborhoods are disappearing."

"And the German Church supports this?"

"Like I said, these are difficult times for Christians in Germany, and throughout Europe. Best we can do is pray… How's it going for you as a Seeker, Walter?"

"I've written down another passage from Scripture I'd like to discuss with you," Walter said, handing Rev. Heilmann a folded sheet of paper torn from Leonard's yellow school tablet. "I look forward to hearing your interpretation of how this Scripture applies to times like this," said Walter. "It's John 16:23."

"We'll see how this unrest in Germany plays out. Remember: America was against involvement in the Great War, then people realized sometimes we have to unite, rise up and fight to keep tyrants from power. Read the Sermon on the Mount in Matthew, where it says that following Jesus can exact a very high cost. Keep seeking understanding from God, Walter.

You have a copy of *Luther's Small Catechism*. You'll find an answer to most any question you may have there. Now I'm sure you must leave to collect Emma and the boys from church… How's she doing?"

"She's still got a long way to go to regain her strength, but we're grateful to have her back with us. Thanks for everything you've done for my family. This church has helped more than we can ever express."

"You're very welcome, Walter," Rev. Heilmann said.

Walter noticed the minister's momentary gaze across the rows of pews, perhaps imagining the expansion that would soon be underway.

"Our church is growing, Walter. We'll be breaking ground this week. Praise God!"

"I agree with Luther. 'Every man must do two things alone; he must do his own believing and his own dying,'" Walter said. "The renovation should serve both nicely."

Walter walked toward the front doors of the church, and flinging them open, he inhaled deeply of the crisp May morning air. Fourth Street was now nearly void of Lutherans. The troublesome words from the sermon yet buzzed in his head. A storm was definitely on the horizon. What would another war with Germany mean for German Americans living in the Midwest? The very thought evoked the painful memory of seeing yellow paint splattered on his family's farm buildings.

Perhaps prison was next… Jail, for being German.

CHAPTER TWENTY TWO

Boxing On The Island Park

For the next few hours that late Saturday spring afternoon, Sweeney planned to sit under some maple tree on the Island Park and watch teenage boys and mature men pummel each other for sport. Charles Grantham had finally reinstated amateur boxing on the island.

Financing for the new cable walk bridge to the island was part of Roosevelt's New Deal, designed to put people back to work. Next year, a concrete dam would replace Oxbow's old log dam.

Sweeney made his way to the island and found a seat on a makeshift bench, rows of planks stretching across cement blocks that encircled a boxing ring made of heavy ropes strung between oil drums. Mostly he was interested in Doc Buckmaster's twin boys from Dunkerton, another small railroad community between Oxbow and Waterloo, but he'd also stick around for the heavyweight matches.

The boxing rules were simple: no cursing, quarreling, hitting with heads and legs, and no hitting below the belt. Each fight went three rounds, or until one of the fighters was knocked down and couldn't stand for ten seconds. A round lasted three minutes, with a one-minute break between. Grantham and his protégé, Frank Miller, owner of Miller Plumbing & Heating and the town's fire chief, kept track of points and decisions to end matches early due to injury.

Goobers! Sweeney thought, eyeballing the long procession crossing the footbridge…men in white shirts, suits and ties; women in dresses and heels. Nice duds, at least on the surface, though he knew much of the clothing was home-sewn, made from plain cloth manufactured in a WPA factory in the South. And a lot of shoes probably still had cardboard linings.

He searched the faces of parents who had the daunting job of keeping the heaviness of hard times away from their offspring. Everybody was here on this Saturday afternoon to be entertained for a few hours, though for the men, boxing just made them feel manly again.

The high school band struck up as soon as Sweeney unfolded the newspaper under his arm. The front page headline hit him harder than he could have imagined.

New Tax Indictment Names Torrio and 4 Others—All to Face This Month for Income Levy Evasion

April 7, 1939—A sealed indictment voted last Friday by a Federal Grand Jury charged Johnny Torrio and four others on charges of income-tax evasion.

The indictment, which contains three counts, accuses the defendants of having defrauded the government of $86,643 owed by Torrio in taxes on his income for the years 1933 to 1935, inclusive. Torrio, according to Seymour Klein, Assistant U.S. Attorney, is the man who brought Al Capone to Chicago. Other defendants are William Stockblower, Torrio's brother-in-law; John D'Agostino of Egg Harbor City, N. J., and Louis G. La Cava. They are scheduled to be arraigned today.

Sweeney stared at Louie's name in the article. What would be his fate—prison? Things could be worse for the guy though. Coulda turned out like Tommy Carroll, shot down and killed in the streets of Waterloo in '34. When police said he was going to jail, Carroll said: "The hell I am!"

Sweeney knew Louie wouldn't be left holding the bag either.

He was suddenly jostled by a man, woman and young child taking seats next to him. As Sweeney prepared to stand, the man spoke.

"Marshal Delaney, I'd like you to meet my wife and son. Phyllis and I were married a year ago, and this is my boy, Mikey—we have another on the way," he said, nodding to the woman's belly.

"Remind me of your name again," Sweeney said.

"Dustin Cobbledick... I guess we never did get formally introduced that night."

Sweeney at last linked the man's face to the Weibel break-in.

"Nice to meet you, Phyllis," Sweeney said, shaking her hand. He turned to the boy, "How are you, Mikey?" Sweeney took a moment to tweak the boy's cheek before continuing.

"I'd like to stay and chat, but I need to go place my bet... Before I go, I'm wonderin' if you got work, Dustin? The town will be doing significant work to the dam in the near future. You should go to city hall and ask to put your name on the work list."

"I appreciate the notice, marshal...and I've wanted to say thank you for a long time for the good word you put in for me, back then," Dustin said. "I was young and pretty desperate. Went about things the wrong way. Glad it was you I ran into in that alley. I've turned my life around."

"That's great to hear. Keep up the good work," Sweeney said, as the crowd filled the seats around them. "Ever thought of giving boxing a try? Winning a bout or two and getting a small purse can put a little something extra in the pocket. Charles Grantham can provide the gloves. You can sign up over there!" he added, pointing to the small table next to the ring. "He'll call your name when you're up!"

"I'd need to take a lesson or two first, get conditioned," Dustin said, grinning, as he held up one of his scrawny-looking arms. "But who knows, I might be the next Gene Tunney!"

Sweeney excused himself as Grantham made a last call for bets on the lightweight matches, which included the first of the Buckmaster twins. He quickly placed a sawbuck on the boy, noticing Cassius Ward standing nearby, a heavyweight who drew one of the largest followings.

"You hittin' on all sixes?" Sweeney said, walking toward Cash.

"Took a couple hard punches to the head last week, still haven't been able to shake it off."

"You should take a break for a while. Too much poundin' to the noggin' can't be good for ya.

"I'll be all right, Sweeney," Cash said. Swinging the cinched pair of gloves over one shoulder, he pulled a roll of tape from a pants pocket that he began to wind 'round the knuckles of his other hand.

The gong sounded from the old navy bell and Sweeney joined the crowd now four-deep around the ring. In one corner, the teenage Buckmaster boy stood confident, his chest bared, toned arms, lean frame, fists gloved with fat padded mittens that he held chest high, unbelted blue jeans loose at the waist, doin' a kinda slow two-step in anticipation of the bout to be underway.

Someone called out from the crowd: "Get 'em Bucky!"

His dancing partner ducked under the rope, a first-timer from Oran… wide grin, mouthful of pearly white teeth, dressed in a white cotton shirt with the sleeves ripped out, belted dark dress pants below. The Oranian soon began to taunt his opponent, extending his left arm as he moved toward the center of the ring, pushing the chubby gloved fist closer and closer into Buckmaster's face.

The boys went to their corners. The gong sounded. Initially they encircled each other, tentatively poking and jabbing like two spring colts in a meadow, both easily avoiding the first swooshes of brown leather passing by their tanned glowing cheeks.

Grantham orbited the two in bowler hat and bowtie, white vested shirt and dress pants.

Nearly a minute passed before Buckmaster landed a serious blow, when the boys really went at it, dancing on tiptoe now, pushing two fists at each other, jabbing left and right, in a head-on frontal assault.

The Oranian reciprocated with a lucky cut just below Buckmaster's right eye. Bucky, surprised, stepped back momentarily. An older boy in the crowd called out, "Take Doc's kid down… My bet's on you, boy!"

Buckmaster followed with combination punches that hit squarely on the Oranian's nose. Blood spurted down onto his shirt. The boy slid a forearm under his gushing nose then stepped back into the fight. A small white Jack Russell dog suddenly emerged into the ring, jumping and biting at the Oranian boy's glove, before retreating just as quickly to the sidelines. A man called to the mutt from outside the ropes, trying to grab hold of the dog as it attempted to return to the ring.

As the bout intensified, the two boys repeatedly locked arms. Each time Grantham split them apart, counted three seconds before they bumped gloves, and the sparring resumed.

The dog materialized in the ring once more, jumping and biting at slugging arms and gloves, obviously hell bent on being the third fighter in the mix. After a few seconds, the mutt again ran off.

Buckmaster suddenly landed a dizzying blow, this time to the Oranian's temple, which sent the boy seeking refuge in a corner. Grantham hurried over to ask if he was able to continue. The boy nodded, and the fighting went on.

The gong sounded, which ended the first round. In the Oranian's corner, Frank dropped the kid onto a wooden stool, handed him a towel and told him to pinch his hemorrhaging nose, while Frank tried to avoid spurting blood on his clothing or the nice white Panama hat on his head. In the other corner, Doc Buckmaster seated his son and smeared ointment on the cut below his eye.

Grantham reexamined the Oranian boy's nose twice before calling out: "I'm calling the match!" then rushed over to Buckmaster and raised one arm. The crowd booed its disappointment.

"And the fights are on hold 'til someone gets that damn dog out of here!"

Sweeney walked to the table to collect on his bet, passing by the Oranian boy, now bent over pulling a Daniel Boone. He continued on to the Baptist church food booth set up on the east side of the island near the walk bridge.

"What can I get ya'? Sweeney?" asked Alice Skinny.

"Give me a bratwurst and Coke."

"Enjoying the fight?"

"My boy won! The other Buckmaster boy's comin' up soon. Cash Ward won't fight 'til later."

"I guess you probably know how I feel about wagering, Sweeney… Got pamphlets here for a missionary at the church in two weeks. Take a few and share them around town, will 'ya?"

Sweeney eyed the brochures as he reached for his brat and Coke. Hearing the cheers of the crowd prompted a glance over his shoulder. The match for the second Buckmaster boy was beginning. He headed for a seat to eat his sandwich.

Once more he picked up the newspaper and spread the front page across his lap. He began to read an article about Hitler's new Germany. The U.S. government had monitored Hitler's rise to Chancellor. He'd sent troops into Austria and annexed it in '38, then made claims on parts of Czechoslovakia. The Munich Agreement, signed a few months later, allowed Germany to claim parts of Czechoslovakia, with consent from France and the United Kingdom. Substantial growth of the German navy then allowed Hitler to take over the remaining parts of Czechoslovakia. Germany and Italy signed the Pact of Steel, and Italy invaded and took over Albania.

This can't be good, Sweeney thought.

The noise of the crowd alerted him "Baby Grand" Cash's match with "Dynamite" Dunn was up. If Dunn was on his game, he'd throw effective combination jabs, crosses, hooks and uppercuts, exactly what Cash didn't need.

Sweeney closed the newspaper and ambled toward the ring. Several minutes elapsed before Cash stumbled across the ropes. Grantham intercepted him, stared into his eyes and deemed him unfit to fight.

Sweeney felt relief: *There's only so long a man can hold his fists in front of his face to protect himself. Cash mighta blocked most of the hits, but some woulda got through. Besides, both Cash and Dunn were favorites, so there was no heavy sugar to be made on either.*

He decided to return home and listen to a radio rebroadcast of the Joe Louis vs. Jack Roper fight, where Louis soundly defended his #1 heavyweight boxing title. Joe Louis was his new American hero.

La Cava again came to mind as Sweeney stepped onto the walk bridge. Too bad he had to miss the first of the boxing matches. Likely, Louie was sitting somewhere on a hard bed in a jail cell preparing for the fight of his life. Might be years before he showed up in Oxbow again… a lot longer if he got a sentence like Capone's.

CHAPTER TWENTY THREE

Guilty Plea

When Johnny Torrio figured out the Feds were closing in, he tried to flee with his wife to Brazil. He was arrested by an Internal Revenue agent the day he went to pick up the passports. For the next three years awaiting trial, he spent days at his home under heavy guard—his nights at the Federal Detention House in Manhattan. The trial finally got underway on March 29, 1939.

Louie, too, had been kept in a secluded location. Midway into the second week he was scheduled to testify. A U.S. marshal and two deputies escorted him into the court room, directing him to a chair in the first row behind Prosecutor Seymour Klein.

Torrio, seated at a table next to his lawyer, Max Steuer, turned in his chair to acknowledge his protégé as Louie entered the room.

Louie made eye contact with the dapper little bald man before taking a seat. Occupying the chair in the row behind Torrio was his dedicated wife, Anna. He'd married her at age twenty-two, an intelligent woman of good breeding from Lexington, Kentucky. Over the next few minutes, Torrio repeatedly turned around to give her reassuring glances.

Louie recalled the last time he and Jess had gone out to dinner with them. Torrio admitted he could get a dozen years in Levenworth. Anna begged J.T....when he got out of prison...to go straight...get out of the business...for good! He promised her he'd go into real estate. But Louie knew there was only one way out of da business. Torrio was a genius, and he could be adviser to the Luciano or Genovese families—or anything else he wanted.

Once he got outa da slammer.

Newspapers had listed a host of witnesses presented by the government during the first week of the trial. Jacob "Yasha" Katzenberg was among them. Louie knew da guy well. He peddled booze and narcotics from Europe to America. "Yasha" was not there.

Louie thought: *After dis trial is over, it best if he disappear from face of earth.*

Reporters also discovered Al Capone had been questioned at Alcatraz about Torrio's finances and his ways for hiding income. Capone allegedly had prepared a multi-page statement.

Dat story is a plant by da Feds, Louie surmised.

And Mrs. Frances Flegenheimer was still due to testify. In addition to tax fraud, the Feds hoped to tie Torrio to the October 23, 1935 assassination of Torrio's business partner, Arthur "Dutch Schultz" Flegenheimer. Torrio and Dutch had owned two-thirds of the Greater City Surety and Indemnity Company and were in position to create a monopoly on bail bonds in the city. Police believed Frances was at her husband's side when he was murdered. Louie knew da Feds hoped she'd cave under oath and finger Torrio. He searched for her face in the courtroom. She was not there either.

The twelve jurors entered the court room. Louie believed they'd been kept sequestered with deputy marshals guarding them day and night.

"All rise!" said the bailiff, as the judge emerged from a side door and ascended the bench.

"The Federal Court presided by Judge Robert P. Patterson will now resume hearing testimony in the case of the United States of America versus Giovanni "John" Torrio," stated the bailiff. "All who have knowledge or wish to give testimony of this crime draw near."

"The prosecution calls Louie La Cava," said Attorney Klein.

Louie walked to the witness stand, raised his hand and was sworn in by the bailiff.

Klein moved from behind the table and stopped in front of Torrio.

"Please state your full name, age, and address to the court."

"Louis G. La Cava, 48 years of age. I live on Greely Avenue, Stanton Island, New York."

"Mr. La Cava, you are called today to give testimony as one of the defendants charged in defrauding the government of $86,643 owed by John Torrio in taxes on his income for the years 1933 to 1935, inclusive. Please tell the court the year you met John Torrio and describe your relationship with him."

"I know "Papa" Johnny mosta my life. He help me getta first job as salesman with Schlegal Lithograph Company in New York when I jus young man. I still employ by dis company."

"Have you ever been in the employment of Mr. Torrio?"

"I help with books for import liquor business."

Louie made a slight adjustment in his chair to look around the prosecutor to see Torrio's face.

Klein likewise shifted his stance.

"Oh, Mr. La Cava, I believe you've understated your long relationship with Mr. Torrio, haven't you?" Klein said confidently. "Isn't it true that John Torrio, once a leader in the Five Points gang in New York City, sought out a gang member, Mr. Alphonse Capone, and invited him to relocate to Chicago around 1918, where Mr. Torrio had established bootleg and prostitution businesses. You, too, relocated to Chicago from New York about that time to assist Mr. Torrio, I believe. Your gift for keeping the books caught Mr. Capone's eye, and you became so entrusted that your name was the only other listed, beside Capone's, on his bank box. And, wasn't it your testimony about Capone's income from his speakeasies, brothels, and booze, so to speak, such that you 'nailed the coffin shut' for Capone at his income tax evasion trial in '31?"

"Objection!" said Attorney Steuer. "Leading the witness."

"I ask the court for latitude, your Honor... I'd like to lay out the role Mr. La Cava has played in John Torrio's businesses, verifiable by the defendant's previous court testimony in United States of America versus Alphonse Capone, October 17, 1931."

"Overruled," Judge Patterson said.

"Mr. La Cava, around the mid-1920s, John Torrio handed over reigns of his Chicago businesses to Mr. Capone and returned to Brooklyn, where

Mr. Torrio reenergized his bootleg and narcotics business...thanks to the services provided by a Mr. Jacob Katzenberg. Before Capone went off to prison, you returned to New York to again partner with John Torrio. Is there any part of this statement thus far for which you care to comment?" asked Klein.

Louie stared blankly at the attorney, discreetly lowering his right hand which had begun to tremble.

Klein quickly continued: "More recently, with the 1935 assassination of John Torrio's business partner, Dutch Schultz, plus several other gang members, a new group of outlaw leaders took control of all the major rackets in New York. With Schultz dead, John Torrio became sole owner of the bond business they had co-owned, and Mr. Torrio became a leader in the Big Six. And you've worked side by side in business with Mr. Torrio all these years, even as a stockholder in his liquor import business. Isn't this a more correct assessment of your business relationship with Mr. Torrio?"

A disturbance behind Klein erupted, prompting him to spin around and gape at the defendant's table.

Louie could see Anna standing next to J.T. The two were engaged in a hushed conversation. Tears flowed down her cheeks.

"Order in the court, order in the court!" said Judge Patterson, repeatedly striking his gavel on the bench. "Attorney Steuer, return your client to his seat or I shall have him removed from the court room."

Steuer finally addressed the judge: "The defendant wishes to change his plea."

"I wish to plead guilty, your Honor!" Torrio stated. "My wife, Anna, say to change plea to guilty."

Louie, stunned, fixed his gaze on Anna and J.T., whose arms now enveloped her petite body to the point that she nearly disappeared within his fine black suit coat.

Several more seconds passed before he finally understood. *Questo è amore*, Louie thought. *This is love. This is love.*

He lifted his gaze to Judge Patterson... *But now what happen to me?*

CHAPTER TWENTY FOUR

Epitome of Evil

In the weeks before Leonard reported for duty at the U.S. Department of the Navy office in Des Moines, he found himself contemplating the word ombrophobia, from the Greek word *Ombros*, meaning "storm of rain." Joining the navy would be the ultimate test of his twenty-one years. For most of his life he had hated being out in the rain and snow. Now he would have to find a way to survive in all kinds of weather, on the middle of some ocean as a tin can sailor on a new destroyer, standing watch as helmsman, performing exterior maintenance, or a gunner shooting a 20mm AA gun at enemy aircraft.

And he thought about Adolph Hitler, perhaps more than most. Why the German people elected him into office was a quandary. Every kid in America knew he and his Nazi cohorts represented the very epitome of evil.

Something else his father told him that was likely true about Hitler—there was no Anna Torrio whispering into his ear, pleading with him to do the right thing.

Now the cold December 1941 morning of his deployment had irrevocably arrived.

He, Walter, Emma, and Samuel converged with dozens of other somber families at the Oxbow depot. Leonard knew his father had dreaded this day, protested, fought against it vehemently—even bitterly, at times.

But Leonard fought to enlist in the Navy, and Walter finally acquiesced.

Father Torpey soon walked toward Leonard with chalice and wafers to give Holy Communion. When Leonard took the host, Father Torpey handed him a rosary, then inquired about the whereabouts of Billy Bundy and Jason McCuniff. Leonard pointed them out in the crowd. The priest walked off in their direction.

Sweeney closed in to say his goodbye, too. "Olivia and I wish you God's safety," he said, extending his hand to Leonard. "We'll be praying for you every day, and Olivia will be knitting sweaters, socks and such for the Red Cross to send to all our boys in the war. We hope these things will bring warm memories of home. I believe Roosevelt will lead our country through the war, just as he has the depression. Look me up when you come home on leave—we'll throw some pitches."

"Thank you, Marshal Delaney," Leonard said, vigorously shaking hands with the man he most admired after his father. "I appreciate your good wishes…and I'll look you up, I promise! Next time I get leave to come home."

Leonard saw Billy and Jason wave at him from across the way. "I'll be right back," Leonard said, "I want to greet some friends."

Leonard made his way through the throng, giving Jason a light smack on the back as he arrived.

"I can't believe we're going to leave on the same train to go fight for our country!"

"I'm taking my catcher's mitt with me. Got it packed in my duffel bag," Jason said. "I hope we're assigned to the same ship so we can throw a few balls when we're off-duty."

"I got my St. Christopher medal," Billy said. "My mother said it would keep me safe… I admit, I'm a little scared."

"I've packed my family's Bible… When I get home, I'm going to study to become a priest, though I haven't told my parents yet," Leonard said. "I'll trust God to keep me safe."

"Let's keep in touch… I'll write and let you know where I end up after basic training… You do the same," Leonard said before walking away.

Leonard hadn't allowed himself to think about the moment he'd have to say goodbye, but he knew it was time. He drew near to his mother, his slender physique now a foot taller than hers.

"Promise me you'll take care of yourself, Leonard," Emma said, her voice still weakened from her war with tuberculosis. "I'm grateful to have you for a son. I love you, and I'll pray for your safety every day. Write as often as you can." Then she grabbed her eldest son around the neck and held onto him in the tightest embrace.

As the train closed in on the station, Leonard and Samuel faced-off.

"Goodbye, brother," Samuel said, giving Leonard a quick handshake and hug. "I'm going to really miss you."

"I'll send you a souvenir from the first exotic place I get to," Leonard said, wiping tears, which had begun rolling unabashedly down his rosy cheeks. "And I'll write and tell you what it's like fighting on a big ship."

Leonard knew his father was awaiting his turn. He stepped in front of him…and saw his father's lower lip quiver.

Walter's voice broke as his first words tumbled out: "Carry this with you every day," he said, placing something in the palm of Leonard's hand. "I'll be carrying the same in my pocket; it'll be our connection during these months we're separated. I love you very much, Leonard… I hope you know that."

Leonard glanced down at his palm then back into his father's moist eyes, and carefully tucked the piece in an inside coat pocket. The two embraced, just long enough for Leonard to whisper into his father's ear: "I do know you love me… and I love you. Goodbye, Father, until we meet again."

He reached down and grabbed his duffel bag next to Emma's feet, turned and made his way through the crowd toward a middle wagon where Jason and Billy were holding a seat for him.

A few moments later the locomotive began to jerk from the station. Leonard got back up and made his way to the rear of the wagon for a final wave goodbye. He stepped out into the crisp winter air onto the small iron platform with a short railing. He saw Walter standing stoically between Emma and Samuel on the station platform, his arms around their shoulders. Emma dabbed at her eyes with a hankie.

Samuel waved and hollered, "Good-bye, Leonard… I'll be waiting every day for a letter from you."

Leonard responded: "I'll send word when I hear the Bismarck's been sunk."

And he knew he'd be back at the depot tomorrow. And the next day. And the day after that.For a very long time to come.

As the train pulled from the depot, once more Leonard gazed upon his beautiful mother. She blew a kiss he knew was intended only for him. He waved heartily again to Samuel, then stared at Walter, wondering if his father would avoid his gaze. At the last moment their eyes met. Leonard half-smiled, then three-finger-waved. Walter didn't reciprocate.

In an instant, diamond-encrusted snowflakes began to fall from the grey heavy sky. Leonard leaned beyond the canopy to look heavenward. In a very short time the landscape would turn into a beautiful wintery painting. A palpable fear pulled him back until his backside comfortably hugged the wagon door.

Leonard remained on the landing until the tracks veered right at the quarter-mile turn, where the terrain's curtain dropped down between them, and home disappeared from sight.

The rear of the caboose nearly out of sight and the fare-welling over, Sweeney glumly slogged through the deepening snow to go home to bed, for now. Though he still had a full day's work ahead of him. Electrical maintenance. Tree branch removal following last week's ice storm. Plus, house meters that needed to be read.

And he knew he'd be back at the depot tomorrow. And the next day.

And the day after that.

For a very long time to come.

CHAPTER TWENTY FIVE

While You Were Gone

With each passing year, Sweeney admittedly missed his squat side-kick. Missed the smell of acrid cigar smoke intermingled with witch hazel. Missed his strut. Likely Louie had come back to the area for a couple days now and then to see Josephine, choosing to keep his visits concealed. He had his reasons.

Neither had Sweeney seen one word about Louie in a newspaper since the Torrio trial, when Torrio got two and a half years in a Federal prison for income tax evasion with probation of ten years. The two other defendants—Louie La Cava and John D'Agostino—received mistrials.

His first thought had been: *So, Louie beat doing prison time again— the man's got nine lives!* He recalled the agreeable feeling that had come over him until he remembered, at the end of the day, he was a lawman and justice must prevail.

Or, perhaps Louie was still a hunted man because of his testimony at Torrio's trial. And perhaps the Feds still tracked his every move, trying to build a case in the murder of Dutch Schultz.

A third possibility was an old problem: Al Capone.

In November 1939, newspapers had plastered stories of Capone's imminent release from prison after undergoing treatment for paresis at a Federal Correctional Institution at Terminal Island in San Pedro, California. Finally, having served seven years, six months and fifteen days, and having paid all fines and back taxes due, Capone got released and moved back into his Miami mansion. Sweeney wondered: *Had Scarface spent his years in lockup fantasizing about how he'd get back at Louie, a star witness at his trial. Would Capone yet put a hit out on him? Was Louie relegated to living out his life in hiding?*

Sweeney believed eventually Louie would show up in Oxbow; after all, Josephine had been staying with family in the countryside since before the Torrio trial. But Louie would definitely return…for his money.

The town's rumor mill maintained that years earlier Louie had moved all his dough to the Oxbow State Bank. Sweeney believed a Main Street businessman initiated the rumor after noticing one morning Louie's car was parked in front of the bank. The next morning the car was back, and the next. Another local, who daily stopped by the bank, reported seeing Louie make trips to the deposit room in the vault. The rumors eventually settled down to a single theory: Louie La Cava went to the bank every day he was in town to count his holdings and make sure the bank wasn't pilfering from him.

Whether Louie was fastidious about counting his money, Sweeney couldn't say. But he was certain there weren't enough hours in the day for the man to count all of it in just one sitting, at least according to Captain Hughes, who said Louie had plenty of money, which he kept in cash so the Feds couldn't track any of it.

While Sweeney hadn't heard much from Hughes since Capone went to prison, a few months earlier the captain had called, said it was to inquire about Sweeney's retirement. He asked Sweeney to let him know when the date was firmed up so he might attend the party.

That pleasantry out of the way, the captain drifted the conversation to a little old business, this time wanting to chat about the wealthy and notorious La Cava family. He said the La Cava brothers had made it into the Feds' "Who's Who of Organized Crime in Chicago" for being deep in the Capone organization and sanctioned gambling under the Thompson administration. Joseph La Cava was hauled in by the Feds in '28 for questioning during a gambling war bombing, though nothing more happened. But definitely the La Cava boys had gotten filthy, stinkin' rich during Prohibition.

Finally, he got down to inquiring about Louie's current whereabouts. Most lawmen had forgotten about "Three Fingers," but Hughes remembered him...remembered he'd never been tried by a court of law for activities as Capone's lieutenant or the *Cosa Nostra* on the east coast. This put Louie on the extremely short list of thugs who'd escaped prison, or a torpedo killing, or cement entombment at the bottom of the Chicago River. Yes siree! The captain remembered Louie. He was still out there somewhere. As free as the wind.

"Best I can tell you," Sweeney had told Hughes, "Louie remains a mystery man. He drops into town from nowhere, then inexplicably disappears for months, sometimes longer."

Sweeney ruminated whenever Louie did decide to show his face around Oxbow again, he'd find much had changed. He'd never forget the fire at the Methodist Church on Sunday morning, November 8, 1942.

Shortly after the sun came up, he'd gone to the well shed to pump water so folks had water for bathing before church. Waiting for the tower to fill, he sat on the bench outside the engine house, relishing the tranquility of an empty Main Street, thinking it might be what he liked best about life in a small town. In many ways, Oxbow still had a Wild West feel: wide barren dirt Main Street with run-down steel bridge crossing the Little Wapsie, and nineteenth century architecture with cloth canopies overhanging a rolling, weathered boardwalk. Four hundred souls already called this place home when the northern part of the township was platted in 1854.

An hour later, he returned to the well shed. Just as he flipped the switch to turn off the pump, the fire siren sounded. Within minutes a few old duffers raced toward the engine house.

"It's the Methodist church!" someone hollered.

Sweeney scanned the skyline above the church, straightaway seeing a thin veil of black haze. He followed the men inside the engine house to help ready the 1928 Model A truck, its sides encumbered with soda-acid cylindrical tanks to maintain water pressure, tanks transferred from the old Maxwell truck. Minutes ticked down before the truck's rounded nose emerged through the double-wide doors and the red beast turned west onto Main Street, siren sounding, yellow rubber-jacketed and black-helmeted men clinging to straps on its sides, their feet planted on wide steel rudders. Sweeney's among them.

At the scene, firemen uncoiled the long flat canvas hose, attaching one end to the firetruck tank, while Fire Chief Frank Miller grabbed the slender black nozzle at the other end. Soon a tenuous stream of water began to flow; but by then a thick black cloud cloaked the white wooden structure built in 1870. More locals arrived—men, women and children—who pulled buckets from the truck and quickly formed brigades. One line extended from a fire hydrant in the next block; a second stretched from the river to the church. Each soon delivered pails of water for dousing the fire. Firemen managed to carry out a few choir chairs and two preacher chairs before brazening unstoppable flames curled around external walls and roofline. The frame hissed and crackled. Stained-glass windows popped.

Sweeney noticed in the middle of the next block, atop the back stairs outside the apartment above Lehmkuhl Hardware, their children looked on.

After the last flames were extinguished, Rev. Winter poked amongst the hot, smoking rubble for any salvageable vestiges. Only the resolute brick chimney stood in the background.

Families continued to arrive for the worship service. A farmer, Delbert Haberkamp, told Sweeney: "My daughter, Carol, said she wasn't coming to Sunday school and church this morning because every week Oxbow has another fire. I guess I'll go back home now and tell her it's a good thing she stayed home...'cause this morning the Methodist Church burned to the ground."

Chief Miller approached Sweeney, saying: "The fire probably started from an overheated furnace. The fire was discovered before the start of Sunday school on the top floor."

Rev. Winter established a church rebuilding fund before the day's end.

Sweeney thought about Louie. *If he'd have been in town that day, he'd have been among the first to make a donation. Anonymously, of course.*

Then, in early '43 fire destroyed the old grist mill, the second nearly ninety-year-old structure gone within a year's time.

The following August came a tragedy of the vilest kind. A three-year old boy, Dale, left in the care of a neighbor, had been at play with two older boys, all drawn to the railroad tracks, as the town's children often were. Perhaps they'd become immersed in a game of hide-and-seek, meandering between parked wagons on the second set of tracks, crawling beneath them, emerging on the other side, before ducking under still another, once more out of sight. Perhaps too consumed with fun to heed initial whistles signaling the approach of the freighter about to come barreling through town, or the shrill whistles following, which locals knew warned of imminent danger.

In the final moments, the train looming down upon them, the two older boys dove into the weeds in the berm to escape. The younger boy, yet on the tracks, the engineer held steady on the whistle. The train came to a stop fourteen wagons later. The engineer descended the locomotive's side ladder and searched along the tracks until finding the boy's limp body in a tender bed of wildflowers. Gently lifting him into his arms, he walked toward the growing cluster of parents and neighbors, asking: "Who does this child belong to?"

The boy's mother hastily claimed the lifeless child and carried him to Youngman's Undertaking. Her screams of agony echoed across town, block by block. His funeral at the Lutheran church followed, then the child in his small casket was delivered to the Protestant cemetery. A newborn at home, the mother never spoke of the tragedy again.

Sweeney knew, if Louie had been in town at the time, a cardless floral spray would've stood next to the coffin. And most would have guessed it came from Louie.

Sweeney also fancied updating Louie about other town happenings.

The August 15th Oxbow Days still included a small carnival on Main Street. Louie loved to take in the girlie show.

And the Wiltse Hotel had come back to life in November '39, when John and Pearl Gipper from Westgate bought the hotel and gas station, filling it with their half-dozen children, and once more the establishment teamed with young life. Within the year, John died. So again, at the helm of the hotel was a strong, extremely capable woman—seemingly the hotel's destiny. While Louie maintained the Wiltse's previous owner, the spitfire Lucy Minton, had meant little to him, Sweeney remained certain the next time Louie was in town, he'd drive by and stretch his neck to check out the Wiltse, now under new ownership.

Plus, Louie always liked to be brought up to date on Sweeney's family.

Vanessa had gotten married to her childhood sweetheart. Her husband worked for the railroad. Their first child was on the way.

And Sweeney's parents' home by the railroad tracks had burned in the fall of '40. His mother was preparing the midday meal when a fire started from the oil stove. The shack was gone in a flash. No one was hurt, but little was saved.

Louie would return to town one of these days. Then he'd tell Louie about everything he'd missed...while he was gone.

CHAPTER TWENTY SIX

Homecoming

December 1944 had been a string of bitterly cold days. Today was no different. Sweeney stood outside the post office building, bracing his back against the seventeen mile per hour icy wind that pushed against his reedy frame in the twenty-degree Fahrenheit morning. With every move, the billy club at his side wobbled like a long icicle.

The whole nation had experienced a particularly hellish year. In September the Great Atlantic hurricane hit nine hundred miles of the east coast; a second major hurricane hit Florida in October; and the Mississippi rose to the highest stage ever recorded, all the while the Ohio Valley recorded one of the worst droughts in years. Now, December in the leap year, the country braced for historic cold and snowfalls.

All the while, the hellish World War II dragged on. The D-Day Normandy landings on June 6th stood out as the decisive battle of the war in Western Europe. Leonard's ship, the USS Glennon off Utah Beach, provided protection for invasion shipping and naval gunfire support for assault troops. The destroyer took a hit from a floating acoustic mine early that morning, causing her to be grounded by the stern. Finally, she sank. Leonard and other survivors went to a rest camp in Scotland for three weeks. In September, he got reassigned to the USS French. Sweeney eagerly awaited another letter.

The squad of women in line behind Sweeney had grown to nearly a dozen in the past half hour. Each held at least one brown-paper-wrapped package in her arms, unmistakably on its way to a son, nephew, neighbor or church member fighting in the war. The lineup was a daily occurrence.

He struck up a conversation with Rev. Clarence Soden's wife, the very capable woman in charge of the sewing brigade at the Baptist church. Only a bare minimum of her face was left exposed to the elements; the rest of her head was swaddled in a thick, drab wool scarf.

"I told Olivia I'd pick up the mail this morning," Sweeney said, expelling a plume of hot smoke from the cigarette between his lips, which, he noticed, hung in the air like a thin film of marshmallow candy.

"Olivia was kept pretty busy yesterday at the Methodist church. Our women and girls spend every spare moment they can find sewing bandages and surgical dressings, as do yours, I imagine… She is speaking at the next Ladies Aid meeting, giving an update on the thousands of Jews pleading to be allowed to come to the United States."

Mrs. Soden responded: "I thought the war might be over after General Eisenhower led our boys to victory at Normandy. But I fear another big battle is coming… I can feel it. Haven't heard anything from my son Jake for months…always means something on a grand scale is about to take place. Last I knew, Jake's troop was being moved to Belgium.

"And as far as the Jews so desperately wanting to come to America," she continued, "I wish someone would explain that to me; surely there are other places they can go that are closer."

At last, Postmaster Bud Murphy appeared inside the glassed-in entrance and unlocked the door.

"Good morning, folks!" Bud said, with his usual cheerful enthusiasm, holding open the door as the first customers entered, then passed through the half-door leading to his station behind the counter.

The lineup quickly wound 'round to the rear of the long, narrow first floor. Sweeney headed to the west wall, where rows of small numbered boxes filled the space floor to ceiling.

"I'll get your mail for you, Sweeney," Bud said, interrupting service to the woman standing opposite him at the counter. Bud pulled the contents from Sweeney's box, wrapped it with a couple of wide rubber bands, and handed it to him.

"Thanks, Bud," Sweeney said.

At the front door, he ran head-on into Josephine La Cava. He held the door open as she entered.

"Good morning, Josephine—any word from Louie? I've sure missed the ol' boy. What's he been up to?"

"I'm hoping for a letter," she said. "I've come to town this morning with my brother-in-law, Joe, who is running errands. It takes a few days longer to get mail delivered to the farm, and I'm anxious to hear from Lou."

Politely she pushed past Sweeney and took her place at the back of the line.

Sweeney found himself wondering what Josephine really knew about the comin's and goin's of Louie. Over the years, he'd watched her grow from a young girl into a beautiful, stately woman. Unfortunately, she now spent her days waitin' for her man to send a letter saying he was comin' home.

He held firmly to the banded mail in his hand as he took a deep breath and stepped back out into the face-numbing winter wind.

Wherever you are today, Louie, he thought, *I hope it's a helluva lot warmer there.*

—

Since America joined the Allies in the war effort in '41, each church in town had held at least two funerals. Sweeney attended all of them. Victory in Europe came with the surrender of Germany on May 8, 1945, though Japan stubbornly refused to surrender, so homecomings for returning soldiers remained on hold.

But Louie finally surfaced, according to a blurb in the Oelwein newspaper. For the first time, Sweeney realized others in the area must have been awaiting word of his return, too.

> *Oelwein, July 27, 1945—Louis La Cava of New York is visiting at the Joseph Levendusky home. Mrs. La Cava has been here for some time.*

Forty-eight hours later Louie showed up on Main Street. The day was not unlike the one in the early 1920s when Josephine and her new husband first arrived in Oxbow. Sweeney had been standing outside the city building on the boardwalk as a shiny black Lincoln crept to a halt outside the Coffin Café, and emerging from the car was a local girl, Josephine Necker, clinging to the arm of a man whom Sweeney would come to know as Louie La Cava. The only difference now was they were both older, greying, and Louie was driving a different shiny black Lincoln.

Sweeney scuttled across the street to catch up with Louie.

"Where ya been? It's been a helluva long time since I've seen your Italian face around here!"

"Sweeney, my friend!" Louie said, as the two firmly shook hands. "Jess sent letters with 'da news…heard you plan to retire! Imma just back in town. Tomorrow I stop by barber shop. Hope see you then. Perhaps we go for ride to Chicago soon. Much to catch up."

"Stop by the engine house—you know where to find me," Sweeney said, then watched as Louie and Josephine hurriedly drove off in the Lincoln.

—

About a week later came news of Japan's surrender, provoked by President Harry Truman's order to drop atomic bombs on two Japanese cities. The man-made devastation was unparalleled. Over the course of the next months, area soldiers began arriving home on trains at the depot, and with each the community celebrated, jubilant that Hitler and the Axis had been defeated.

Then came the first staggering reports out of Europe on the discovery of thousands of Jewish corpses in Nazi concentration camps.

"You know what?" Sweeney said to Olivia one morning in early 1946.

"These world events have knackered me. I think it's time for me to retire. I'd like to spend my days with you and playing with our grandsons. The rest of the time, I'll hunt and fish and ice skate with the town kids on mill pond.

"And maybe the town council will let me continue to play Santa Claus at the engine house at Christmastime. Of my duties as marshal, most enjoyable was seeing that long line of children, and the look on their faces when I handed each a brown bag of nuts and candy, all their very own.

"But I wonder sometimes, Olivia… What kind of a job did I do as marshal? I've tried to serve this town well."

Olivia responded without hesitation.

"You upheld the law in this community, which wasn't always easy, as you were surrounded by childhood friends.

"When the town got electricity, pretty quickly residents started bringing you their broken-down appliances, and you never charged a dime to fix any of it.

"And remember how everyone wanted to be connected to the new water mains—immediately?

"But I suspect folks are gonna miss seeing you walk around town reading water meters, hearing you belt out verse after verse of 'Big Rock Candy Mountain.'"

"You really are not a very good singer, in case no one ever told you, dear," she added, staring endearingly into his smoky-blue moist eyes.

CHAPTER TWENTY SEVEN

Redemption and Grace

SIXTEEN YEARS LATER

The Florida license plate first appeared on Louie's car in '48, the year after Capone relocated from Miami to Mount Carmel Cemetery in Chicago. Sweeney might have missed that detail as a rookie, but not as a seasoned marshal. Now Louie drove a new '61 black Cadillac DeVille. Still a luxurious automobile, but not a Lincoln.

"It's been a while since we made a trip to Chicago," Sweeney said, removing his jacket, carefully folding it in half and placing it neatly on the back seat. A cloud of harsh smoke from Louie's cigar swirled out from under the roofline to greet him as he climbed inside and situated himself on the grey leather bucket seat, which, he said, hugged his old bones like a soft fur coat. He gave a gentle tug to the passenger door handle and listened for the crisp, clear sound of the door closing.

"I take few back roads today… Chicago trip take little longer, if thatta be okay with you," Louie said. "You inna rush get home?"

"It's your nickel, Louie. Olivia's taking the Dinky to Waterloo this morning, I'm just along for the ride… Plan to lie back in my seat for the first hour to get some shut-eye. Old men like me aren't used to getting up this close to sunrise… Who knows? this may be our last trip together."

"Fine, Sweeney… You ramble whenna you talk, so will enjoy some peace."

Sweeney reclined the seat, pulled the brim of his newsboy hat low on his forehead, leaned his head against the side window and closed his eyes.

He could hear the roar of the 325-horsepower engine as Louie floored the accelerator and the sleek Caddy sped east on Grove Street, soon veering onto the smooth blacktopped Highway 281 leading to Oelwein. The car moved deftly, like she had the route memorized. He felt the morning sun pierce the mammoth windshield that cocooned his body in warmth. One final time he lifted his cap to peer out a side window to glimpse the car's long black shadow trailing along the southern ditch, passing over tall green grasses and squalls of the last blooming iris.

"I believe this is about as comfortable a ride as exists, Louie," he said, his final words before drifting off to sleep.

Louie fidgeted with the radio dial, knowing Sweeney's snoring would soon reach full throttle. At KOEL-AM out of Oelwein, he heard the sweet twangy voice of Loretta Lynn. He had met her backstage at the Grand Ole Opry in Nashville a year earlier and could still visualize her on stage in a homemade cowgirl outfit, long auburn hair framing her beautiful face, and poor-girl's guitar strap hanging around her neck as she played and sang "I'm a Honky Tonk Girl." Content the radio signal would carry for a good portion of the trip, he returned his leather-gloved hand to the steering wheel.

A dozen miles later at the Highway 281/150 intersection, he turned the Cadillac south. The 190 Club used to sit at that corner. It burned to the ground in the middle of the night a half-dozen years back. Police never did figure out the cause of the inferno.

Just beyond the intersection, he spied a thumb in the air. Nimbly he swerved around the pretty young thing and brought the sedan to an abrupt stop along the shoulder. Within seconds, the girl tramped past the large rear black fin and the door behind Sweeney flew open.

Louie turned toward the entering passenger: "Where 'ya headn', doll?"

"Chicago, if that's as far as you're going," she said. Pushing Sweeney's coat aside, she dropped a small canvas backpack from her shoulder onto the expansive rear seat. At last, her tall slender body positioned, with a delicate hand she pulled the heavy door closed.

"I'm Gracie...Gracie Failes," she said exuberantly.

Louie gawped at the girl's flawless face and wispy blonde hair pulled back into a long ponytail, tied up with a thin pink scarf.

"Nice meet you. I—Lou..." he stammered. "And that's Sweeney," nodding at the lump with his face hugging the window.

Sweeney let out an earth-shattering snore, and the girl giggled with abandon.

"Oh, my God! What's that noise?" she said. "I guess I better get used to that—huh? When you get a free ride, you get what comes with it."

The Oelwein Methodist church pastor had replaced Loretta Lynn on the radio, and after offering a word about the Sunday service, he began to pray: "Oh, most gracious, loving Father, we beseech you—"

Louie turned forward, reached for the volume button, and immediately the sound of the praying pastor dropped off.

"We go Chicago today...anna you welcome join us!" he said affably, positioning the rearview mirror to garner a fuller reflection of her angelic face. Again, he floored the accelerator and the wheels sprayed gravel as the auto bounced back onto the road. A second later he powered down the side window halfway and tossed out his cigar stub.

"You from dese parts?" he asked, waving residual smoke from the car's interior.

"Sure am, and I'm leaving for good! Nothing here to come back to."

Likewise, she lowered her window by several inches then sat silently staring at passing farm fields of maturing crops—*everything she'd probably known slinking from sight,* he surmised.

"Folks know where ya headin'?"

"Nope...and if that's a problem, you better stop the car right now!"

"Fine, I no wanna get nosy."

Sweeney shuffled in his seat and uttered in a low moan: "But Olivia, I told you..." before repositioning his face up against the glass.

"Where you from, Lou?" she said.

"Florida, now... I move 'round some. Salesman by trade."

Louie could feel her eyes on the back of his head. At one point their eyes met as he checked her out in the mirror.

"So, you're gone from home a lot, I imagine."

"Over forty years a salesman...this my craft, how earn living," he said, reaching over to turn up the radio a bit to hear "Stand By Your Man," sung by Tammy Wynette. He felt his upper arm drag slightly as it passed over the piece under his jacket.

"I no wanna pry...but you runnin' 'way from home?"

"Whattya got under your coat, Lou?"

His eyes flitted to the mirror.

"I carry piece. Issa for protection—I onna road lot."

"I figured you for a gangster! I'm a fast study of people, got a real knack for it."

"Why say that?"

"This car! And you just have the look. I bet you got at least a couple more guns on you...and you've used 'em, right? Maybe I carry one, too... Don't I look like the kind of girl who needs protection? Got it right here," she said, patting the backpack on the seat beside her. "I grew up on a farm. I know about guns."

His mind drifted to another day, time and place...only the sound of gravel kicking up inside the wheel well brought him back from the stale memory, and the DeVille to the roadway.

A minute later he came upon a slow-moving tractor pulling a wide flat wagon. He slammed on the brakes. A second later he nosed the car out into the left lane to check for oncoming traffic, only to jerk it back again behind the wagon just as a grain truck growled by.

"You know what's wrong with this world, Lou? she continued. "Character...nobody has any. Take my father, a real religious man. High up in the church. He stands and reads Scripture at church services on Sundays. He's high up in the Masons, too, but it's all for show when it comes right down to it. He's a mean-spirited SOB every chance he gets... I could tell you so much more..."

The sound of the backpack being moved caused his eyes to jettison again to the mirror. An instant later, she stopped, as though frozen in place, her eyes seemingly focused at the back of Sweeney's seat. A few wispy hairs loosened from her ponytail fluttered from the draft of air coming through the window.

At last the tractor veered off the highway onto a gravel road. Louie trounced on the accelerator to separate himself from the vehicles stacked up behind. At the town of Independence, he turned east onto Highway 20, where he knew the long automobile could zoom along the paved roadway with few twists and turns for miles.

She went on: "In the end, there's no real difference between a gangster and an immoral man hiding under the veil of religion—is there, Lou? Both do the same stuff... Kill people. Kill dreams. Kill...just because they can. Only one is labeled a bad man... The other never gets the label but does the same bad stuff. That's why I'm leaving home."

Sweeney stirred and raised his head. "What did you say, Louie? Were you talking to me?"

"No, Sweeney—not talk to you! We gonna stop in hour or so... Go back sleep. I wake you."

A voice on the radio announced top of the hour headline news. Louie fidgeted with the dial to get a clearer signal: "Sources say East Germany has begun to build a barbed wire and concrete wall which appears will separate East and West Berlin..."

"Are you Catholic, Lou?" Gracie said, raising her voice to talk over the radio. You know we've just elected a Catholic president. God, is that freakin' out the Protestants. They think he's gonna make everyone in America convert to Catholicism. Tell me, does your religion really mean anything to you? I mean, why bother, if you don't let it change you? But for some, I suppose, it's all about puttin' on a good face. I so hate pretense!"

Louie eyed Sweeney sound asleep.

Another glance into the mirror and he noticed she had reclined her head against the seatback and closed her eyes. *Perhaps she will sleep,* he thought. A minute later she sat back up to fish amongst the contents in her backpack and retrieved a compact mirror that she held up to her face. With an index finger, she cleared smears of mascara from the corners of her eyes and tucked loose hairs back into the ponytail.

Sweeney changed position and his lower jaw dropped, releasing a deafening rumble from deep within his throat.

"Oh my God! do something about that noise!" she shrieked.

Louie reached over and nudged Sweeney. His head gently clunked against the window and the snoring moderated.

"You hungry, doll? We stop for breakfast at Center Grove...issa not too far."

Gracie leaned forward in the seat, then paused, as though considering her next words.

"Lou, did you ever figure out why you became a gangster?" she began. "Did your dad do bad stuff to you...abandon you as a boy, and now everybody has to pay because of the rage you carry inside? Or maybe you were a poor kid and decided when you grew up you were gonna be rich, have money, no matter what you had to do. Maybe your mother was weak, and you felt you had to one day turn into a big, bad man, so you wouldn't feel weak like her."

Louie looked down at the steering wheel at his leather-gloved hands. They felt heavy against his skin. A restlessness came over him. Twice his chest heaved. He waited for the feeling to pass.

"My wife leave home when young girl... Imagine she issa lot like you, Gracie Failes," he finally said calmly. "Imma concern—what happen if you got nowhere to go in Chicago. I have friend can stay with."

"Thanks, Lou, but I got friends in Chicago, too," she quipped.

Again, he felt her eyes burning a hole in the back of his head. He heard her fidgeting in the seat. Finally, she continued.

"By the way... Are you from these parts? Now that I think of it, I may have seen you around Oelwein. Wait! Are you the gangster who's married to the girl from Oxbow?"

"Got lotta friends inna Oelwein...go there often."

"Did you know John Dillinger, too?"

Involuntarily his eyes rose to the reflection of the lovely creature in the mirror, which was followed by the compulsory flutter of a cheek muscle; then his head began to nod, ever so slightly, side to side.

"Oh, my God! Are you on your way to Chicago to kill someone?" she gasped.

He considered pulling the car off to the side of the road. Instead, he gunned the accelerator and turned his head to stare at the passing scenery to his left.

"You're getting' up there in years for a gangster... I've always wondered: whatcha gonna say to God to explain all the bad stuff you've done? And Just once I'd like to listen in when you go to confession. Doesn't the priest tell ya to stop all the killin'? Give back the money ya took? I believe in forgiveness, Lou... I believe there ain't nothin' so bad that God can't forgive... But you won't be able to forgive yourself 'til you make it right with the people you've hurt."

Not hearing a response, she nuzzled her face up to the window. He could hear her taking in deep breaths of fresh air.

"Think there issa God, Gracie Failes?" he said slowly, matter-of-factly.

In the next instant, he felt her hands grasp the front seat and she pulled herself forward.

"Can't say there's a real God, can't say there isn't," she said. "All I know for certain is it sure feels like there's a positive force in this world trying its damnedest to help us out from time to time."

"My life made by fate. I soldier inna Great War. What issa war anyhow but organized killing? Lotta bad people get what comin' to 'em. Then there issa street war... Government start dis war, too. Lotta guys get paid to take down criminals... And dey jus' leave 'em to die inna gutter. I not feel guilt about killin' dose guys; I figger, issa dere blood, or mine. If God exist, Gracie Failes, he make my life go bad long time ago. I not 'fraida God."

From the mirror, he watched as Gracie slid back in the seat, her mouth wide open. He stared at her and she at him.

Expelling a loud belch, he reached across the front seat to jostle Sweeney from slumber.

"Wake up... We almost to Center Grove... Stop for breakfast now."

Sweeney slowly lifted his head.

Louie glanced in his direction, then over his right shoulder.

"We pick up hitchhike, Sweeney. Meet Gracie Failes. She goin' all da way to Chicago with us," Louie said, noticing that Gracie's expression still hadn't changed.

Sweeney looked at Louie, then back at Gracie.

"I musta been really out! Nice to meet you, Gracie," Sweeney said, still in a fog.

A quarter of a mile later, Louie pulled the Caddy onto a gravel lot and parked outside Sadie's Café. He twisted the key in the ignition, and the engine and radio fell silent.

Gracie latched onto Sweeney's arm as she exited the car.

"I've pretty much got Lou figured out," she said, ignoring Louie's enduring stare in her direction. "Now I'd like to hear your story."

Louie held the café door open for Sweeney and the girl. Inside, the homey place smelled of hot coffee, bacon and pancakes. The trio walked toward an empty corner booth. Hardly anyone in the place noticed an Italian and old Irishman with a blonde Scandinavian girl in tow, her in denim jeans, white blouse and canvas shoes.

"I'm going to the back room," Sweeney announced, walking away as Louie claimed the seat facing the front door. "Order me some coffee."

"Be with you in a moment," called the waitress from across the room.

Gracie scanned the room for the daily specials before taking a seat across from Louie.

"The menu's written up there," she said, pointing to the chalkboard along the back wall.

"I'll bet this was a famous gangster stop in its day... I can just imagine Capone stopping here, sitting down with his mobsters for a meal after committing murder and mayhem," she continued, looking around the room as though imagining the scene. "I guess that would include you, Lou."

"They need eat, too—imagine," Louie said.

"I'll bet there are some back roads around here, a way to cross the river into Illinois, besides the main highway... Know anything about that?"

"Probably other route," he said, pulling a spicy-smelling cigar from his coat pocket and lighting up. Seconds later, he placed the roll of smoking tobacco in the ashtray and pushed it toward the center of the tabletop.

The waitress arrived at the booth and dumped a newspaper and three white coffee-stained cups onto the tabletop. "Someone left a newspaper, if you're interested... Three coffees today?" she said, pouring black steaming hot coffee into the first cup.

"Three—fine," Louie said, as Gracie reached across the table and stole the front page of the newspaper from his hands.

"Do you mind? I like to read the news, though I prefer to get mine on television... Never know, I might see some gangster I met while hitchhiking."

Sweeney dawdled over to the booth. "I'll take No. 3 Special," he said, seating himself next to Gracie while dropping his hat on the table. "Eggs scrambled, crispy bacon, and don't burn the toast. Just lightly browned will do."

Louie removed his gloves and held up an index finger, "*Uno* for me."

"And I'll order toast with peanut butter," Gracie said, reaching with one hand into the back pocket of her tight jeans to retrieve a few wadded-up bills and a few coins that she deposited onto the table.

"Is that all you brought with you for the trip?" Sweeney said.

"Got enough to last a couple days... I'll get a job in Chicago and be on my feet in no time."

"This meal is on me. You're a damn fool to be reliant on anyone for a hot meal or a warm place to stay in a new place. There are people who'll take advantage, if you know what I mean."

"I've got this, Mr. Sweeney... I do!" she said.

"How long you been planning this trip? Doesn't appear you're very prepared."

Gracie rolled her eyes as she counted out the correct change with tip, then pushed the pile aside and pocketed the remaining money.

Sweeney added: "Are you sure you're ready to do this? You could catch the trip back home with us later this afternoon and make your move to Chicago in a month or so, when you're ready. It's a good option—think about it."

Louie lowered the newspaper in his hands enough to scan the room. "Sage advice, Sweeney," he muttered, before disappearing again behind the sports page.

"The point is, you don't get do-overs; life's fragile, and you'll find that you can't turn back the hands of time. I know a man from Oxbow who killed a young woman in his youth— it was an accident. He was drinking. Ran her down one night on a side street when he was driving home from a tavern. The man spent time in prison and when he got out, he started his life over, with new purpose. Gave up booze, got married, had children of his own. But there are things that can never be expunged from one's life's record. So that's how he lives his life every day. Don't know if you're into boozing or drugs... But even if that's not the case, the moral to the story still stands."

"Food's up!" the waitress said, approaching the booth. One arm supported a large platter for Sweeney and Louie and a smaller one for Gracie. "I'll be back with a pot of hot coffee in a second... Get you anything else right now?"

Louie grabbed the front page from Gracie's hands, folded the newspaper in half and handed it back to the waitress. "This fine," he said.

Sweeney pulled a paper napkin from the silver holder on the tabletop and delicately unfolded and spread it across his lap.

"I'm hoping you'll be in Louie's back seat on the return trip from Chicago today. We can drop you off anywhere you wish. It's up to you, Gracie—it's your life."

"Who'd you say you are, Mr. Sweeney?" she said, dragging the plate with the buttered toast and side of peanut butter in front of her. "Have we ever met?"

"My Christian name is Sweeney Delaney. I was Oxbow's town marshal for over thirty years, and on occasion I've bemoaned the fact I didn't help more young people when I saw them goin' down the wrong road. Ultimately, their bad decisions proved a hardship for themselves, and their families. Let's just say...if I can get you to change course, then I'll feel I've earned some redemption and grace from God Almighty. And who can't use a bit more of that?"

"Tell you what, Mr. Sweeney... you let me know what time you and Lou will be back at the corner where you drop me off in Chicago this morning, and if I'm standing there, then slam on the brakes and take me back home, but I sure wouldn't count on it."

"Sorry to hear that... Sometimes I think I'm a good judge of character; guess I was all wrong about you, Gracie Failes. Sounds like you just like to give advice," Sweeney said.

CHAPTER TWENTY EIGHT

A Long Shadow

FOURTEEN YEARS LATER

Vanessa had heard an axiom repeated many times since she was a young girl: "The shadow should be the same length as the body," and Sweeney Delaney had cast an appropriately long shadow. After his stroke, her father was diminished physically, but it didn't affect his bellowing bass laugh or his spirit. In the months that followed, many longtime friends came by to talk about old times, and to play Five Hundred.

On a winter Sunday morning in 1962, Sweeney died. Vanessa had gone to the Methodist church to practice on the church organ before the morning service. She thought it odd at one point when her husband and Rev. George Gaide arrived and sat in the front pew. As soon as she lifted her foot from the pedal, the last note falling silent, they told her Sweeney had just passed away. Everyone says death is inevitable, but there comes a point in life when it's reduced to a cold hard fact. Her father always said the Chesterfields would one day catch up with him— and he'd bought an awful lot of them over the years. But he lived his life on his own terms, and she guessed that was the best anyone could ask.

At his funeral, the congregation sang "Amazing Grace" as Sweeney's casket was laid out in front of the altar of the Methodist church. Vanessa took Olivia's arm and the two followed the casket down the center aisle. Vanessa noticed all the Protestants and Catholics crowded shoulder to shoulder in the pews. What a sight.

As Sweeney wasn't as much a church man as a community man, Rev. Gaide used those very words in his sermon and eulogy. He talked about poker nights at the engine house, and Sweeney's forgetfulness, like the countless times he'd flooded Main Street when he forgot to turn off the water pump for the water tower. Baseball remained his favorite pastime, and ice skating was never far from his thoughts. Rev. Gaide spoke of Sweeney's more sensitive side, too, particularly his innate understanding of how children required intentional teaching to guide them.

Reverend Monsignor Leonard Bierkoff, now serving St. John's Catholic Church in Independence, also spoke at the service. He talked about his brief baseball career under Sweeney's tutelage and of how Sweeney had been a faithful supporter when he served in World War II—just two examples of the marshal's selflessness. Sweeney was the other man who'd given spirit and direction to his life, second only to his father. And Leonard told the mourners how Sweeney had helped his whole family through tough times when Emma was at the sanatorium. His father always said that Sweeney was a man who brought sunshine and shade to his life.

The service concluded with the singing of "Blest Be The Tie That Binds," Olivia's favorite hymn. During the final verse, members of the public school board and fire department carried Sweeney's casket to the Woods Funeral Home's black hearse parked out front of the church, which delivered him to the Protestant cemetery. It was a bittersweet day; so many dear friends, such a loss to the whole community.

Back at the church for the noon luncheon, Vanessa and her mother spoke with Captain Michael Hughes who'd driven up all the way from Chicago to offer his condolences. He said he and Sweeney had worked together on police matters, and that Sweeney was an honorable law official and man.

While Agnes Triggers spoke mostly of the mutual disdain between herself and Sweeney, she confessed: when he could've come down hard on her for listening in on his official phone calls, his soul showed up and he stopped short of insisting that she be fired.

Stories from others confirmed Sweeney's was a life well-lived, though, admittedly, Vanessa found George Weiland's comment a bit mystifying, a story she'd follow-up with him about later...something about George stumbling upon Capone's hideaway in a drunken stupor one night when visiting family in Wisconsin. George said he'd completely forgotten to tell that story to Sweeney, the man who ultimately supported him to sobriety.

A few years after Sweeney's passing, Olivia died. Vanessa said she had shared a wonderfully close relationship with her mother, the kind most mothers and daughters only wish for. At her funeral, she recited a saying that best described her mother: "Do good, then do it again," a quote from the Wesley brothers who'd founded the Methodist denomination. Olivia had taken being a Christian and Methodist to heart, in words and actions.

The last time Vanessa saw Louie La Cava alive was the fall of '79. He, too, was alone now. Josephine had died in '78 at their Florida residence, though she was brought back to Oxbow for a funeral Mass at the I.C. Church with burial in the Catholic cemetery.

On that September day, Vanessa observed Louie from the vegetable garden next to her house. Louie walked south on the sidewalk along Fourth Street, smoke from his thick cigar trailing behind his short, pudgy body. His attire: a classy polo shirt, khaki pants and black cabby cap. Though she couldn't recall the exact timeframe, at some point over the years his strut had turned into swagger, that of a satisfied man.

She noticed his swagger again that morning. She surmised Louie had probably just left the house he and Josephine had built in '68 on the north end of town. When word got out the La Cavas were planning to build a home in Oxbow, most folks took it with a grain of salt, as nearly fifty years had lapsed since he'd first stepped foot in town. Only a few old-timers even remembered his alleged ties to Al Capone, or the fear Louie's presence once evoked. The La Cava home, with attached garage, was much like other newer homes in the township, though a few people who got inside reported a few unique characteristics: a half-dozen dead-bolts and locks on every door, a set of double locks on every window. Even the outside garbage can had a lock on it. Another inside feature: a huge crystal chandelier hanging in the entrance, one more befitting a Manhattan mansion.

Vanessa surmised that Louie was on his way to play cards downtown at a tavern with the regulars. Likely he'd stop by the old McKee Drug, now Welsh's, where he usually picked up his witch hazel aftershave or grabbed a bite of lunch. Wilma Welsh told of the day Louie stopped by and suddenly began to recite a recipe for coleslaw dressing: "One cup vinegar, one cup sugar..." for the benefit of anyone listening. He was like that, Wilma said. Real chatty, though never about anything of a personal nature.

Bob Maricle, who owned a body shop on Main Street in the sixties, said Louie used to drop off his car for repairs. Louie never gave a tip for work well done, though he did invite Bob to stop by the house to see his nice chandelier once. Bob said he wasn't much into chandeliers.

And young Kurt Lehmkuhl, Louie's paperboy at his new house, told about knocking on his door to collect, always finding a note directing him to the thirty-five cents on the porch windowsill. He never did meet Louie.

And a couple neighbor lady friends called on Josephine from time to time. She was fun to be around, and loved to cook and chat, they said.

Vanessa first learned of Louie's death through a small obituary in the Oelwein newspaper. Like Josephine, he died in Florida and his body was brought back to Oxbow for Mass and burial.

> *April 15, 1980—A former Oxbow resident living in Vero Beach, Fla, Louis G. La Cava, died Sunday evening in Florida. He was 91. Funeral services will be held at 10 a.m. Friday at Immaculate Conception church in Oxbow with burial in the IC cemetery. Visitation is after noon Thursday at Woods Funeral Home in Oxbow where a rosary will be held at 8 p.m. Survivors include two brothers, George La Cava, Staten Island, N.Y., and Rocco La Cava, Daytona Beach, Fla; one sister, Mrs. Pauline Myers, Staten Island, N.Y.; and several nieces and nephews.*

Curious about whether an obituary for Louie had appeared in a Florida newspaper, Vanessa contacted the *Oelwein Register* to see if they could find one. The idea reminded her that she'd perhaps inherited some of her father's propensity for police work. She found Louie's Florida obituary included a few more details:

> *April 15, 1980, Vero Beach, Fla, Press Journal—Louis G. La Cava, 91, of Riverview Apartments, 2333 Indian River Blvd.,*

Vero Beach, died Sunday in the Royal Palm Convalescent Center. He was born September 17, 1888, in New York City and moved to Vero Beach 32 years ago from Staten Island, N. Y. He was a World War I veteran and a member of St. Helen's Catholic Church of Vero Beach. He was a retired salesman with a lithography company in New York.

Survivors include two brothers; one sister; and several nieces and nephews. Repose and visitation will be at the Cox-Gillford-Baldwin Funeral Home from 9 am to 9 pm on Tuesday. Christian Wake services will be at 7 pm at the chapel of the Cox-Gillford-Baldwin Funeral Home with Monsignor Irvine Nugent, pastor of St. Helen Catholic Church, officiating. The remains of La Cava will be sent Wednesday to the Woods Funeral Home, Oxbow, Iowa. Mass of the Resurrection will be at 10 am Friday, Oxbow, Iowa, with interment to follow in the I.C. cemetery.

Vanessa attended Louie's funeral, then followed the procession to the cemetery. As people departed the gravesite, she heard a new rumor about Louie: He'd given all his money to the I.C. Church.

If he did, she thought, Louie wouldn't be the first to give money to the church in the hope of securing a little extra redemption and grace. Still, she knew better than to place much stake in the rumor.

Louie had been a mystery man most of his life, and that's exactly the way he intended to keep it.

CHAPTER TWENTY NINE

Face In The Crowd

Samuel increasingly took over his father's farming operations after graduating from the engineering program at Iowa State University. He married within the year. Eventually he, his wife and two children bought a neighboring farm. In his spare time, he worked on medical inventions and had a couple patents pending; one was for a mechanical patient lift machine.

Walter remained on the home place after Emma's passing, maintaining there was only one way he'd ever leave.

In the early spring of '81, Walter received an invitation from the Oxbow Commercial Club, asking that he and Maggie honor the community by serving as Grand Marshal in the Oxbow Days Parade, still held every year on August fifteenth. He was delighted to accept, and a month before the parade, Samuel prepared the Model T—checking her tires, oil and engine, and starting her up and taking her for short rides. He remarked to Walter that Maggie still had a lot of life left in her for her age.

On the morning of the parade, Samuel arrived early at the farm. He parked Maggie next to the house and gave her sleek black frame a thorough dusting. Walter's frail frame soon appeared through the old screen door. The stroke a few years earlier had left a stagger in his gait, but untouched was his positive outlook on life or boundless wisdom. He pushed open the screen and gingerly descended the wooden steps, one hand holding firmly to the steel hand rail recently added by Samuel.

"Have we left enough time to visit your mother before the start of the parade?" Walter said, his once thundering voice now breathy and husky. "I don't know if she'll remember about the parade... I thought I'd tell her again."

"Yes, Father, we've allowed time... The parade doesn't start until nine. Are you feeling well enough to participate?"

"You and Leonard will be with me; I'll let you know if I tire too much."

Walter walked to the driver's door, where he fingered the two long red ribbons hanging from the handle, a deep love story encapsulated in each. Samuel helped him into the car, then walked to the passenger door and got inside. Samuel knew his father could no longer tell the car smelled musty and of vermin who lived and played amongst her skeletal frame, long ago retired to the back of the corn bin. Nor would Walter notice the cardboard in the dashboard dials had yellowed, or the dullness at the ten o'clock and two o'clock positions of the once shiny black steering wheel. His hands at the helm, he surely felt a surge of memories flowing back and forth between his fingertips and toes—like it was the '20s and '30s all over again. Walter maneuvered the handbrake lever to neutral, advanced the spark, and the four-cylinder engine jerked to life. His face lit up like a child at a Fourth of July fireworks display.

The two traveled in silence on the smooth blacktop highway into town. Walter observed the fields as he drove. Some had long rows of yellow-tasseled corn stalks—others, populated with knee-high bluish-green soybean plants; and still others held round, buttery-colored hay bales dropped carefully onto the short, prickly brown grass. He waved to farmers, many of whom were the sons and grandsons of childhood friends. He was on his way to a parade, and they all knew it from an *Oelwein Daily Register* article published earlier in the week.

At the western outskirts of town, Walter turned Maggie north, passing by I.C. Church on his right, then followed the black dirt road for a quarter mile before taking another right onto a crushed gravel driveway. A couple hundred feet later, Maggie's tires slowed to a stop. He stepped from the car onto the parched green carpet, not another soul in sight besides himself and Samuel on such a bright sunny summer morning.

Approaching Emma's grave, a swarm of field sparrows lifted from the ground and flew to leafy vegetation nearby. He walked to her modest tombstone and gently leaned a tiny bouquet of lavender flowers against it.

"Hello, my beloved," he said, waiting patiently for Emma's kind, gentle smile to appear in his mind's eye. Samuel set a folding chair in the grass and helped Walter to the seat before returning to the car to give his parents some privacy.

Walter began: "I miss you every day on the farm... The sunny parlor is as it was the day you departed. I go there in the evening before retiring, still able to sense the warmth of your final breaths...to feel your presence in the living space you last filled...though it's been a year.

"And I remain grateful the boys and I had several days to say our last goodbyes, lucid until the very end you were. You know how the boys looked up to you, mothers and sons...there's no relationship like it."

Walter paused. The warmth of the early sun swaddled his body in light, and a tepid breeze pushed gently against the cover of the book he'd brought with him. He lowered the book to his lap and opened it, carefully exposing an earmarked page.

"I've started reading the writings of Dorothy Parker. I got her book, The Portable Dorothy Parker, from the Oxbow library. She was a flapper! One of the best writers of her era, but she isn't one I'd normally be drawn to. Initially I looked for her book after reading somewhere that her mother and step-mother died when she was young, then her uncle went down on the Titanic in 1912. There's much to learn from people who've gone through hard times.

"But it was this saying of hers which first drew me to the book, because it reminded me of you." Lifting the book from his lap, he read from the page: "Men seldom make passes at girls who wear glasses."

His face glowed as he listened for her lighthearted laugh, weakened though it had become in her latter months.

"That sure wasn't my case with you, now was it, dear?" he said. "I saw in those eyes of yours, in your bespectacled face, such a deep well of love that I was very soon quite smitten."

Walter stopped as a half dozen sparrows swooped low overhead, one alighting on her headstone, tilting its head as though attempting to listen in on the conversation.

He glanced over at Samuel who'd opened Maggie's hood and was now folded in a sheath of black tin. And across the way, he spied the gravestone of Louie and Josephine La Cava.

"I've wanted to tell you, Emma... the other day I dug out my Capone journal. I thought I'd made my last entry years ago until I remembered I didn't write about the day I traveled with Louie to Chicago. As you'll recall, it took me quite by surprise that I'd even agree to go—such contempt I had for this man, wishing there was a way to rid the community of the foul air he brought with him. Then, when he invited me to accompany him, and knowing Sweeney and a couple others who played cards with him at the tavern had already done so, I quite enthusiastically replied: "I'd love to go!"

"Most of the way I listened to Louie talk, about his travels, the places he'd seen, and heard him spout off the names of people he'd met in big business or at lavish parties, the race track—even Hollywood stars. He was an extremely intelligent and knowledgeable man, on a certain level.

"By then I knew Louie about as well as any other local, but it wasn't until that day in his Oldsmobile I noticed the unease in his chatter. Underneath the fine suit and veneer of confidence, I sensed a brooding darkness there.

"I still wonder about Louie... How does a just, loving God forgive the most calamitous sins? And how does God judge society's complicity in creating men like him?"

He looked over at Emma's grave once more... Almost hourly he thought about dying and joining her. For much of his life he'd considered himself a sojourner, first going down a path, the one his parents had chosen for him; then as a young man, he sought to make his own way in the world. And now, all these decades later, he remained unsure of exactly why one pathway was chosen over another, or of what still might lay ahead. Hardly a day passed by that he didn't wonder exactly what the Creator God required of him—at times feeling completely in step with the Universe, when what he needed for that exact moment suddenly appeared like manna from heaven; as though someone knew ahead of time what he was going to need. And other times, feeling as though the God who'd launched this place called Earth out into the cosmos so very long ago—like a woman pushing a baby from her womb out into the world—stood off in the distance, peering from the thin spaces, watching the creation He begat and not lifting even one finger to help, when help was needed most. Those were the times he felt alone. Abandoned. Helpless. Orphaned. Life's a mystery, he'd concluded. Faith's a mystery... along with the Creator God.

Three constants had sustained and given his life direction: seeking God's wisdom; striving to become the best person he could be; and trying to make it right with folks whenever he'd knowingly failed. He was especially fond of the prayer of St. Francis of Assisi, "Lord, make me an instrument of your peace"; and from Luke 10:25-37: "Love the Lord with all your heart, and your neighbor as yourself."

And sometime over the span of his life's journey he'd learned that giving up resentments, and the like... Takes away the sin of the world.

Walter raised his face to gaze heavenward. At one time he feared retribution for his failings. Surprisingly, he'd found redemption and grace. And inexplicable peace.

Noticing that his shadow on the ground had shifted, he closed the book, rose from the chair, the signal to Samuel he was ready to go.

"I do hope you remember, Emma, that Maggie and I are leading the parade in town today—and I must go soon. Noritta and Ed send their love, my dear. They've sold the farm and are enjoying retirement in a small house in Oxbow. Victor continues to work on the farm with Samuel; he's prompt, hard-working and courteous, though Samuel tells me he must prepare Victor well in advance of any changes to the farm's schedule. That income, along with what Victor earns at the grocery store in town, allows him to live independently."

He walked to Emma's headstone, raised his right hand to kiss the tips of his fingers, then tenderly touched them to his wife's name.

"I still think I see you in crowds, my dear. You were a fine woman, as strong a woman as there ever was. I'm honored to have known and loved you."

At the public school, Commercial Club President Earl Bellis greeted them with a wave, and directed Maggie to the spot at the front of the parade. Two volunteers draped a GRAND MARSHAL banner across her grille.

"It would be my honor to drive Maggie today, Walter—will that be all right with you?" Earl said.

"Fine by me," Walter said, sliding to the passenger side of the bench seat. "It's a beautiful day, and our town is teeming with new people and new possibilities. Let's get this parade underway…just as soon as Leonard arrives."

"Hurry, the parade's about to begin," Walter said, waiting for Leonard to take his seat next to Samuel.

Walter turned in his seat and stuck his head out the side window far enough to view the lineup behind Maggie. He saw a flourish of homemade family and commercial floats carrying the mayor, members of the town council, or lovely young girls in beautiful gowns—likely, the county pork or beef queen with her attendants. The floats were followed by the public school marching band, clad in smart school-colored uniforms, sounding out their last warmup notes. Next was a small band of Veterans of Foreign Wars members—old men dressed in snug military uniforms, each with a rifle over one shoulder, a designate in the first row proudly carrying the American flag, all standing in formation awaiting the order to march. Following was a long string of antique and new farm tractors, their engines bombarding the air with the rattling din of firing cylinders. Fire and ambulance vehicles with their crews, men and women of every age, brought up the parade's rear.

Earl got behind Maggie's steering wheel and slowly crept her forward to Main Street. They were met by the first throngs of people lining both sides of the wide, concrete thoroughfare, some standing, some seated in colorful webbed folding chairs, many waving small American flags; young children crouched along the curb, awaiting the first hard candy thrown from floats passing by.

"Throw those kids some candy," Walter said to Leonard and Samuel.

As Maggie passed by the middle of the first block, random recollections washed over Walter. He recalled when the Texaco station on the corner had been Park Gas. Across the street, Chapman Lumber was now Midwest Lumber Co. The big empty lot in the next block had once housed the grand Wiltse Hotel, torn down in the early '60s. Only half of the Brick Hotel remained—recently turned into a flower shop. In the next block,

Miller Plumbing & Heating still proudly maintained a presence on Main Street after seventy years.

As Maggie neared the barber shop, he remembered most mornings he and Maggie lingered long enough for Walter to peer inside to see who was sitting in the barber chair. Louie La Cava went there for his daily shave whenever he was in town. Eventually, he told a few people he was a book-keeper for Al Capone's charities, but largely folks believed he did a lot more than that. And most chose to steer clear of him, thinking that at any time of the day or night their lives might change drastically, should some goon follow him to their community and a shootout ensue on Main Street, with perhaps their children in the thick of it.

Marshal Sweeney had told a few friends about going duck hunting with Louie. He said once Louie pointed his shotgun at Sweeney's chest, and Sweeney thought he might die that day in the blind next to the Wapsie. Louie's admonition to "watch your back!" stuck with Sweeney for a while, too.

Nonetheless, Louie lived and dwelt among the people of Oxbow for sixty-plus years. And there wasn't one thing anyone could do about it.

One question yet remained: What did Louie think of Oxbow? *Mostly we're ordinary, messy people,* Walter thought, *who choose to live in this small town, interacting day to day with one another as human beings. Louie must've cared something for the people, 'cause he's still here with us—albeit six feet under.*

Walter rested his head against the back of the seat and listened to the sound of Maggie's chatter. Her engine hummed like the lady he'd first courted some fifty years earlier, still able to strut her stuff. Frequently he lifted a weathered hand to wave to familiar faces in the crowd. Many he knew were from the churches in town, each holding a special place in his heart. He saw farming friends, owners of century farms: Beierschmidt, Gallup, Goeller, Kane, Niebuhr, Neil, Shields, Siggelkow, Trebon, and others. It was hard not to detect all the new faces, too. He realized that he was running out of time to get to know them.

"Go real slow when we pass by the Island Park, Earl," Walter said. "The place holds dear memories... Emma, the boys and I used to spend a lot of time there...picnics and such."

Walter turned around to glance at his two grown sons, waving and laughing together.

Leonard caught Walter's eye.

"You never did tell us the rest of the Louie La Cava story, Father... What was he doing for those thirty years in Florida after Capone's death? Did he retire? Give up the gangster business?"

"Remind me another time to tell you... Once a gangster, always a gangster."

Walter then abruptly turned around in the seat.

At that moment, he thought he'd glimpsed Emma's face in the crowd.

—

AUTHOR'S NOTE AND ACKNOWLEDGEMENTS

My primary family moved to Fairbank, Iowa—a small town much like Oxbow—in the mid-1950s. The idea for Gangster in our Midst came when interviewing former school teachers, town councilmen, and other locals for my second book (We Are Eight, a Memoir, 2015)

Several people provided stories about the decades they watched us eight Brandt kids grow to become solid members of the community.

Plus, they made references to the town's alleged gangster, Louie La Cava, though he had died in 1980.

Largely, they said La Cava first showed up on Main Street after marrying an area girl in the early 1920s. Over time, they came to believe he worked for Al Capone as his bookkeeper. But ninety years later, no one knew for certain.

In the back of my mind I tucked away the thought: This could be an interesting story to tell in a future book.

During the spring of 2016, ready to embark on a third book, I returned to these same people, asking: "What made you think the town's mystery man was a gangster? Did he rob the bank? Did he show you his guns?"

"No!" came their replies. "We thought he was a gangster because of his mannerisms, like the way he walked downtown on Main Street, surrounded by the children of the town; and because he refused to let the barber turn his chair facing away from the front door."

Others said the gangster story was folklore, and there was nothing more to it.

At that point, I thought there might not be a story to tell.

I was pleasantly surprised when an initial Internet search for a connection between Al Capone and Louie La Cava provided two credible sources. The first was an 89-page filing by Special Agent Frank Miller, Bureau of

Internal Revenue, who'd been assigned by Bureau of Investigation Acting Director J. Edgar Hoover to investigate Capone on tax evasion. Miller mentioned Louie La Cava early in his December 21, 1933 official report filing, posted by www.wikileaks.org.

Another was a book written by *Chicago Tribune* Reporter, Fred D. Pasley (Al Capone: The Biography of a Self-Made Man, Garden City Publishing Co., 1930), which came out just as Capone was about to begin serving his 11-year sentence at the U.S. penitentiary in Atlanta, GA. The name Louie La Cava appeared within the first forty pages.

These discoveries encouraged me to believe a lot more information probably existed—and I was right. Through FBI and police reports, newspaper accounts, and stories from the town's people who knew the gangster best, I've been able to tell this story.

—

The list of those I wish to acknowledge is long. First, thank you to the five Fairbank historians who participated in this book-writing project from its beginning: Howard Durham, Bob Maricle, Arnola Siggelkow, and Maurice and Wilma Welsh. Indispensable is the best way to describe their willingness to be of help in any way possible. And most knew the gangster personally and shared their stories.

Verlie (Hahn) Trower, at one hundred years of age, her mind still sharp as a tack, generously granted several interviews. Born in Fairbank, she never left. Verlie is the eldest daughter of Charles William "Bill" Hahn, Fairbank town marshal from 1916-1949.

Leo Beierschmitt, Mary Ellen (Klenzman) Youngblut, Helen (Chase) McSweeney and Lois "Lo-E" Miller, too, opened their hearts to share personal stories of the town and its people from so very long ago.

Finally, Geraldine "Deane" (Lehmkuhl) Fink and Gayle Lehmkuhl gave unsurpassed support in helping track down resources, people and documentation, of the town's businesses from years gone by. Deane's family lived on the second floor of their family's hardware business on East Main Street. Her personal stories were unlike any other I came across.

Personal friends from Minnesota and Indiana read chapters as they were written and provided general feedback. They included Noritta Carter, Ward Denaway, Robert and Lornell Kopp, Rev. Dr. Frank Nelson, and Mary Schacht.

Those who helped scour national and local newspaper archives, periodicals, and other records included: Pam and Michelle at the Archive Center and Genealogy /Department of the Indian River County Main Library, Vero Beach, Fl.; and Cathy at Century College Library, Maplewood, MN— but there were others at various institutions.

Early in the project, I published an invitation in a Fairbank area newspaper, plus posted on the town's Facebook page, a request for anyone who wished to participate in the project to "come forward." The number of participants grew, most of whom are/were current or former Fairbank area residents. Again, many knew the gangster personally or garnered secondhand stories of him.

I'm grateful for the manuscript critique from Erin Hart, editor from The Loft Literary Center, Minneapolis, Minn., who helped draw out the story that lived inside my head. And for Janet Joslyn, a dear friend I met along the way, who worked tirelessly with me to the very end, helping to edit.

Finally, a special thank you to my dear husband Jonathan, the only person who really knows all that went into writing this book. He's my Walter, a wise man who tells me: "Writing books is not for the faint of heart." I'm also fortunate to have the love and support of our children and their spouses, and grandchildren: Jeffrey and Adela Maurer, Mekhi, Alex and Stephen; Greg and Tamara Kokinos, and Brittany. But there were other unnamed family (and friends) who listened to me go on and on about the new book I was writing…and offered encouraging words.

It's important to also acknowledge that in the writing of any book (this is my third) a certain amount of good luck comes into play. It's not enough for a worthy story to present itself; one must have time, energy, perseverance, patience and dedication to invest in finding the people who know the story. If one is lucky, an author will cross paths with the right people.

Writing books take more research and resources than one ever anticipates. I came across the "Keefer sisters murders" at the end of my research, quite by chance. The story really helped pull together one chapter.

Fictional characters were needed to tell the story. For me, some came to mind by fluke during a Sunday morning Presbyterian worship service; another was a name overheard in a conversation across the aisle on a flight to Las Vegas—just two examples.

At some point, I had enough assembled pieces, scattered like jig-saw puzzle pieces in paper and computer files, to begin to make the story take shape—a beginning, a middle, and an ending.

I experienced bouts of vacillation, of course...moving from... I'm not sure if I'm the right person to tell this story to... This is turning out to be an amazing, interesting story, and I'm happy to be the person to tell it.

In the end, if one is lucky, a well-written and edited story gets told. Really—it's a miracle that any neglected story gets told.

I definitely had a little luck in telling this story.

In August 2017, through perseverance and a wellspring of community spirit, *Gangster in our Midst* came to fruition.

I hope you enjoy this neglected TRUE Iowa story.

COMMENTS

"Your coverage of Louie La Cava facts and your story of his connections with Al Capone is factual and fascinating reading."

—Verla S., Fredericksburg, Iowa

"I enjoyed meeting the characters—the families, and even the gangsters! I think you nailed the time period for small towns in the Midwest during Prohibition. I loved all the history, and I think you did a great job."

—Sharon O., Estancia, New Mexico

"Loved the book. It was an easy read...great details, and I didn't want to put it down. I got to really know the characters, and the story line brought me to tears a few times. I look forward to future books."

—Lori K., Rushford, Minnesota

"You captured in your descriptive writing the feel of time and place in the story... I was transported back to the time of both my grandfather and father! I could almost see them with their cars, going hunting, and playing card games."

—Kathy M., St. Paul, Minnesota

www.ingramcontent.com/pod-product-compliance
Lightning Source LLC
Chambersburg PA
CBHW021009120726

47905CB00009B/2932